ERASING MEMORY

ERASING MEMORY

A MacNeice Mystery

SCOTT THORNLEY

RANDOM HOUSE CANADA

PUBLISHED BY RANDOM HOUSE CANADA
Copyright © 2011 Scott Thornley

www.randomhouse.ca
Random House Canada and colophon are registered trademarks.

This book is a work of fiction. Names, characters, places, and incidents either are
the product of the author's imagination or are used fictitiously. Any resemblance to
actual persons, living or dead, events, or locales is entirely coincidental.

Lyrics on page 2 from "War" by Edwin Starr.
Lyrics on page 161 from "Montana" by Frank Zappa.
Lyrics on page 304 from "Good Vibrations" by The Beach Boys.

Library and Archives Canada Cataloguing in Publication

Thornley, Scott
Erasing memory / Scott Thornley.

Issued also in electronic format.

ISBN 978-0-307-35925-4

I. Title.

PS8639.H66E73 2011   C813'.6   C2010-901432-4

Design by CS Richardson

Printed in the United States of America

2   4   6   8   9   7   5   3   1

For Jude and Shirley—thank you for being in my life.

PROLOGUE

—

THE BLACK SUIT JACKET was folded neatly on the bed. Beside it were two black metal suitcases, one open, the other closed. On the closed suitcase sat a smaller black case, big enough to hold a flute, which was open. Inside was a black Styrofoam nest. It was empty.

In the bathroom, the tap was running. A tall man in a white dress shirt and black trousers stood at the sink, humming, then broke into song.

"War. What is it good for?"

He took the hotel shampoo container and emptied it into a stainless steel cylinder, then placed the cylinder under the flow from the faucet till foam came up over the lip. Once the cylinder was clean, he took the last of the towels, smiling at the easel card that spoke about saving the environment by using your towels more than once, and dried the outside of the cylinder. He then took the hairdryer and blew the interior dry.

His eyes were dark and gleamed with intelligence. The skin was drawn tight over his angular cheekbones. Below them, his face narrowed so much that in certain lights you could see the embossing of his teeth on the skin of his cheeks. Even clean-shaven, he was cursed with a dark beard line that only served to make his face seem more sculpted and severe.

When his cellphone rang on the bedside table, he carried the syringe out of the bathroom, placed it in its black nest and closed the case before he answered the phone.

"Yes, it's done. A policeman arrived within minutes of my call. Immaculate? Yes, like the conception. Send the wire transfer now. We are finished."

He hung up. Slipping off the back panel of the cellphone, he pulled the SIM card and laid it on the ceramic floor by the straight-backed desk chair, then slammed the metal glide of one chair leg down on the card. Picking it up, he bent it in half and went into the washroom, where he dropped it into the toilet and flushed. Returning to the bed, he placed the syringe case and the cellphone in his suitcase and snapped it shut. Humming again, he rolled his sleeves down, buttoned them and put on his suit jacket, tugging each cuff sharply so that it hung a half-inch lower on his wrists than his jacket's sleeves.

He wrote a note on the single piece of hotel stationery and propped it against the new vacuum cleaner by the bed. *My wife liked the suction but she didn't like the colour. Please enjoy.*

Picking up his luggage, he opened the door and left the hotel room.

"War," he sang. "What is it good for? Absolutely nothing."

ONE

—

I T WAS THE SAME as it always was, chamber music driving up and jazz driving back. But this time he'd asked her, "Why do you want to be buried so far from town?"

Kate had smiled and closed her eyes—for such a while that he thought she'd fallen asleep—then softly, but with some strength, as if to ensure that the point made it through the haze of morphine and fatigue, she said, "It's beautiful there. It's a lovely drive. Not too far. I know you'll visit. And"—breathing deeply—"if it was in the city, I doubt you would. Anyway, it'll get you out of your head for a few hours."

She was right. He'd been up once a month for the past thirty-eight months. When he'd looked at her ashes, he couldn't see the difference between them and the ashes he retrieved from the fireplace to sprinkle on the garden—he couldn't reassemble her. And yet, below the ground, beneath a headstone that bore only her initials, KGWM, he could imagine her on her side with her legs slightly tucked up—asleep.

And it did get him out of his head. A cemetery in the city could never do that—the sound of sirens, the headstones of people they'd known, the buzz of traffic nearby would distract from the solace of being near her.

HE STAYED THIS TIME, as always, past sundown, reading, watching for birds and announcing each out loud for the odd comfort it gave him—cedar waxwing, swallow, cardinal, chickadee, a rare ruby-throated hummingbird—not because he truly believed she would hear, but because he didn't entirely disbelieve it. The kitchen of Martha's Truck Stop stayed open till ten, and on the way back he stopped and ordered the same thing he always did: a hot beef sandwich with gravy, no fries, followed by apple pie and coffee.

He was just cresting the Canadian Shield above Lake Charles when the call came over the radio. "All units. All units. We have an anonymous call about a fatality in a beach house on Shore Road, Lake Charles."

MacNeice pressed the hands-free button. "The caller—male or female?"

"Male. Over."

"Did he sound agitated, Sylvia?"

"No, Mac. Cool as a cucumber, not hurried or concerned. Over."

"Describe his voice—north-end, west-end, local, foreign?"

"I'd say foreign, but very educated in English. You can judge for yourself when you hear it. Over."

"Thanks, Syl. I'm about five minutes away from the cut-off to Lake Charles."

TWO

—

H<small>E COULD APPRECIATE THE</small> rare beauty of it, the ice-blue chiffon of her gown spilling about her, the white sheers from the window billowing with the breeze off the lake, almost touching her legs, which were still and slightly—but not unnaturally—akimbo. But what stopped him, arresting all the clock wheels of his experience and wisdom, was the way her right arm rested, the hand dangling above the tone arm of the pale green Seabreeze, which soldiered on—the second Schubert Piano Trio, music that had formed something of a through-line in his life—skipping each time it hit her hand, then going back to the beginning. *That's persistence*, he thought as the familiar melody began again. *We're both just trying to do our jobs.*

He slid the sheers aside and looked out over the lake, which was romantically perfect. The music swelled and the breeze lifted the waves, spilling small shells and tiny pebbles onto the shore with a soft hiss and sigh.

Soon enough the scene would become the macabre job site of the professionally detached. But for these moments he allowed himself to listen, to absorb the inglorious end of a clearly glorious young woman. No blood. No obvious trauma, needle marks, coke residue—she had been a healthy woman, until the moment she wasn't anymore.

Reaching down, he lifted her hand as a gentleman would to usher a lady onto the dance floor, then lowered it again as the needle passed by. The music continued as if nothing had happened, but his own blanket of forced detachment was already descending. "We're all machines," he said wearily—he wasn't sure to whom—as he rose again to survey the room.

When the Schubert ended, the yellow plastic arm rose to return to its cradle. Once again he lifted the cold hand so the cheerful arm could pass underneath, but instead of settling into its cradle, the arm paused as if considering what to do next. The black vinyl slowed, hesitated, then kept spinning, and the needle eased down, caught a groove and began playing the music again. It had been set on repeat. MacNeice let her hand descend to where, in roughly fifteen minutes, the skipping game would begin again.

In law enforcement an established mantra was applied to every crime scene: look at the big picture. And yet every success in his life had occurred through an intense scrutiny of detail. Only recently had it occurred to him that the thrilling intensity of life close-up was what made him effective as a cop. For better or worse, that was his "big picture."

He knelt down and leaned forward, supporting himself with one hand on the wall, to study her face, looking for a sign of trauma or fear, but nothing was revealed. Her skin, slightly olive, was without blemish. Her eyes were closed as if she'd fallen asleep watching a movie—or listening to Schubert. He leaned closer and inhaled the remains of a floral perfume. With his nose less than an inch from her chin, he let his face glide slowly up hers, inhaling deeply to the hairline. There a subtle but sharp smell invaded his nostrils; he rocked back on his heels, put his hands on his thighs and exhaled before standing up. In an hour or so this young beauty would be transformed into something awful on the olfactory, overpowering her perfume and that pleasant scent of the night coming in off the lake.

No signs of strangulation or that broken-chicken look of a snapped neck. But high up under her chin was a bruise, an old, brownish mark like a three-day-old hickey—a conclusion he was sure the Young Turks would jump to when they arrived. But he knew this style of bruise; it was identical to the mark tattooed on the neck of a girl he had loved. She'd been proud of her bruise-in-training even when it was still pink.

This woman's mark had the look of permanence, of someone deeply committed to practice. She had been a violinist. He bent down to look at the soles of her shoes—no sand. She hadn't walked up from the beach. He turned back to the front door and examined the carpet, expecting to see the imprint of her high heels. Other than the impressions of his shoes, only the track patterns of a vacuum cleaner marked the carpet.

He began moving about the room. To the right of the bar was a component system that in its brushed-silver coolness made the Seabreeze look childlike and simple. There were no CDs, however, no stacks of 45s or LPs, and while the jacket from the Schubert appeared to be missing, its inner sleeve was on the sofa within reach. That the Seabreeze was on the floor and not neatly set up on one of the tables suggested that it had been brought here for the occasion.

He stared down at her. *Was this piece going to be your first triumph? You could be wearing your graduation gown.*

He took the latex gloves out of his back pocket and slipped them on with a snap. His wife had hated that he always carried these things about. Whenever she'd be searching for the car keys or milk money and felt the powdery latex on her fingers, she'd let loose a stream of furious cursing, which he always recalled when he reached for them. The memory of her exasperation briefly warmed him.

Time was running out—soon the Turks would arrive and the scene would dissolve in a wave of sick jokes. And then the baggie-footed, gloved-hand, plastic-bag-toting, Tyvek-clad forensic nitpickers would take over and she'd cease to be "human" forever. He asked himself what was missing, then thought, *Even a violinist has a purse.*

He searched the hall closet and the two bedrooms. Nothing out of place, nor any indication that anyone had been living here. But he found no vacuum cleaner either, though the cleaners could have brought their own. On the balcony, the sight of the lake rippling in the light of the half-moon, silhouetted by pine and birch—the music, the chiffon gown—made him realize what an exhaustingly sad scene this was. Standing at the railing, he looked down towards the blue grass and sand—nothing.

Turning back to her, he paused to listen, as if an answer would come from her lips. Squatting down, he reached under her shoulders and, lifting her up slightly, slid his hand beneath her. There under her ribcage was a small, glittering evening bag, not much bigger than his glasses case. He retrieved it and gently let her shoulders fall.

The magnetic clasp gave way with a little pop, but he had already felt its contents through the sequined fabric. It was full of optimism but little else. No wallet, no credit cards or identification, just a key and a lipstick—Barely Cherry. He looked at her mouth and said respectfully, "God bless the innocents, for they will be first to the slaughter."

The key, on a small roundel fob, was for one of those locks guaranteed to be burglar proof. More optimism. On its brushed silver head were the letters *LT*, engraved with serifs and a slight descending flourish. That was all she had with her.

On cue, the heavy Chevys pulled up outside—two cars. Three doors opened and slammed shut. His time alone with her was up and he still had no clue, no idea and no advantage that his age and experience could produce, beyond knowing what the music was on the turntable and recognizing the bruise on her chin.

He heard one of the Turks ask, "Whose rig is that?"

"Judging by the stuff on the seat, I'd say MacNeice," came the response.

MacNeice remembered that he hadn't put the CD wallet away, and the volume of e. e. cummings was on the front passenger seat too. He was putting the key back in her bag as the three cops came in.

"That's not your style, Mac. Too many sequins—wrong colour too."

"I know," MacNeice said. "I'm told I'm a winter, but I still prefer spring, don't you, Swetsky?" He set the purse down beside the girl.

"Smartass. Whaddya got?"

"Well, she's beautiful—and dead. There's no apparent trauma. She just looks like she fell asleep and didn't wake up."

MacNeice reached over to the outlet and pulled out the plug of the Seabreeze. The needle ground to a halt in one of the grooves.

"Who placed the call?" Swetsky asked.

"Anonymous. Male. Gave the address. Said we'd find a body and hung up."

One of the other Turks, Palmer, was already in a semi-squat with one arm down for balance. He leaned towards her face. With his free hand he pointed to the bruise under her chin and said, "I used to give hickeys like that, but I just don't have the suction anymore."

Swetsky, Palmer and Williams—the only black homicide detective in their unit—cracked up. MacNeice began removing his latex gloves. He sighed, discreetly, he thought, but Swetsky picked it up. "Come on, Palmer," he said, "show some respect for the lady." Palmer stopped sniggering only when he tried to stand up, his knee complaining.

"Right knee blown, Palmer?" MacNeice said.

"Yeah, but I get by, thanks for asking." Palmer shifted his massive bulk over his hips to find the sweet spot where the pain would subside.

"That hickey is no hickey. The girl was a violinist." MacNeice folded his gloves, shoved them into his back pocket and stepped onto the balcony.

"Where ya off to, Mac?" Swetsky asked.

"I'm going to check out the beach."

At the top of the stairs down to the beach, he heard Williams say, "What's his problem, Swets?"

"No problem. Check the bedroom." He heard them snapping on the gloves, getting to work. Latex—the ubiquitous protector of evidence.

———

THE STAIRCASE, AN ENAMELLED metal job intended to look clean and modern, shivered under his weight. The shore grass was soft and damp and the coarse sand beyond dark. The water was black, the waves a lazily undulating silver. Someone was already out in a motorboat, trolling for pickerel by the sound of it. There was a slight breeze, pleasant for a mid-June night.

"Seabreeze," he said out loud. Why would anyone own a Seabreeze in a digital age? He turned away from the water and began to follow the shaft of light from the living room window. At the foot of the stairs he stepped sideways to position himself just under the leading edge of the balcony. Sighing again, he put his hands in his pockets, closed his eyes and dropped his head.

For a few moments he drifted, swaying—not to any music in his head, just swaying. He listened to the heavy feet moving slowly across the cottage floor twelve feet above him, until the sound of squealing brakes announced the arrival of the forensics team.

The balcony above him sagged under the weight of two more men, baggies on their feet, scanning the beachfront with flashlights, the cones of light crossing and seeking like searchlights in old war movies. The men didn't speak, and just as silently they soon went back inside.

His eyes having adjusted to the dark, MacNeice turned his attention back to the beach. The smell of the grass, lake and pine carried by the breeze was like scented silk on his face. Roughly fifty feet or so to the right, over on the dark and dimpled sand, was a triangular shadow. He moved slowly towards it, putting on the latex gloves again.

He realized what it was well before he reached it—the Schubert jacket. He picked it up by the edges, blew off the grit and turned towards the yellow slice of light coming from the cottage. When he got there, he squeezed his palms together and peered inside the elliptical opening, expecting to find it empty, but there was something inside: a neat white rectangle with a deckled edge. He flipped the jacket over and tilted it so that the paper slid closer to the opening. A photograph.

A smiling brunette, maybe fifteen or sixteen years old. He took out the photo and held it up to the light. The girl in the image—the woman who now lay dead in the cottage—was sitting on a beach recliner in a one-piece; another recliner was off to the side with a towel and beach bag beside it. Two pairs of flip-flops lay between them. On the back of the photo there was handwriting in pencil, too faint to make out in the dim light. He turned it over again to look at the girl.

She had the figure for a bikini but she was wearing a one-piece, modest by the standards of a decade or so ago, when, he assumed, the photo had been taken. Her legs, firm and tanned, were closed—not forced together by modesty or shame, just gently together. He had a photograph of someone he loved in that same pose—all smiles and sunshine—it was somewhere in the mess of his desk drawer. That drawer was a stark contrast to the cottage above, so neat that even a corpse couldn't mess it up.

The place had been built with money but in haste, as if more attention had been given to the idea of a beach house than to building it well. It looked as if it had never been lived in. The nearest neighbours were out of sight, a hundred yards in either direction. They'd be interviewed, as would the person trolling around in the outboard, but MacNeice guessed that no one would know the people who owned this cottage.

He made his way up the stairs to the balcony and, preferring to avoid the swarm inside, walked around to the breezeway and into the garage. Through the window he could see that Williams had assumed a position at the bar where he pretended to ignore the forensics team. Swetsky, catching sight of MacNeice, came out the side door to meet him. "He's sulking."

"I can see that." MacNeice was holding the album and the snapshot the way choirboys do their hymnals.

"Whaddya got?"

"Schubert. A piano trio. It was on when you arrived." MacNeice held the jacket up so Swetsky could read the title, careful to tuck the snapshot behind it.

"You don't say."

"Swets, do me a favour—get that key from the purse and bring it out here for a minute."

"Sure, but why not get it yourself?"

"I need to get some things out of the car. While you're in there, push the button to open the garage door, okay?" As Swetsky went inside, happy to have a mission, MacNeice propped the Schubert jacket against the wall of the cottage, wedging it so it wouldn't fall, then slipped the snapshot into his jacket pocket.

As he cleared the breezeway, MacNeice could see that the small turning circle among the pines was now lined with vehicles, including the pathologist's black Suburban. Palmer was sitting in the passenger seat of one of the Chevys, talking on his cellphone. He glanced vacantly up as MacNeice went by, then turned his head away to continue the conversation. From the look of it, he was getting into something hot and heavy. He had a reputation with women—often somebody else's. Maybe another cop's wife or, like the last time, a firefighter's. That one had ended with his Indian motorcycle—the real love of his life—going up in flames at 4 a.m. outside his apartment. When the pumper truck arrived, the first firefighter out of the truck was the woman's husband. No charges were ever laid, and Palmer was still paying off the bike.

From a weathered black Samsonite case in the trunk of his car, MacNeice removed a Sony digital camera, one of those little black jobs that clock in at ten megapixels and can capture almost as much as the Nikon SLR the crime-scene boy was currently clacking away with inside. MacNeice closed the lid and laid the photo on top of it. He took several shots, zooming in for detail, and then turned it over to take several more of the back, making sure the flash wasn't bleaching out the writing.

The garage door opened so smoothly and quietly behind him that it was only the sudden wash of light that gave it away. Swetsky appeared, latex gloves on, purse in hand. MacNeice stifled a grin.

"There were prints and partials on the clasp, lipstick, key and fob," Swetsky said. "No idea yet what killed her."

"Poison, or something worse. As for the cottage, it was cleaned before we got here."

"Why do you figure poison?"

"Something about the way she smelled—up close, I mean."

As Swetsky handed over the purse, MacNeice passed him the snapshot. With a wry smile, Swetsky said, "I knew you had something else, dammit. I knew it." He stared at the photo for a long moment, losing the smile. "Shit, she really was a beauty."

MacNeice took a tin of putty out of his case. Taking the key, he pressed it into the putty. "These types of keys are registered. We might as well find out to whom before the Tyvek boys do. The company's Lock Tight." Swetsky watched him remove the key and put the tin back in the case, next to a bar of seventy percent dark chocolate. As MacNeice was photographing both sides of the key and fob, Swetsky noticed Palmer, still on the phone, and shook his head slightly.

"Strictly speaking, Mac, this isn't kosher." Swetsky wasn't referring to Palmer.

MacNeice put the key back into the purse. "Neither are you. Neither am I. You are a second-generation polack and I'm a Glaswegian thrice removed . . . not that we couldn't be all that and kosher too, mind you."

"*Thrice*. Christ, that's nice."

MacNeice took back the photo, dropped the purse into Swetsky's hand and said, "I'll grab the Schubert jacket from the breezeway—the snapshot was inside it. We'll give them both to the nerds."

Walking through the garage to the breezeway door, MacNeice couldn't take his eyes off the snapshot. The play of light seemed to animate it somehow. He wasn't listening when Swetsky said, "Did ya notice? No oil stains, no tire-tread marks, no nothing. We're walking on virgin concrete here."

Turning the photo over, MacNeice finally registered what it said: *Lydia and Margaux. Friends Forever. 7.00*

"Am I talking to myself here?" Swetsky said.

MacNeice glanced at him standing under the twin fluorescents, the tiny clutch bag at his side. "Don't get used to carrying that thing around, Swets." He slid the snapshot back into the sleeve, then handed them to Swetsky and said, "Would you hand this stuff over? I'll put where I found it in my report, but I've seen the beach and now I'm going home."

Swetsky nodded, and as he turned towards the breezeway door, stopped to say, "Mac, how'd you get here? Or better still, why'd you get here? You're not on shift, and this isn't your usual territory."

"I was coming back from the cemetery when the call came over the radio." He hesitated. "I'm going to request the lead on this, Swets, if that's okay with you."

"Sure, no problem. But d'ya mind telling me why?"

"Let's just say I have a soft spot for violinists. I'll call it in to Wallace on my way back to the city."

Swetsky nodded again. "I'll get Palmer and Williams to talk to the neighbours and I'll check the ownership on this place. We'll walk copies of this snapshot around too."

MacNeice had stopped listening again, so Swetsky headed back through the door to the cottage.

AT HIS CAR, MacNEICE pulled the keys out of his pocket, happy that he'd parked close to the road and wasn't blocked in. He glanced back once at the cottage, and through the open front door he could see four Tyvek-covered nerds—three men and a woman—working closely around the body. They were quiet and thorough, using gadgets only they knew the purpose of.

So there it was, he thought: the dream cottage on the lake all lit up with more people in it than likely it had ever seen, and he thought of the young violinist in the chiffon gown who had become the centre of attention. Unlocking the car, he glanced at Palmer still sitting there on his cell, talking the talk to someone who'd regret it later. Wearily he opened the car door and sank behind the wheel.

He picked up the CD wallet from the passenger seat, flipping through the sleeves until he found one of Kate's favourites—*Ascenseur pour l'échafaud*—a soundtrack by Miles Davis for an old French film. When she'd brought it home, he'd pointed out her resemblance to the blonde in the liner notes. "Look, it's a very sexy picture of someone who looks like you, with Miles." And she'd smiled a smile that took several minutes to wear off.

He turned on the ignition, then slipped Miles into the dashboard player. He tucked cummings into the glove box beside his holstered weapon, removed the camera from his pocket and tossed it onto the passenger seat, then buckled himself in and listened for a moment to the low, comforting rumble of the car until the deep opening bass notes of the CD took over, Miles's horn mellow in the early morning.

The digital clock on the dash read 5:31 a.m. and the sun was minutes away from its big ta-dah of the day. MacNeice ached with fatigue, and something deeper. He eased his old Chevy out of the circular drive and over the grated ditch that ran alongside the road to keep the cottages from sliding into the lake when the November rains came. The chassis groaned as the wheels took on the uneven surface. Three times he'd been offered one of the new fleet cars and had declined. "As long as there's a mechanic willing to keep her going, I'll stick with her." There was a willing mechanic, though the man suspected, rightly, that MacNeice's loyalty to his ride was all about the CD player and the superior sound system that had been installed in a factory error.

MacNeice drove south on the road that skirted the lake for a few miles, the distant ridge of maple and pine backlit by the deep purple of pre-dawn. Accelerating onto the four-lane highway, he appreciated the way the slow, languorous rhythm of the CD seemed in synch with the pale yellow sodium lamps flashing over the hood. He glanced over at the camera and suddenly regretted not taking photographs of the dead girl. Then he thought how strange it was that she'd become a girl to him, no longer the woman he had first encountered. The effect of staring at the snapshot, no doubt.

There would be no shortage of clinical photos, of course, but he would have attempted to capture her beauty. He was convinced that insights would come as much from those images as from the other. And if images needed to be shown to the family—but then again, maybe that was just him.

Soon he was approaching the cut-off to Greater Dundurn— if he took the exit to the right he could come into town along a treed Victorian promenade with a manicured park on one side and a 2,700-acre nature reserve on the other, conceived and built by a people certain of an industrial future that promised prosperity for all and forever. While the golden era of heavy industry had passed, the trees, plantings, stone crown-adorned abutments and ornate balustrades of the bridges high above the bay were still elegant symbols of a long-forgotten optimism.

He chose the other way, powering the Chevy towards the great soaring bridge that separated the lake from Dundurn Bay. Built in the late 1950s, the Sky-High Bridge allowed both access to the inner harbour for what had been an endless parade of lake freighters and uninterrupted flow of traffic to and from New York and Ohio to the city of Toronto. To MacNeice, taking the bridge was simply the best way to get a view of everything.

Though he'd lived here all his life, it was still a thrill to see the sun rising over the lake and shining across to the old steel mills and factories that lined the bay. Most visitors thought Dundurn was ugly. MacNeice could never understand that. The harbour was inspiring to him—even the smokestacks, the towering cranes and the enormous rust-coloured, dust-covered buildings with long piers that clawed like fingers into the bay towards the few freighters that still eased their way in and out.

THREE

—

THE CITY, LIKE ALL CITIES, measured its prosperity geographically. With Dundurn, the best measure was how far you lived from the plants that provided its robust economy. The north end—closest to the factories and the bay—was the poorest and toughest, its houses forever coated in red dust. Depending on the prevailing wind, residents rarely knew anything but the smell of sulphur in the air. The sweet spot in Dundurn was still the west end, farthest away from the prevailing breezes of the steel plants. And the sweetest spot of all was close to the escarpment that ran the length of the city, referred to by everyone as "the mountain."

The city's crime played out the same way. The white-collar stuff was almost exclusively a west-end affair. In the north end, violence was frequent and always visceral. As Swetsky, who had grown up in the north end, put it, "If your everyday vocabulary includes the words *blast furnace*, you can expect some

spillover in the kitchen at night." When MacNeice was walking a beat there as a new recruit, people would joke that the
local rats were bigger than the local cats, and more numerous.
His sergeant told him that in the old Mafia days of the 1920s
and 1930s, bodies wearing cement overshoes were dumped in
the bay by the dozens. They were probably still there.

Slowing, MacNeice moved to the inside lane of the bridge,
lowered the volume on the music and switched on his two-way.
Within two connections he was speaking to Betty Fernihough,
the head of the precinct's IT unit. After a brief exchange of
pleasantries—Betty liked it that way, as did he—he asked,
"Have you found out who owns the cottage?"

"Yes, I gave the name to Swetsky about ten minutes ago.
A Dr. Michael Hadley—he has a dental clinic in the west end.
We think he may keep the beach house as a rental property."

"Swets hit you early, Betty. I'm sorry."

"It's okay, Mac, I'm an early riser anyway. I was in at five
thirty this morning."

"Can you do me a favour, then? Look and see if you can
find any images of young women just graduating or beginning
their careers as violinists. First name Lydia. She was probably
in her mid-twenties."

"Christ, Mac, how the hell did you come up with that?"

"Just a hunch. Look at the university, the Conservatory of
Music, chamber music societies, orchestras and soloists between
here and Toronto. You'll know this girl when you see her—tall,
brunette, beautiful, and blessed—or cursed—with an optimistic
smile."

"Whatever the hell that is," Betty said distractedly. If it
weren't for the road noise and the faint bluesy Miles, he was
certain he'd be able to hear her already clicking away on her

keyboard. "Get some sleep, Mac—you're sounding borderline crispy. Swets told me how come you got there first."

MacNeice eased the Chevy off the highway onto Mountain Road South, cranking down both driver and passenger windows to breathe in the early morning air. The sun was streaking through the houses and trees on his left, flickering through the car. The stripes on the road unfolded; the streetlights had gone out, but he couldn't remember when. He wound the fingers of his left hand through his hair—it was long for him, and showing signs of grey.

As the wind blew the strands out of his grasp, he realized he was falling asleep. "Two hands," he told himself sternly, shoving his butt into the back of the seat and pulling himself erect. He glanced down at the Sony. "I would love to have seen you play."

The sun was already warming up the hill below the escarpment where the hundreds of happy-looking houses of Pleasant Park defined the eastern end of the city. Beyond it lay the town of Secord, as quiet and bucolic as ever. PP, as it's known over the two-way, had been finished three years earlier, and from a distance it admittedly looked lovely spread along the hillside. The development had been the subject of a community brawl between those who wanted the hill to remain a place of quiet beauty, of songbird, deer and fox—MacNeice's perspective—and those who saw it as the best opportunity to expand the city and "take the pressure off the inner core." He knew little about the design of successful cities but had assumed that compression was one aspect that made them work. In his travels with Kate to France and Italy, he'd never once felt that the narrow streets, or the shops, apartments and houses that had been built around and above them, lacked for anything, least of all space.

MacNeice made a hard right up the long, winding lane towards the Cedarway Estate, which had sat for almost a century on a vast property that crested the escarpment. Easing to a stop in the gravel drive of the Gatehouse, the Edwardian folly a hundred feet below the top that he called home, he put the car in park and turned off the ignition. Electronic rolling fences and video security systems had long ago made the gatehouse redundant to the estate above, which suited MacNeice just fine.

As a young patrolman he had arrested the gateman several times for drunk driving. Coming here each time to inform the man's wife, he had grown to admire the solidity of the building. When the gateman and his wife retired and moved into town, the owner carved the building and the quarter-acre stand of pine and cedar that adjoined it from the main estate and put it on the market. MacNeice and Kate had put up everything they'd saved to make the down payment. The owner likely remembered his name, or his father's, from the MacNeice Marina on Raven Lake, where as a kid Mac had pumped gas into the tank of the man's sleek twelve-cylinder mahogany motor launch. Or perhaps he had a soft spot for young cops or violinists, because the estate agent told MacNeice and Kate that theirs wasn't even close to the highest bid—it was just the one he accepted. They took that as a good omen for their lives, and for the most part it had been.

Leaving his keys on the table inside the door, MacNeice went to the living room to set the Sony camera next to his computer. He looked out the large window at the trees. Its mullions broke the scene into a soft grey grid—good for a moment like this.

The window—ten by six, with an industrial frame—was something he'd seen while checking out a wrecker's yard on

Harbour Street after the owner had been found—cold as slate, crack pipe in hand—sprawled on the floor of the yard's office. Next to him was his Doberman. It had guarded him right up to the point when hunger overtook its desire to serve and protect. Most of the wrecker's face and neck were gone, and when the first officer opened the door, the animal, presumably now protecting its food source, lunged at him. He put it down with two rounds from his service revolver.

When MacNeice arrived, the young patrolman was leaning against the railing in front of the office, having a smoke. After warning him about what he was going to see, he said, "You know, I've patrolled by this yard so many times and that damn dog would always come snarlin' and snappin' to the fence, but he never came at me like that before. He knew he had some good eatin' in there."

The yard was the resting place for most of the doors and windows, wood panels and plaster mouldings, cornices and ironwork, and even flooring of the century homes and factories torn down in the city. For anyone wanting to recreate the town the way it was, this yard was one big erector set. But then, no one had ever wanted to do that.

He'd found the window that now occupied most of the eastern wall of his living room rusting away underneath the stair to the office. When the wrecker's estate was settled, MacNeice purchased it for a hundred dollars, which, the wrecker's widow told him, would go to the local animal shelter, because "no animal should ever go hungry."

JUNE WAS GIVING WAY to summer, and the dappled light through the stand of trees outside was so intense it made the whole room dance as if it was the happiest place on earth.

MacNeice went to the kitchen, took out the grappa, poured a shot and took it back to the window. Through the trees he could see fragments of the deep blue lake in the far distance. He was aware of the birds, especially the swallows that came every spring to the birdhouses his father had built and mounted on the trees as a house-warming gift. But after the long night he found the light too much, and slowly he drew the drapes on the scene.

Grappa. Even the word was comforting to him. He'd first tasted it in Italy with Kate, but it was years before he tasted a smooth grappa like the one he now enjoyed just before bed or occasionally combined with espresso in the morning. Easing into the old club chair he'd rescued from the lobby of an abandoned theatre, he held the narrow shot glass to his right eye. The details of the room twisted into vertical streaks—tall Giacometti shafts. MacNeice emptied the glass and, letting his hand drop, allowed the heavy cylinder to swing gently between his fingers before putting it down on *Birds of North America* on the floor next to the chair.

He took out his cellphone and found Wallace's number. It rang three times before he heard a voice say crisply, "Deputy Chief Wallace."

"Good morning, sir, it's MacNeice."

"What can I do for you, Mac?"

"I am requesting the lead on a case I responded to last night—the young woman found dead in the cottage on Lake Charles."

"I'm just reading Swetsky's report. What's so special about this one?"

"I'm not sure, sir. I just think I have a feel for it." MacNeice wasn't sure that made a convincing argument but waited for a response, which came moments later.

"Swetsky thinks you do too. I'm fine with that." It sounded as if Wallace was outside, being buffeted by the morning breeze off the lake.

MACNEICE NEEDED TO SLEEP. He switched off his cellphone and put the glass in the sink on his way through to the master bedroom.

In the three years since Kate had died, he had yet to sign a truce with the place. The rest of the house and property held traces of her—the garden she had planted and he maintained, the dishes and assorted cutlery, the painting she'd bought at auction because it reminded her of the lavender fields in the south of France—but they all co-existed with him. The master bedroom, and especially the bed, had betrayed him—comfort and intimacy stripped from them both—and only when he was exhausted, like now, would he go there.

He opened the window by the bed so he could hear the birds calling as he fell asleep. Lying on his side, staring at the sky above the garden, MacNeice looked for patterns in the clouds going by. When he was eight, or maybe twenty, he'd imagined clouds as forms swimming in a superior sea while he, and everyone and everything he knew on earth, existed on the bottom of this ethereal ocean. He wondered how many people had fantasized in the same way about clouds.

As exhausted as he was, his eyes refused to close, and images of the girl back at the beach house seemed safer to him than everything he feared in sleep. Panic hit him—he'd left the camera in the car—and he bolted out of bed, reeling slightly from grappa and fatigue, and ricocheted out the bedroom door and down the hall. Grabbing his keys, he opened the front door to full-on sunshine and realized he was wearing only the

T-shirt he slept in. Ducking like a freshman sneaking out of the girls' dorm at dawn, he made his way to the passenger-side window—the camera wasn't there. Then he remembered that he'd dropped it beside his computer, and he rushed back inside, feeling foolish.

He went to the Mac and pushed the flat silver button, and in the promising blue light of the screen, took the firewire from the drawer. He loaded the images from the long night onto the computer, hit print, and then realized there were several still in the camera that he'd taken on a trip earlier in the year to visit Kate's mother, Jo, in Suffolk, and downloaded them too. He hadn't looked at them since, but he took the time now. He'd borrowed his mother-in-law's car to go off to Butley Low Road, where Kate had once taken him to see the colonnade of ancient beech trees that lined the road. The trunks bore scars dating back three hundred years, telling brief tales of love certainly, but also of the sea, of beautiful women and sailing ships, or just initials or the year. These were surface scratches, tattoos that didn't impede the health of the tree any more than the gouges on the sides of a whale appear to shorten its life. Each trunk, like a fingerprint, was unlike any other. The trees showed where people had passed, recording their passions and failures to be viewed from the safe vantage of years.

MacNeice knew about passing—it was part of the job—and though he had put away most of the evidence of Kate's passing, he knew on which shelf it lived. He'd made certain it was in a place he had no need to visit from day to day, so he wouldn't make the mistake of stumbling upon it while looking for something else.

The photo albums, bound by cloth and wire against decay, were gathering dust on top of the bookcase. Tucked into one was a legal-size creamy vinyl zipped envelope with FARNHAM FUNERAL HOME on it in gold letters, which contained all the formal words spoken at her service by friends and family—but not by him. The funeral director had handed it to him, saying, "Mr. MacNeice, you may not want to look at these now perhaps, but with God's help, I believe someday you will." *Not fucking likely* was what he'd wanted to say, but instead he'd simply thanked the man. If God or the vinyl envelope was calling, he could not, or would not, hear.

The mechanical wheezing of the printer—four tiny jets of ink painting pictures of a snapshot—stopped. Its miniature wheels kept spinning for a moment, cleaning the heads, and then it was silent.

FOUR

—

WHEN MACNEICE AWOKE, twilight was coming on. Shreds of cirrus clouds edged in burnt orange were racing across the sky. He recalled loading the images from the scene onto the computer but not actually seeing them, and he couldn't remember falling asleep. Closing his eyes again, however, he could see the one photo he hadn't taken—a beautiful woman's hand suspended above the arm of a Seabreeze. He threw off the duvet and swung himself around to sit on the side of the bed.

The clock radio read 9:30 p.m.—Swetsky would already be back on the job. He hated that he'd slept through his entire shift.

By 10:21 MacNeice was in the car on Mountain Road, feeling strange to be dressed for work and heading to the morgue. He turned on the radio and put out a call for Swetsky. Several minutes later the big, brusque detective barked, "MacNeice, are you cruising for my job or what?"

"No, Swets, I just thought I'd come out and see what the nightlife is like. How far have we gotten with this?"

"It was like you said—the place had been swept before we got there. Not a speck of dust on any of the surfaces in the kitchen, bedroom, living room or toilet. A cleaning rag under the sink was still damp. There was a small pool of water in the kitchen sink—the taps aren't leaky, so something had been poured into it. The nerds found patterns on the floor consistent with a vacuum cleaner, but the vacuum cleaner was missing. It pissed them off that we'd been walking around 'naked'—that's a quote."

"Yes, well, that was a mistake. Tell you the truth, Swets, I didn't think of that till I was down on the beach. . . . What else?"

"We're pulling up the plumbing as I'm talking to you. Also, up the road about sixty yards, in the bush, Williams found a broken Champagne bottle. Several feet away were two shattered long-stem glasses—I think a sophisticated guy like you calls them flutes. They're with Forensics now. Oh, and apparently there was a drop or two of bubbly left in the bottom of the bottle."

"Anything more on the girl?"

"Not yet."

"Betty find out what I asked her?"

"Dunno. Whadya ask her?"

"To dig up photos of the graduating classes or debut performances of young violinists."

"Nope, haven't heard anything. But I can tell you something interesting."

"What's that?"

"It looks like nobody, and I mean nobody, has ever lived in that cottage. There's very little shit in that tank."

"I don't know what to make of that."

"Me neither. The cottage is at least a few years old, wouldnya think?"

"Judging by the garden and the weathering of the breeze-way and balcony posts, yes, I would think. But remember the garage? Nothing had ever been parked in that space."

"I thought you didn't hear me say that, Mac."

"I always hear you."

"Yeah, anyways, where are you headed now?"

"I'm going over to see the pathologist."

"Surprised she's still there at this time of night."

"So was I. Said she'd hang in for me though. Is Forensics done yet?"

"They're still upstairs. No idea what they're doing. They're up there with their lights and gizmos and shit while we're down here opening up an empty crapper. Have you considered it might be suicide?"

"I'm certain it wasn't."

"How come?"

"For starters, a suicidal girl doesn't lie down on her purse. She doesn't arrange her body artfully over a record player and turn on the machine. And she doesn't float to the floor with-out leaving a footprint anywhere. I mean, she can't sweep the room after she's dead."

"Right."

"Call me if something breaks tonight. And I'll do the same for you tomorrow."

"I don't mind waking you up, you sleepless fucker, but when I get off here, the last thing I wanna hear is this shit. They don't pay us for 24/7. I'll hear soon enough."

"Later, Swets."

"Later, brother."

———

WALKING ALONG THE subterranean corridor from one pool of fluorescent light to the next, MacNeice felt slightly claustrophobic. The glossy white concrete walls and grey tiled floor that led to the autopsy room made for as unforgiving a space as any he knew. He tried deep breathing, but the more he thought about breathing the harder it was to breathe, and of course there was that awful resident smell that clung to the clothes and in the nostrils and hair of everyone who spent more than an hour in this place. He paused for a moment before pushing the stainless swinging door, pulling his sleeve down so he didn't have to touch it with his hand.

The pathologist's assistant, wearing calf-high rubber boots and an apron like a fishmonger's, was hosing down the tiled floor. He looked up at MacNeice, nodded slightly and directed the hose away from the entrance. The stainless table was clean, thank God, and the body on the gurney next to it was covered by an opaque white plastic sheet. The pathologist, Mary Richardson, a tall, slim British woman in her late forties, was writing something on her clipboard. After checking her watch and marking down the time, she glanced over at MacNeice.

"Is that the young woman from the beach house?"

"Yes, it is. I've had a first look. I'm just making some notes before we put her away for the night."

"How did she die?"

"A needle in the ear. It broke through the canal into her brain, filling her temporal lobe with acid," the assistant interrupted. He could never resist the gory details, and the pathologist took on a look of resigned familiarity—like a mother listening to her son being rude at the dinner table.

Wedging his squeegee handle into the valley of plastic sheeting between the girl's feet, he pointed to his left ear. "The needle was eighteen gauge and at least three and a half to four inches long. Whoever did it had to puncture the tympanic membrane"—he motioned with his index finger, a sharp jab that made MacNeice flinch. "That's poetic, I think. The killer took out her eardrum first. Then he had a choice: go down the Eustachian tube or up slightly to the cochlear organ. Either way he'd have to punch through bone to enter the skull. He took the Eustachian route." Again he jabbed at his ear, and this time his head recoiled as if it had taken a shot. "Once inside the temporal lobe, he squeezed the syringe, and the rest . . . Well, sulphuric acid's like shoving a hungry rat into a bucket of burger meat—the rat keeps right on eating."

"Junior, that's enough." Richardson looked over at MacNeice, who was paler than when he had arrived, then shot a stern glance at her assistant, who nodded several times, picked up the squeegee and returned to his cleaning.

"Jesus Christ," MacNeice said. "Sulphuric acid—you mean the same as in a car battery?"

"Exactly. Garden-variety battery acid," Richardson said. "The likelihood is she didn't feel a thing; she'd been knocked out with something. Hopefully we'll find some residue in the Champagne glass or the bottle—they're with the toxicologist. But there's something else. . . ."

"What else could there be?"

"The diameter of the needle would suggest a veterinarian more than a medical doctor, but he or she knew exactly where to insert it. Not one false start, no torn tissue other than along the track of the needle."

"Who do you think would know how to do that so pre-cisely, other than a doctor?"

"Certainly not a GP, and in truth, I don't believe a vet. Even very few neurosurgeons would know how to hit this target as precisely—there's no reason to go into a brain that way other than homicide. Whoever did this has had practice, and I'd start there. Check and see if anyone else has had a brain melted by acid."

"Why didn't I see any blood? Wouldn't it have come back out the ear canal?"

She reached over to a rolling table and picked up a small steel object, examining it over her glasses. "It's brilliant, in a sick way," she said. "This is, in effect, an earplug. If it had any other function I cannot imagine what that would be. Once we pulled it out—you wouldn't have been able to spot it, Mac, the way it was placed—the ooze started, like pulling a finger out of a very nasty hole in a dyke. It was a first for both of us."

She was looking in the direction of her assistant, who was now leaning on his long-handled squeegee. Both sides of his mouth were curved down, but his eyes were smiling—he enjoyed grossing out cops.

"If you'd opened her eyelids," the young man volunteered, "the whites of her eyes would have been slightly grey, but by the time we got her, they were black. This is some new terri-tory we've entered here."

The pathologist had lifted the plastic sheet and was look-ing down with disbelief and maybe even wonder. Fortunately for MacNeice, she'd only lifted it on her side. He had no inter-est in seeing what had happened to the girl since the cottage.

"But wouldn't the killer *have* to be a medical guy?"

"Not necessarily," she replied. "He—and I'm almost certain

it's a he, as I don't believe a woman would have the strength in her hand and arm to be so precise with the insertion—could be a watchmaker or a diamond cutter. This was precision work, and when I think about it, it doesn't strike me as medical. And more to the point, Mac, a doc would have dozens of ways to kill her—a needle up the nose to the brain, for instance. No, this was deliberately, diabolically elegant. The acid took out the temporal lobe, then it ate through the midbrain, and that took out the heart and pretty much everything else. The heart stopped pumping in seconds, but the acid just kept going. If you had arrived an hour or two later, the acid would have been on the outside as well. She would have dissolved before your eyes." Richardson lowered the sheet.

"Rats in a bucket. We've flushed most of the acid out, but it'll continue to eat away at her," the assistant said.

MacNeice couldn't bear to look at him. "Any idea of the kind of syringe?"

"Not yet," Richardson said, "but I can tell you the acid would have dissolved anything plastic, so it must have been glass or stainless steel. Secondly, the amount of acid injected is more than most syringes would hold, and he couldn't have changed cylinders easily without wriggling the shaft. The shaft went in, it stayed in and then it came out. One deft move—no hurry and no hesitation whatsoever."

"Is there any medical application for a syringe like that?"

"No. This was a custom instrument with no other use for human or animal. It's hard to believe the damage done. Even when she arrived here, she looked like she'd just fallen off to sleep."

MacNeice said, "That was the plan, I guess. Laying her on the floor, starting the record player, placing her hand just above the turntable—and he knows we're all playing our part now. It's theatre." He turned towards the door, determined to get away from the smells, the stainless steel, the lighting and the constant dripping of—what? He didn't want to know. But then he paused and turned back to her. "Why the temporal lobe? I mean, why would he take out the temporal lobe? Why not the heart?"

"I have no idea. The temporal lobe is key to phonological recognition—language, sound. The acid he injected would have quickly wiped out the cortex and everything above and below. She was already unconscious, so she wasn't going to scream. That's the riddle, Mac. There are six other orifices, all untouched."

MacNeice tilted his head slightly as if cradling a violin between his shoulder and chin. "This was the ear positioned just above the violin."

"Oh yes, Swetsky told me about the 'hickey'—very funny. Yes, I suspected this was a violin player."

"So this wasn't just about killing her," MacNeice said. "That much would have been easy. This was a message for someone still alive—that's why the bother. And the real pain for that person or persons will begin when we break the news. We're the messengers."

Mary Richardson offered him a slight, sad shrug.

MacNeice nodded and put his shoulder to the door.

A LIGHT RAIN WAS FALLING. Caught in the triangular spill of the parking lot floodlights it looked more like mist, an unnatural yellow-white at the top of the cone, fading to a silvery blue where it met him. MacNeice looked up and closed his eyes for a moment, letting the rain kiss his face. He needed to go home and pour a grappa, listen to some music and try to forget until morning that someone out there had a mind more twisted than any he'd yet encountered.

Somewhere a dog was barking, a series of short warnings to something or other.

FIVE

—

MacNeice knew the value of exercise and had kept his regimen going even as his wife was dying. It was somewhat shy of spectacular but well above the level of essential. At forty-five vanity was waning for him, but he had structural issues—a knee, a shoulder—that if ignored would mean pain and dysfunction, and the latter was too humiliating to contemplate. The next morning he was up with the sun and on the stationary bike for an hour, pushing it, focused on speed and tension and sweat and escaping the memories that kept grabbing at him.

He'd gone to a dinner a few nights earlier with Vic Tanaka, his old high school football teammate, who had taken it upon himself to represent the opinion of several of Mac's friends: it was time for him to move on, to try to leave the past behind.

MacNeice had suspected that a mission like that was the reason for the dinner, which was why he'd put away more than his share of two bottles of wine before the subject hit the table. Leaving things behind had worked whenever they'd had a bad game, but sitting in the back booth of Marcello's after a fine dinner, Mac went on the offensive. "I listened to Louis Armstrong and Ella Fitzgerald singing 'Stars Fell on Alabama' on the way over here. On the way home I'll probably listen to Miles Davis—hell, I may even listen to Ama-fuckin'-deus Mozart—and no one would tell me that I had to turn those dead fuckers off and listen to someone who's still alive. But when it comes to someone who meant the world to me, who meant something to you too, Vic, you think it's time that I should just leave her behind?"

It had taken him two days to calm down enough to call his friend to apologize—not that he really needed to. All he could say was, "I can't let her go. I don't know how."

But now he had a purpose. He needed to find out who had created a needle that could puncture tissue and bone and inject sulphuric acid into a girl's brain. He should have told Vic that nothing gives a man new purpose like catching a killer.

THE FIRST THING HE DID when he got to work was log on to his computer and Google "manufacturer precision instruments Dundurn." Six names appeared; one he recognized as the tool-and-die maker who'd testified as an expert witness in a case involving the gift of a custom-made handgun that had come apart in the owner's hand the first time he attempted to fire the weapon. The single-cartridge split barrel had exploded backwards, slicing through the man's cheek and tearing off the hard-shell hearing protectors—with his right ear inside them—before embedding itself in the firing-range wall, next to a poster that read SAFETY FIRST. UNLOAD AND LOCK YOUR WEAPON AWAY AT HOME.

Certain that, since his wife had hired the handgun's designer, the bolt had been intended to take off more than his ear, the man launched a civil suit against the gunsmith, a seventy-year-old Spaniard who insisted that the malfunction had occurred because the bolt had not been in the "lock and fire" position. Intrigued by the case, MacNeice had sat in on the tool-and-die maker's cross-examination. He had proved the Spaniard's assertion by rigging up the weapon in his own range. With the bolt locked, it fired perfectly. Unlocked, the rear end of the split barrel had disappeared into a six-foot Plexiglas cylinder full of rigid Styrofoam, captured from all angles by three separate video cameras. The charges were dropped and the wife of the scarred and earless gun collector sued for divorce the same day.

There were three other names, and two corporate entities that sounded too large to be creating syringes out of stainless steel. The Spaniard, who would now be in his eighties, wasn't listed. He called the expert, Donald Ferguson, first.

"Hello. Ferguson Engineering here."

"Mr. Ferguson?"

The refined English voice on the other end took his already cheerful greeting to a new level. "The very same, sir. How can I help you?"

"It's Detective Superintendent MacNeice. I watched you testify in a civil case involving a malfunctioning handgun some years ago. Do you remember the suit?"

"I remember it clearly. Miguel Figuero's fancy firing tool, the one with the split barrel. How can I help you?"

"If I can swing by this afternoon, say two p.m., I'd rather speak to you about it in person."

"Two is fine. I'll be in the shop out back of my house. It's 32 Glen Avenue."

"I'll see you at two."

MacNeice checked his watch—9:42 a.m.—and thought about another espresso. His passion for espresso had risen to a new level once he and Kate had moved to the gatehouse and the nearest decent espresso bar was miles away. The department had chipped in for a machine after Kate's death, as a way to show him they cared without having to say so. Swetsky had suggested that the real reason they had bought the machine was so they could keep him from disappearing for an hour just to get a coffee at Marcello's. It was Marcello himself who had arranged the purchase: "Buy Swiss—don't buy Italian. Trust me, I'm Italian."

The machine sat next to the regular coffee maker like a Ferrari parked next to a Dodge minivan. But other than MacNeice and Michael Vertesi, a second-generation Italian, and Fiza Aziz, the division's only homicide detective with a doctorate in criminology—and its only female—no one touched it. That was just fine with Mac; he'd taught both Michael and Fiza how to clean and backwash, how to grind and pack the coffee, what was great crema and what was burnt crema. Both of them loved coffee as much as he did.

He picked up the phone to retrieve his messages, the first of which was from Swetsky. "The owner of the cottage is out of the country golfing in Palm Springs. He's due to arrive home Sunday and no one at his office knows his exact whereabouts. So, short of doing the legwork to find him, that's all we've got at the moment."

The telephone rang a second after he hung up the receiver, the call display reading "DC Wallace."

"What can you tell me? I've got a press conference at ten thirty."

"Only that a young woman was murdered in a beach house up on Lake Charles and her identity has not been confirmed. Pathology and toxicology analysis are underway as to the exact cause of death. We are actively pursuing leads as to the identity and whereabouts of her killer or killers."

"Okay, and what can you tell me that I can't say out loud?"

"She was likely given a spiked glass of Champagne to knock her out, followed by a needle inserted in the left ear and an injection of battery acid directly into the brain."

"Christ almighty. What do you need?"

"I'm fine for now with Vertesi and Aziz. Swetsky's offered to pitch in when he can."

"Do you think this is someone who's likely to go for two?"

"I don't believe so. It was such a theatrical display of confidence, even arrogance, that I'm fairly certain there won't be another like it."

"You make it sound perfect."

"No, it was clean, but it wasn't perfect." Though MacNeice wasn't sure at the moment what the imperfection was, he was certain he'd find it.

"I hope you're right," Wallace said, and hung up.

The phone dead in his hand, MacNeice set the receiver back in the cradle. David Wallace was considered by both the city and the upper echelons of the force to be a serious and capable professional with no lack of ambition. While he likely knew that MacNeice had been offered the job of deputy chief just after he'd lost his wife and had declined, he'd never shown anything but respect for the older detective. This was due in part to the fact that MacNeice had the highest solve rate in the region for homicides. For his part, MacNeice considered Wallace to be a brilliant political strategist as well as a capable administrator. He respected his boss, and most of the time his boss left him alone to get on with things, which was what he needed.

MacNeice stared thoughtfully at the desks around him. The only thing he liked about the low partitions that had turned the squad room into a cubicle farm was that they could pivot. For more intense investigations he could swing them inwards and create a semi-enclosure. The power, Internet and phone cables all ran along a raceway underneath the raised floor; if you took your shoes off—as MacNeice often did—you could feel it vibrating very slightly with the constant hum of words and images being transmitted to and from the unit.

THE TWO YOUNGER detectives knew some of the details of the events at the lake, the most salacious involving injection of battery acid into the brain, and thought they knew why MacNeice had requested command of the case. When he got up out of his chair and came around the corner of his partition, both of them instinctively stood up. Vertesi, not wanting to appear that he was eavesdropping, picked up a file on his desk and flipped it open.

"We're on," MacNeice said. "Vertesi, grab one of the large whiteboards from storage and some black, red and blue markers."

When Vertesi had rolled in the whiteboard, MacNeice began his debriefing, handing each of them a set of images of the snapshot and the key. Then he took up a black marker and made top-line notes on the whiteboard of what he knew, then, with the red marker, all that he knew he didn't know. When he was finished, he sat down, saying, "It's not much, but it's a start. We should be getting Palmer and Williams's report from the neighbour interviews today, but I'm not optimistic for two reasons—"

"Because Palmer's a dick?" Vertesi often reached for a gag. Aziz and MacNeice usually ignored him unless it was really good, in which case they both cracked up. His Palmer shot was not good. "Sorry, sir. Two reasons?"

MacNeice began again. "It's a cottage screened from the road, spotless inside and out—not a grease stain on the garage floor, a scuff on the drywall, a worn bit of flooring, nothing. I'll be surprised if the neighbours have ever noticed anyone living there. Secondly, the other cottages are at least a hundred yards away on either side, with bush in between, and while sound carries near the lake—the guy who was out trolling had to be a mile away—this girl didn't scream; she just went to sleep. Though, I'll grant you, someone may've heard the Schubert."

"I'll find the landlord," Vertesi offered. He loved his work, but more than that, he loved that Swetsky hadn't taken the trouble to track down the owner, wherever he might be. "I'll also put out a feeler internationally to check for any similar killings, and I'll see what I can find out from Lock Tight about that key."

Aziz swung her chair back towards her desk. "I'll get onto the forensics team for their image bank and information about anything else they may have found. I'll also find out what Toxicology has on the contents of the Champagne glasses and bottle." Aziz was the only person in the unit who got respect from the forensics team. Vertesi was convinced it was because she had a better education than any of the propeller-heads in the lab.

"When is the pathologist's final report coming?" Vertesi asked.

"Tomorrow, but given that the brain was liquefied and there were no other signs of trauma on what was otherwise a very healthy young woman, probably the only thing we don't know yet is what the specific sedative was. Dr. Richardson was somewhat doubtful that Toxicology would be able to identify it precisely."

"If the glasses are connected to this and Toxicology can identify what was in them—other than bubbly—then we may have found the first imperfection," Aziz said.

"Possibly." MacNeice rolled the whiteboard off to the side of his desk. "But to toss the glasses into the bush, where we'd be sure to find them, could also be part of the plan. . . . I'm off to see Ferguson, the tool-and-die maker who made mincemeat of the malfunctioning-handgun civil suit several years ago."

Aziz looked at Mac hesitantly, then made a suggestion. "When you meet with Ferguson, ask him if he knows of any precision instrument freelancers who happen to be from the former Eastern Bloc."

MacNeice loved how Aziz's mind worked, how she was learning. It was as if she were leaping across a stream, landing on all the expected stones, then suddenly jumping to one not so obvious that gave her access to a shorter, surer route. "What makes you ask that, Fiza?"

Both Aziz and Vertesi were aware, perhaps more than MacNeice himself, that when he used their first names, it was a form of praise. Aziz smiled as she replied, "It just seems like something that would come from there. They developed a killing game of lethal subtlety during the Cold War, and skills like those don't disappear just because a wall comes down."

MacNeice picked up his notebook and jacket. "Aziz, when you're talking to Forensics, ask them for the designer label on that gown. Track down where it came from and find out whether the store clerk knows anything about the big night it was purchased for. I'll be off the radio, but you can reach me by phone or email on my cell."

On the way to the stairs, MacNeice heard Vertesi say quietly to Aziz, "'Lethal subtlety'? The Wall? You're a gen-i-us, Aziz, a freakin' gen-i-us."

"Why, Michael, my dear boy," Aziz replied, channelling the Queen, "you're too kind."

FIZA AZIZ AND MICHAEL VERTESI couldn't have been more different, and maybe that was the magic of it. Aziz had been born of Lebanese Muslim parents who had escaped the inferno of Beirut to move to the U.K. in the 1980s. Her father was a mechanical engineer and her mother, a professor of biology. Their families had lived for generations in Beirut, where Christians, Muslims and Jews rubbed shoulders to such an extent that their many differences seemed to have worn away. Her parents were shocked when their world of peaceful co-existence dissolved, seemingly overnight.

Fiza had been eleven when her family emigrated to North America so her mother could accept a senior post at Queen's University. By September 2006 Aziz had earned her doctorate and, with her parents' support, she entered the police academy's officer training course as its only female devout—as far as anyone knew—Muslim.

What sustained her, MacNeice imagined, was her sense of humour, which he took to be British. But there was something else about her, a quality he found both rare and fascinating.

She was elegant even in cop clothes. Though her demeanour was somewhat distant, the smile that had briefly lit her face just now was a moment of surfacing beauty.

As remarkable as Aziz's journey had been, it wasn't pre-ordained that Michael Vertesi would become a cop either—far from it. His father was a Sicilian who had come to North America as a child after the war. Michael had been born about two miles from Division but still considered himself to be Sicilian. He had run with a tough crowd as a teenager, one that saw three of his best friends incarcerated before they were nineteen. Vertesi was saved from a similar fate only by excelling at football.

MacNeice remembered the time another second-generation Italian had arrived in the department and Michael had asked him where he was from. The sleepy-eyed young officer had smiled and answered, "Napoli. Where are you from?"

"Head office, Calabria." Michael had shaken his hand, but neither man was smiling.

When MacNeice asked him later about the remark, Michael said, "Calabria, the toe of the boot, home of the families. I'm the only cop there's ever been in my family. My pop loves that."

Slightly younger than Aziz, he had joined the force at the same time. Michael had been with the department for six years and had distinguished himself not only as a uniformed officer but also as a student of officer-training courses with a focus on homicide investigation. His application for promotion to detective had come with a request: "If I'm chosen, I'd like to work with MacNeice."

MacNeice took lunch alone in the bar of a restaurant down the street from the division office. The television was on but he paid no attention to it until the local news program cut away to Wallace's press conference.

"Please turn it up a bit, just for this."

"Sure thing." The bartender aimed the remote at the screen hanging behind him.

MacNeice put his fork down and listened as Wallace made his scripted announcement. It was more or less precisely what MacNeice had given him during his call, but he added, "Our department is following several leads at the moment and we hope to make an announcement soon."

MacNeice winced. He hated overpromises, particularly when they involved him. The reporters pressed the deputy chief for more details but Wallace deflected their questions easily and ended the press conference. The network already had cameras at the beach house but they were being kept at a distance; they could capture only the roof and part of the garage through the trees. He looked at his watch—1:32 p.m. He pushed the rest of his salad aside, paid his bill and walked out into the sun, heading to the parking lot behind the division.

As he turned onto South Shore Drive, something snagged him like a hangnail on a sweater. The spotless garage, as far as he could tell, had never seen a car, but at the beach, always changing, traffic could be coming and going and you'd never know. The thought that sent a chill through him, causing him to pull over to reach for his cellphone, was the boat—the trolling fisherman.

"Vertesi, get over to the beach house. Check the shoreline for any hull marks in the sand that would indicate a boat—maybe a sixteen- or eighteen-foot runabout—being pulled up on shore."

"You thinking about the troller, Mac?"

"That and about how the girl got to the beach house. Go to every cottage around the lake and find out if anyone was out fishing in the early hours of the morning or if they saw anyone on the lake. There are two marinas nearby; see if either of them rented a boat to someone. And ask Aziz to give me a call."

MacNeice just had time to open his notebook before his cell rang. "Aziz, I'm about twenty minutes away from Ferguson and I haven't spoken to Betty yet. Please see what she's got."

"Okay. Vertesi just shot out of here—is this something to do with that?"

"He's gone to see a guy about a boat. What if someone took her on a boat ride? A bottle of Champagne, two flutes, a moonlit lake in June . . ."

"After I call Betty, I'll get down to Forensics and see if there's any sand, grass or marks on that gown or on her shoes. Of course, if it was really romantic, he might have carried her to and from the boat."

"Or if she was asleep. I checked her shoes at the scene and didn't see any sand, but they may have found something."

"Right."

MacNeice pulled into Ferguson Engineering, parking next to a fading burgundy Jaguar with a small plate on the back that read RIGHT-HAND DRIVE. As he paused for a moment, peering inside to admire its worn tan leather seats, he heard Ferguson's chipper voice. "It was my father's pride and joy. When he died, twenty years ago now, he left it to me. It sat in a rented garage in Pelham until I had enough money to bring it over."

"It's a beauty. It truly is."

"Yes, it is, but it's a heavy responsibility too. The electrics particularly, but I've rewired everything from stem to stern and I can't complain about her now. It's good to see you again, Detective MacNeice. Come back into the shop, where we can chat. The kettle's on—would you join me for a cup of tea?"

"I'd like that."

They walked by the kitchen window of the house, where a woman appeared to be washing vegetables. Ferguson nodded towards her and said, "The missus. We won't disturb her, though; she's preparing dinner for the grandchildren. I think I actually make better tea in the shop."

MacNeice met the eyes of the woman in the window and nodded to her. He followed Ferguson to a garage that he'd doubled in length and skylit so that inside it seemed almost brighter than outdoors. A desk, several filing cabinets and a bookshelf were next to a window that looked out onto the garden. The window was a security marvel, likely made of Lucite and trimmed with security tape.

He took his seat opposite Ferguson's chair and used the time while Ferguson was making tea to check out the other security measures. The skylights were rimmed with the same silver tape, and at several points along the walls infrared sensors were mounted that when activated would crisscross the workshop's interior.

"Milk? Sugar?"

"Only milk, thanks."

"You're wondering, no doubt, why all this security? And there's more than what meets the eye too." Ferguson handed him a cup and sat down.

"I was actually wondering what there is to steal."

"Ideas. Ideas are worth more than the equipment I have in

here. I enjoy the reputation I have with my neighbours—as old Donny who likes to putter around in his tool shop—but there are others who'd love to have a go at this place. What brings you here today?"

MacNeice took the snapshot of the girl on the beach out of his notebook and handed it across the desk. "Late Wednesday night or early Thursday morning, this young woman was killed by someone with a hypodermic. The needle was inserted in her left ear and pushed through the canal into her brain. Then the killer injected sulphuric acid. When I arrived, there was no indication of any trauma to the body, and only a faint acrid smell to indicate that anything had happened to her."

"For the love of God." Ferguson put the photograph down, staring at it a moment longer before looking up at him.

"It would take skill to do that, and a precision instrument. No plastics, and no small-gauge needle either, given the density of the acid."

"The needle was eighteen gauge, I'm told. What I'd dearly love to know is what it was made of, and where in the world—or rather, who in the world could make it."

Ferguson moved his teacup to one side of his green desk pad and took out several sheets of tracing paper, retrieving a mechanical pencil from a cup where it was nestled among pencils and pens of different shapes and sizes. He inserted a graphite lead and began rotating it in a small sharpener as he looked out the window. "Here's the problem: The acid, as you can imagine, will eat away anything that isn't steel, so stainless steel was likely used. The shaft must be long enough not only to hold the acid but also to allow him—we'll assume it's a male—leverage for the task of plunging it into the brain. Given the average male hand, the shaft would need to be four or five inches long."

He was now drawing as if he were at a seance producing names on a Ouija board—shaft, plunger, needle. "The interesting thing about the vial, or canister, is how he'd seal it. After it's sealed it's much easier to imagine puncturing for the kill, so to speak, but filling it—I think he'd have to do that on the spot. Your other question, about who could have made it, is also interesting."

"Could the fabricator be someone from Eastern Europe?"

"You're imagining the remnants of the KGB, the chaps who offed the fellow in London with the poison-tipped umbrella. . . . Yes, I'd say that's a possibility." He kept refining his drawing, giving the device form and shading, even marking the dimensions. "And finally, since there were no outward signs of violence, he'd have to allow for, you know, filling the hole once the job was done." Ferguson looked up at MacNeice.

"He did. There was a small metal plug made of stainless steel."

"It would only be a stopgap, of course, because the acid would eventually erode everything around it." Ferguson was now drawing a plug that looked vaguely like the one MacNeice had seen.

"It was more like a nipple than a cone."

"I see. Well, yes, with some force and speed, I can see that might do the trick. But back to the whodunnit. The former Soviet Union had several people who could pull this off, but they've either scattered to the winds or remained in the employ of their various governments and are likely still active over there." He put his pencil down and looked up at MacNeice again. "I can do this for you: I'll enquire with friends abroad, and through a nephew I have in MI6, about who is active and where. It may not produce results, and certainly won't overnight. One other thing I know—or believe I do—is the quality of the metal and who might supply it, so I'll make some discreet enquiries there. Until then, you're welcome to my sketch." He began rolling up the drawing.

MacNeice picked up a pencil and scribbled down his number on a scrap of paper. "Here's my cell. Call whenever you get something." He drained his cup and took the rolled-up drawing from Ferguson. As he stood up, he said, "Damn fine tea, Donald. Thank you."

"I'll tell my wife you said so—she thinks I make terrible tea. But when I mention your last name, I'm certain she'll say, 'A Scot. What does a Scotsman know about tea?' She can be prickly, my girl. Funny thing is, she's from Edinburgh." With that he laughed heartily, and together they walked down the driveway to the car.

STOPPED AT A TRAFFIC LIGHT, MacNeice checked the time on his cellphone—3:37 p.m. He speed-dialled the office. "Aziz, have you got anything for me?"

"How far away are you?"

"Seventeen minutes, maybe a bit less. Why?"

"Let's not talk over your cell. Come as quickly as you can. It's all good."

He drove with the lights, which were timed to keep traffic flowing east along Main Street—one of the more intelligent initiatives brought forward by the city's engineers—and arrived in sixteen minutes. He walked briskly to the stairwell, inhaled deeply and bolted up the staircase two steps at a time, almost bursting through the second-floor door. He checked his watch:

twenty steps in seven seconds. He exhaled and walked to the cubicle where Aziz was waiting for him, smiling.

"Betty came through," she said. "Lydia Petrescu, twenty-four, just graduated from the professional program of the Conservatory. Her father is Antonin Petrescu. He deals in European rare papers—diaries and letters mostly—and fine antiques in the Biedermeier style. There's apparently more about his shop on the Web, but Betty did all she had time for. I was going to get onto it but I haven't had a chance yet."

"I assume we haven't had any missing-person calls for a Lydia Petrescu?"

"I checked—not yet. I did look up the number of Petrescu's shop and called it from the payphone downstairs so he wouldn't pick up a caller ID, but I got a recording—a male voice— 'Petrescu. Leave a message if you wish.' In the background was a violin playing something lovely. I rang off."

"If she were my kid I'd be using her for phone messages too."

"But there's more. The nerd in Forensics who checked the dress for me said it was a rental. When I asked how he knew, he said, 'It says so. *Oscar de la Renta*.' When I asked him what he meant, he said, 'Like, *Oscar of the Rental*,' as if it should be obvious to anyone with a modicum of language skills."

MacNeice appreciated the humour. "A designer label. That's got to be what, a few thousand?"

"Well, I haven't had the pleasure personally, but I'd be surprised if it cost less than five or six thousand."

"At least she graduated in style. Anything else?"

"You were right, there was no sand on the shoes. But they found a very small smear of something silvery on the dress around hip level. That's with Toxicology now, but they think it could be bait."

"Bait?"

"Yes, like fish bait. The little fish you use to catch big—"

"Funny, Aziz. Yes, I get it—bait. From the seat of the boat."

"And last of all, there's this." Aziz sat down and woke up her computer screen, which revealed a photograph of a flower showing leaves and a partial stem. "Valerian."

"The stuff you use to go to sleep—if you don't use grappa."

"The very same, but the flutes revealed a strain of valerian stronger than anything you'd find in North America, but still not strong enough to knock her out. There was something else in there that they haven't identified, which, it appears, acted as an agent to fuse the Champagne and the valerian into something much more potent. They think she wouldn't have detected it because it wasn't dissolved in the Champagne; it was in a transparent coating on both flutes. The bottle was clean."

"Both flutes?"

"Yes."

Aziz looked up at MacNeice to confirm that the same switches had been thrown for him as for her.

"Eastern European," MacNeice said softly.

"All the way, in my opinion." Aziz printed out the valerian image and took it to the whiteboard. When she'd finished taping it up, MacNeice handed her the tracing and said, "While you're at it, you can put this up too."

She unrolled it and looked at the sketch and then back at MacNeice.

"Ferguson drew it for me over tea. He's more or less certain the device we're looking for will be similar. He says he doesn't know anyone who could do it but he does know people who might know. And keep this one close. Ferguson won't want his involvement getting out."

"Does he agree with the theory, though?"

"He does, which is probably why he doesn't want anyone to know he's involved." MacNeice sat down on the edge of Vertesi's desk. "Have you heard anything from Vertesi?"

"No. He was going to call after he checked the beach."

"Last question, Aziz: Petrescu—that's Romanian, isn't it?"

"I believe so, but I'll confirm that. And Property Records have promised to get us his home address within the next two hours."

"If they do, we'll go tonight. It's hard to imagine Lydia Petrescu not being missed by someone."

"They said their server was down and the technician has to come in from Toronto, but that he was on his way. I'll let you know."

"Romanian. Eastern European."

"Before you go, I found out who at the Conservatory is responsible for the graduation ceremonies. Apparently there was a graduating class performance schedule with a list of invitees. I tried to call but the office is closed. It's on my to-do list for the morning."

SIX

—

VERTESI ARRIVED AT THE beach house at 3:10 p.m.
The patrol car and the abundance of yellow tape
stretched across the driveway made it easy to find.
Parking behind the cruiser, he took his digital camera and notebook from the glove compartment. As he was closing the door
of the grey Chevy, he heard the power window up ahead whir
down and then the familiar voice of Peter Stankovics. "*Ciao,*
Vertesi. *Come sta?*"

"Hey, Stinky, how'd you pull this one?"

"I'm in the shithouse for using excessive force two months
ago with Danny Roberts. You remember him?"

"Yeah, mangia-cake. Always talkin' a better game than he
played."

"The very same. He punched his old lady in the face, broke
her nose. One of the kids called the cops, and I had to be the
first fucker through the door."

"I remember now. You and him had a thing for Beth Kemp, that English girl who came in our last year at Central High. You put Atom Balm in his jockstrap just before a game. What a fuckin' great moment in sport that was."

"And now he sucker-punches me right there on Barton Avenue. I took a lot of abuse getting him into the cruiser. I had Lucy Tomassi with me—she was ready to pop him—but the real shit began when we got to the station."

On the seat next to Stankovics was a half-empty box of mini-doughnuts and two extra-large coffee cups, one empty and lying on his daily report binder. His radio barked to life with a flow of static, and he reached over and turned it off before continuing.

"Lucy's opening the door to the station. I'm pulling Danny out of the car—he's all 'fuck you, you piece of shit'—when suddenly he spits at me. Catches me right on the cheek." He put his meaty paw on the spot where it had happened, as if nursing a bruise. "A big phlegmy goober, right here."

Vertesi's face screwed up at the thought of it.

"Exactly!" said Stankovics. "So I head-butted him and split his nose wide open. Apparently I said something like, 'You've always been a snotty piece of shit, Roberts, but that should help your head cold.' Anyway, I shove him, all bloodied up, through the door, and I look up and the shift sergeant's standing there with a slice of pizza and a Coke. He saw the whole thing."

"Is the cake suing?"

"No. Apparently his wife gets wind of this and says to him, 'I'll drop the assault charge against you if you drop yours against Stinky.' It was a classy thing to do, even if it doesn't help her in the long run, but the sergeant put me on a three-month rotation of shit details anyway. I got five weeks to go. Luce has been amazing, though. She's been getting guys to swing by with doughnuts and caffeine, so I'm set."

"What's happening here, anything?"

"Forensics guys just left, media vans were here earlier, but other than that, nothin'."

"Anyone been down to the beach lookin' around?"

"Nope. We restricted the news teams to the road above. I've been taking my leaks in the bushes, but the whole area seems quiet. You goin' in?"

"No, just want to see the beach."

"Well, you came at a good time. Shit, you could strip off and take a swim with the weather up here. Been tempted to myself, but I'd probably come out and find the sergeant standin' there with my uniform."

"Stink, I'll catch you later."

VERTESI CLIMBED OVER THE TAPE and walked through the breezeway to the deck. He turned to look inside the cottage; everything was just as MacNeice had described it, except of course that the girl and the Seabreeze were gone.

The call of a gull pulled his attention back to the beach and the lake. For a moment he couldn't help imagining himself as the owner, surveying all that's lovely about the world. Then he snapped out of it; this would never be the life he'd have. Looking to the left, he could see the leading edge of the neighbouring cottage; to the right was a dock with a small, red-hulled sailboat moored at the end. "Beautiful. Like he said, a hundred yards in either direction."

He sat on the bottom step, untied his shoes, took his socks off and rolled up his pant legs. He folded the socks, put them in the shoes and set them on the step. Retrieving his camera and notebook from his pocket, he took off his jacket and folded it neatly, then set it on the shoes and placed his notebook on top. Picking up a branch that had fallen from one of the birch trees, he stepped over the yellow tape and walked towards the water. The grass was cool under his feet, and the transition to warm sand made him pause for a moment, then shimmy his feet deeper into the sand.

The surface of the lake was almost still; the water lapped half-heartedly at the shore as if it had to keep up appearances. Vertesi walked slowly along the dry sand just above the waterline. He could see the bottom: a shoulder of hard sand that ran the length of the beachfront, extending a few feet into the lake before dropping off a couple of feet or more. He could see the silver slivers of minnows darting about in the deeper water. "What one thing . . . ?" he said to himself as he looked back at the cottage nestled cosily among the trees.

He thought about the boat, about how, if you were going to land it in order to carry someone to the cottage, you'd likely choose your spot so it was more or less in line with the stairs. He walked to the point opposite the bottom of the steps. Squatting down, he peered beneath the surface. Sure enough, there was a groove in the sandbar; it had been softened by the wavelets but was still a distinct V. He drove the stick into the sand just beyond the waterline to mark the spot. He took the camera out of his pocket and framed several shots of the V, checking each time to make sure it registered. It did, but because of the glare off the surface, only faintly. He rolled his pant legs above his knees and waded into the water several feet beyond the groove. "Fucking freezing," he muttered. With the sun at his back he framed several more shots; the V was now more apparent.

Vertesi looked down at his feet in the water, all greeny blue, the minnows racing around him. He was losing the feeling in his toes. He waded a few yards over, parallel to the shore, then came out of the water. Up and down the beach in either direction there was no sign of life, and other than a sail going by on the horizon, there was no sign of life on the water. He thought it weird, but then, considering it was a weekday in the middle of June, maybe not.

He sat on the stairs to let his feet dry and made his notes— all of his observations and random thoughts, just as MacNeice had taught him—before wiping the sand off his feet, putting his socks and shoes on and climbing the stairs. Stankovics was dozing at the wheel of the patrol car. *Too many doughnuts*, Vertesi thought to himself, as he got in the car and drove off towards the next cottage down the lake.

SEVEN

—

DRIVING ALONG KING, which ran west parallel to Main, MacNeice thought about the statement that this killing made. In an age of bombs, assault rifles, IEDs and an endless variety of automatic pistols, who'd go to the trouble of creating a syringe and then use something as crude as battery acid to erase someone's brain . . . and why? That was it, he realized. Lydia Petrescu had been erased, just like wiping out a computer's hard drive—the shell still intact but the device empty and useless. Who was this message intended for?

He'd spent the rest of the afternoon fielding telephone calls, the first of which was from DC Wallace, wanting to know if there was anything new to report. He told him about the tentative identification of Lydia Petrescu and about her father and the weapon. Following that conversation, his phone began ringing with requests from the media for interviews. He could hear

in the reporters' voices the familiar frenzy that always surrounded a homicide, but he reminded them that Deputy Chief
Wallace was the media contact; he had no information to report
beyond what they'd been given by his senior officer.

Slipping the Chevy into the spot reserved for Marcello's
father behind his old friend's restaurant, MacNeice looked at
the time on the dash—6:23 p.m. He turned off the ignition but
left the switch on Auxiliary, as he needed to decompress before
he ate. He reached over to the glove compartment and took
out the wallet of CDs, flipping through till he found *Lush Life*.
Slipping the CD into the player, he put the case back in the
glove compartment; as he did so he remembered the cummings.
He lifted the place-marker ribbon and opened the book to the
page he knew was waiting like an old friend, or a pusher of
pain—over time it had been both. He looked down and spoke
the words that greeted him there: "I carry your heart, I carry
it in my heart."

No one could remove Kate from him, no one could erase
her. Lydia Petrescu had undoubtedly left memories with her
family as well as the voice-mail message with her playing in
the background, but something made his insides ache at the
thought of her being erased from within in an instant. The
idea that the attack had obliterated her talent—the thing that
he imagined she loved doing most of all—seemed the point of
her death. She was beautiful, but the killer hadn't splashed
her face with battery acid, hadn't taken away her physical
beauty. Instead he'd taken the thing that gave her life meaning, then laid her out as if the crime scene were a shoot for a
fashion magazine.

Realizing how miserable he was becoming, sitting in a parking lot with Strayhorn's phantoms playing in his ears and a

poem he knew by heart in his hands, MacNeice closed the book, put it back in the glove compartment, turned off the CD, grabbed his keys and went inside.

Marcello's back door, available to staff, family and only a few friends, led straight into the kitchen, where his wife, Chris, was the chef. Amid the clattering of dishes and the hum of exhaust fans, the happy chatter, laughter and occasional singing, MacNeice always felt at home. Usually as he passed through, Chris would tell him what to order and remind him that if he didn't like it, he should just send it back and she'd make something else. This last was always delivered with a smile; for the decade that Chris had been feeding him, MacNeice had never sent anything back.

As he eased onto his stool at the bar, Marcello himself, a pocket-bull of a man with a ready grin and an endless supply of jokes, wandered over, looking somewhat conspiratorial. "I've got something new for you," he said. "Chamomile grappa." Seeing MacNeice's eyebrows rise, he added, "Trust me, it wakes you up before it puts you to sleep." Then he cracked up, slapped MacNeice on the shoulder and turned towards the shelf for the bottle.

It was perhaps the smoothest and certainly the sweetest grappa he'd ever had. Before he could say anything his eyes had not already expressed, Marcello whispered, "I've got two bottles for you. Give me your keys and I'll put them in your trunk."

"You read my mind, March. *Grazie.* Put it on my bill."

"You got it. Sparkling water, and I've got a nice Shiraz."

"Sounds perfect."

Before he turned away to pour the drinks, Marcello put the daily paper in front of him. MacNeice scanned the front page without interest before pushing it aside and looking up at the television, where a hockey game was in progress.

"A rerun from last week," Marcello said. "Tonight, though, the Leafs play Chicago. That's always a great game."

Marcello and his father both loved hockey. Before he got married, March had been a decent goalie. The position of the television, high up and angled towards the espresso machine, made it a bit difficult for anyone but the bartender to watch it without getting a stiff neck. MacNeice's bar stool afforded the next best view in the house.

Neither of them took his eyes off the screen, but MacNeice had already begun to drift back to Lydia, or more specifically, to her father. While he was obliged to inform him of his daughter's death as quickly as possible, MacNeice decided that he and Aziz would not pay the man a visit until the morning. Apart from Betty's identification, which could not be considered irrefutable, the girl's identity was officially still a mystery. Things would be better for everyone if it was done in the morning.

A bell sounded in the kitchen and one of Marcello's cadre of beautiful, bright young wait staff went to retrieve his first course, *zuppa di pesce*. Placing it in front of MacNeice with flirty efficiency, she asked, "Pepper, Mac?"

"Does it want it?"

The waitress and he both looked to Marcello, who drew down the sides of his mouth in consideration. "Naw, not this one. Go without."

As MacNeice was finishing the soup, his cell rang. It was Vertesi. "Well, sir, nobody knows the guy who owns the cottage. . . ." Vertesi paused, maybe because of the music, the background noise of the place, or maybe it was MacNeice's greeting, a kind of throaty "mm-huh."

"You're at Marcello's. Cool—say *ciao* to him for me. Yeah, so they know the name of the doctor but nothing about him. And sorry, Mac, I didn't nail his whereabouts today as promised."

"No problem, Michael. I'd given you a lot to do."

"Well, here's the thing—I just got home and I'm downloading the images from my camera. They're not exactly *Time* magazine but you can clearly see a groove in the sand. I shot it every way from Sunday and marked it with a stick, but if the wind is up tomorrow it may all be gone."

"Not bad for a dark-horse theory. What did you find out about the troller?"

"That's the thing—no one heard the boat. And everyone I talked to said they'd look if they heard a boat out at night, 'cause I guess that's what they do. One did suggest that if the breeze was coming down the lake, like towards the scene, and apparently it was, there's a likelihood they wouldn't hear it at all if it was revving low for trolling."

"And the marinas?"

"The first had shut down for the night, but the guy who works on the motors at the second one was still there. He says he thought they did rent out a runabout, a cedar-strip job that he didn't see come back. When he walks me around to its berth, which is empty, he says, 'No way that was an overnighter, since it has no running lights on it at all.' He scratches his head and says, 'Some of the day trippers up here are city-stupid, though.' Even with a moon, the lake can be tricky at night—a lot of shoals and rocks. He figured maybe the guy ran aground and took off without letting them know.

"So then I'm walking to my car when he calls, 'Chief, check this out.' I go back to him and he points to a beat-up Dodge pickup. 'That's been sittin' here for two days. It must be the guy who rented the runabout. Can't think of anyone else who owns it.' And so I call in the plate and it turns out it's a guy I know—Ronnie Ruvola, a twenty-eight-year-old from the west end with a record ranging from B and E to dope dealing."

"Don't know him. Is he a serious player?"

"I don't think so, but I'll find out. I got the mechanic to take me to the marina's tuck shop and office. The owner, John Gibbs, wasn't there, but the mechanic pulls up the receipt from the credit card. The card says 'Robert Raymond Walters,' but he gives me a description that matches Ronnie. He also rented a tackle box and fishing pole and even added live bait to the credit card. Gibbs was apparently pissed because that boat had been rented for the following day to some day fisher. He had to upgrade him to a Boston Whaler. I've had the pickup taken in to the pound and I'll go back to interview Gibbs."

"A good day's work, Michael. Aziz and I have news too, but not to be discussed, as she says, over a cellphone. I'll see you in the morning."

Marcello came over, martini shaker in hand. "Anytime I see you on your cell here, I'm concerned. Everything okay?"

"The soup's terrific and, yes, all's well. Say, March, before the place gets into all that thumpa-thumpa stuff, can I hear 'Nun Ti Lassu'?"

"No problem. Chris'll love it too. But one of these days I'm gonna teach you that not all Sicilian songs are sad."

EIGHT

—

SATURDAY MORNING CAME EARLY at the lake. Tim Bookner and his four-year-old son Aidan were sitting on the rear deck of Tim's handsome twenty-four-foot Limestone, *Book's Boat*, designed for heavy weather on Georgian Bay. Anchored fore and aft, the boat bobbed gently in the breeze coming off Billings Island. Tim had been fishing on this lake since he was Aidan's age. He knew where the pickerel and bass were, and he was proud to be introducing his son to his heritage.

For the first half-hour Aidan ate animal crackers. When he was full, he threw one towards a gull that was hovering over the boat. The small cookie barely had time to hit the surface before the gull swept it up and banked high overhead before returning for more. Excited, Aidan pointed up at the bird, calling out in his high-pitched outside voice, "Dad, the bird just ate a lion! A *lion*!" Father and son howled with laughter, and they kept howling as one by one Aidan tossed up the remaining lions, monkeys, giraffes and elephants. In less than five minutes he'd fed half a box of safari wildlife to five gulls and was spent from laughing.

Though they both had lines overboard, Aidan was more interested in looking over the side, hoping to catch the moment when a fish would grab hold of his orange and yellow rubber wiggly. His life jacket was tethered to the rail surrounding the engine housing, so there was no chance he could fall over.

"There's someone looking at me, Dad." The boy was staring directly down.

His father turned slightly towards him and said, "Where?"

"Waving at me—down there, in the water." Aidan waved his small pink hand, hesitantly at first but then vigorously up and down, the way he did when he was glad to see someone.

"Maybe it's a mermaid. Does she have a fishy tail?" Tim kept his attention on the end of his rod, waiting for any movement that would indicate the big moment he was looking forward to—when he and Aidan would land tonight's dinner and return home triumphantly.

"No. His hair's like mine, only longer. Dad, he keeps waving at me."

"Maybe you're seeing your own reflection, like in your mirror at home."

"No, Dad. He's in a boat."

There followed a silence that made Tim uneasy. He looked over at his son, who was still waving, slowly now, hesitatingly, downward. Tim put his rod in the white vinyl tube and went to sit on the cushioned bench beside Aidan, who turned to his father and said, "See, Dad? See him there—he's waving at me."

Tim looked down. "Oh fuck! Sorry, son. Oh my fucking Christ—oh sorry, Aidan, sorry Daddy's swearing. Oh shit, oh shit!"

Tim covered his mouth, then grabbed at his hair. He quickly undid his son's tether, took Aidan by the arm and put him in the wheelhouse seat, snapping his shoulder and seat belts on. Aidan had no idea what was going on but was awestruck to see his father so excited by the man in the boat. Tim went back and leaned over the side again. "Oh fuck. Oh shit—sorry, Aidan, Daddy's bad language." He retrieved both rods and tucked them into the hull rails.

He turned the key with the happy-face float fob and the powerful Swedish diesel rumbled to life, sending two small clouds of black smoke out of the stern's twin exhaust pipes. Running forward, he pulled up the anchor and stowed it haphazardly on the deck. As the boat began to drift, he hauled up the stern anchor, laying it and its line across the blue vinyl bench. In the wheelhouse he threw the transmission into reverse and powered the craft backwards with such force that the water crested over the swimming deck at the stern. He spun the wheel hard to starboard and swung the boat around, shifting back to neutral, then dropped the red ball gearshift down. The bow lifted so dramatically that Aidan wasn't sure whether to be filled with fear or glee. He chose the latter and started squealing as if this was the best day of his life. The deep V of the hull settled down as the boat gathered speed, scattering the gulls that had been resting on the water as they digested their crackers.

Turning around for a moment to watch the white wake breaking the stillness of the lake, Tim picked up his radio microphone and called, "*Book's Boat* to Hangdog Marina." Clicking off, he waited, but only static came back. "*Book's Boat* to Hangdog. Come in, Hangdog."

"Hangdog. What's up, Tim? We're just getting started here. Over." It was Kathy Doolittle, who ran the tuck shop.

"There's a fucking awful problem out here, Kath. You need to get the marine unit on it right fucking now. Over." Tim dropped his speed to ten knots, but he couldn't drop his heart rate. Suddenly he thought, *What the fuck, I can hardly breathe. What if I have a fucking heart attack out here and I'm plowing ahead with Aidan wondering what the fuck!*

"Ah, Tim, don't be messing with me now. I've got Walter here and I don't want any guff—or foul language—from you. Over."

"No guff, for chrissakes, Kath! Walter, get a unit out here— just off the leeside near the end of Billings Island. Look down, twenty feet. There's a guy in a fuckin' boat! Over." Looking over to his son he mouthed another apology for the swearing. The boy had never heard these words before, so the apology was somewhat lost on him.

"You mean on the bottom? Over."

"I mean he's lying in a cedar-strip, one of Gibbs's, I think. It's got a tank, a freakin' motor—and this guy. He's waving his right arm, waving! Over." Tim slowed to six knots.

"Walter here. I've radioed the marine unit, but you'd better not be messing around, Tim. This is some serious shit. They'll charge you and me with mischief and I could lose my licence. Over."

"Do me a favour, Walt. Call my wife, tell her we're coming in. Ask her if her mother could come over this afternoon and take Aidan to the movies. Over."

Hearing this confirmed it—Aidan *was* having the best day of his life. He began his happy chant: "Oh yay, oh yay, oh yay."

———

"HANGDOG TO *Book's Boat*. Over." It was Walter again, sounding more sober than Tim had ever heard him.

"It's me, Walter. Over."

"Well, there'll be a uniform waiting for you when you dock. I let your wife know. She wanted to know what was wrong. I didn't say. She's on her way over too. Over."

"I'm fine with that, Walter. See you soon. Ask Kath to grab an Eskimo Pie out of the freezer for Aidan. Actually, I'll take one too. Oh, and last thing, maybe call Old Man Gibbs and ask him if he's missing a runabout. Over."

"Roger that, Book. Over and out."

The marina's slips were coming into view on the port side. Tim looked back but could no longer see the island, and he began to breathe easier. He reached over and tousled his son's hair just to hear the practised big-boy response, "Dad . . . stop!"

Aidan couldn't believe his luck. Usually he had to beg for an Eskimo Pie. "Did you ask Mr. Doolittle for Eskimo Pies?"

"Yep. After all, we've run out of animal crackers." As Tim reduced his speed for the no-wake zone, they both focused on the marina directly ahead, for different reasons.

"USUALLY WITH A FLOATER, they float." His thermal diving suit rolled down to the waist, the burly young firefighter from the marine unit showed no sign of being impressed, either by the orange body bag being lifted out of the large idling aluminum-hulled cruiser or by the cedar-strip runabout that swung gently from the cantilevered arm above the stern deck.

"This guy was tethered, and not just by the neck to the motor lock. His feet were tied to the oarlocks. I can't tell you whether he drowned or was strangled, but when that ten-inch hole got punched in the bottom, that boat just floated down with him in it. As for the waving that freaked out the dad, that was caused by the current coming around the island. His other arm was pinned behind him by the gas hose, or it would have been waving too." He made a crazy stop-the-train, two-arm wave to mimic what Tim and Aidan Bookner might have seen had both arms been free.

"It pretty much did the same for the diver who went down first. He's in the cabin forward, sucking up ginger ale and trying not to puke." He motioned with his head to the bag being laid on a rolling stretcher by the paramedics. "That guy had his eyes open, looking up and waving."

Vertesi closed his notebook and climbed onboard, steadied by the firefighter's grip on his arm. He walked aft and stood directly under the cedar hull. Just off the left side of the beam in the centre of the boat was a neat hole with blue sky showing through. It wasn't a bashed-out "oh shit, we hit a rock" hole but looked as if it had been cut by a very large drill.

"What do you think made that hole?" He turned to the firefighter standing beside him, hands on his neoprene hips, squinting as he looked up at the underside of the boat.

"No fuckin' idea, pal. But it wasn't anything out there." He nodded in the direction of the lake, as if lifting his massive arm would take too much effort. They both looked up at the hole again. "You see, it went right down through the floorboards." He pointed to the edges of the hole. "The only thing I know that could do that is a circular jig, but I've never seen one that big—other than the ones they use for ice fishing, and I've never seen one of 'em for real, only on the fishing channel."

"How can I get up there to take a picture of the edges of the cut?" Vertesi was looking around the deck and saw there was nothing to stand on. "Can you bring it down a few feet?"

"No can do. The marine cops over there can do that, but I can't. Not even for a cop." He smiled. Seeing that Vertesi was still looking for a way to get up there and that the method he'd likely choose would be to stand on the rail in his loafers, the firefighter said, "Get your camera ready, pal."

Within seconds he had grabbed Vertesi below the knees and was lifting him straight up towards the hull. Vertesi struggled to hold his balance; though he could hear laughter and wise-cracks from the cops and paramedics onshore, he aimed his tiny camera and took several shots of the cut edges of the hole. He was close enough to see the interior ribs of the boat and to smell something stronger than cut cedar.

"Okay, that's enough." Vertesi tapped him on the shoulder and the firefighter let him down gently and stood up.

"Get what you wanted?" He smiled at Vertesi, who tried to relax his body enough to recapture his dignity.

"Yeah, and then some. Weird smells."

"Oh, for sure. The guy had been in there a day or so. He'd evacuated, he'd begun to rot, and that shit all smells—well, like shit."

With that the firefighter gave him a hand getting back on shore. Vertesi thanked him and made his way past the marine cops, who eyed him the way territorial animals do. One said as he went by, "Enjoy the ride, Detective?"

Vertesi stopped. "Yeah, actually I did. It's only ten in the morning and I've already been to the circus. Did you get any-thing from the guy who found him?"

"No, not really. We'll send you what we have, but basically he was just a dad out fishing with his kid."

"Was the kid freaked?"

"Anything but. I think he loved it. Apparently his father"—
he looked down at his notebook—"Tim Bookner, started swearing like a bastard and cranked up that Limestone so he came
howling around the head of the island, and the kid loved it—
the swearing and the going fast."

"But did he see anything else out there?"

"Nothin'. That's him over there in the white job—*Book's
Boat.* His wife got here just after we arrived, seriously pissed,
like he was the one who put the fucker down there. She
grabbed the kid and tore outta here spitting gravel as she
went. I'm thinking, *Hell, the fun never stops for this kid.* Dad
was here when they brought in the cedar-strip, but he's not
showing any signs of interest. I suspect he's had enough for
one day."

"You guys cool if I speak to him?"

"Be my guest, brother. He won't tell you much. He's probably scared shitless that he'll head home, get everything smoothed
over—like, 'Hey, babe, what a day that was'—and the kid sits
down to dinner and lights it up with a stream of 'fuck, fuck,
cocksucker.' Explain that, sailor."

VERTESI STEPPED DOWN ONTO THE floating dock and tried
to walk naturally on the slightly pitching deck.

"Tim Bookner?"

The young father was sitting on the stern bench, trying to
unravel a mess of fishing line caught in his reel.

"That your son's?"

"Actually, no. I got his in okay; this is mine. I was too
freaked and . . ." His voice trailed off and he turned his attention back to the reel.

"Mind if I come aboard?"

"No. Yeah, sure. Sorry, who are you?" Bookner stood up to meet him as he stepped onto the deck.

"Detective Inspector Michael Vertesi. I'm with Homicide in the city."

"I told the marine unit everything that happened, Officer—"

"Detective."

"Yes, well, there's nothing I can tell you that I haven't already said, and to be honest, I'm really confused myself."

"No doubt. You go out with your kid—what's his name?"

"Oh, Aidan. His name's Aidan. It's Irish. And you can call me Book—almost everybody does."

"Why?"

"Why what?"

"Why do they call you Book?"

"Well, besides its being my name, I'm an accountant."

"Right. . . . So you just want to go fishing with your kid, land a big one, and suddenly it's all gone to hell." Vertesi moved into the wheelhouse and looked into the cuddy cabin below. "Can you do overnights in this thing?"

"Sure, there's a head down there and the bed's fine if you don't mind the hum of mosquitoes all night."

"I do. Mind, I mean."

"Yeah, me too. Worse, my wife. She kept me up all night the one time we tried it. That burn in the decking underneath you was the result—a mosquito coil fell over and burned the fibreglass."

"Are you heading home now, Book?"

"No. I mean, I don't know why she blames me for this but she does, and I think I just need to let her chill out. You know what I mean?"

"I'm not married but I think I know."

"Yeah, well, it's great, really. But boy, around Aidan this is, like, freakin' unforgivable or something. Like he's going to be scarred for life."

"From what I've heard, he had a blast."

"I've been sitting here thinking exactly that. I was freaked, but Aidan—shit, he was laughing and waving his hands around like it was all fireworks and candyfloss."

The Limestone rocked slightly as a boat passed, coming into the marina. Vertesi held on to the wheelhouse door frame. "If you're up to it, I'd appreciate it if you could take me out there, to where you saw the guy in the boat."

"Seriously? Like, right now?"

"Well, yeah. You see, this guy may have had something to do with another death, Friday night, up the lake. I want to see just where this site is in relationship to that."

"Somebody else died on the water?"

"No, this was in a cottage. So what do you say, are you up for it? I'll understand if you're not, and maybe I can get the marine unit to take me out."

"Naw. No, this is perfect. I can tell my wife that I haven't just been sitting here untangling a fucking fishing line; I've been assisting a detective from the city. Do you want to go now?" He dropped the rod into its slot and let the knotted line dangle down beside it.

"Yes, now's a good time."

Tim Bookner pulled up his white shorts a bit and moved into the wheelhouse to turn on the engine compartment exhaust fan. He went to the stern and undid the mooring line, then asked Vertesi to unhitch the bowline. Within five minutes they were out of the no-wake zone and headed back to the far end of the lake where Bookner's morning had begun.

Vertesi held on tight to the roof of the wheelhouse. He was enjoying the wind through his hair and even the noise of the engine and the slight bounce, but every time Bookner corrected his course, the boat's sideways pitch made him uneasy. He was also aware that his jacket was flapping in the breeze, exposing his holster and service weapon. He wasn't sure why but he was embarrassed about it, but not embarrassed enough to let go of the frame long enough to button up his jacket.

When Bookner moved the throttle forward to glide into the area where he'd sighted the body, Vertesi hit his forehead on the edge of the wheelhouse roof. The moment the boat had stabilized, he ran his palm over the skin to see if there was blood. There wasn't.

"When we're exactly where you were early this morning, can you drop your anchors just as they were, more or less?"

"Sure thing."

Within a few minutes Bookner had cut the engine. Moving with great agility in the still rocking boat, he dropped the stern anchor and then scampered along to the bow, where he tossed the second anchor some distance away from the hull. He returned to the rear deck to stand next to Vertesi, hands on hips, looking fore and aft. "This is it. Well, pretty much exactly."

"You got binoculars, Book?"

"Sure do, Detective." He leaned over the captain's chair and opened a small teak door to retrieve them.

Focusing on the far shore, Vertesi could see several cottages sandwiched between the dark treeline and the lake, but it was the yellow police tape that caught his eye. Scanning in both directions from the cottage, he could see clearly the distance between them. "They're very private beach houses. I'm surprised there aren't more jammed in there, the way they are on other lakes in the area."

"Yeah, well, that whole beachfront belonged to one guy, William Ingram. He built a meat-packing plant in the late 1800s, and by the time he died he'd locked up most of what you're looking at. His family, who own that huge summer house in the small bay to the left—well, they've parcelled out bits of it over the years, but not much."

Vertesi followed Bookner's line of sight with the binoculars until he could pick out a dock shimmering in the reflected light of the lake, an aluminum mast and a low-slung hull partly obscured by the dock.

"What do you figure the distance is from here to that shore?" With the hand holding the binoculars, he pointed in the direction of the police tape.

"Oh, it's gotta be a half-mile or so, give or take."

"Yeah, that's what I figured too."

"What happened there?" Bookner sat on the blue cushion and took up the knotted fishing line.

"I can't tell you much, but a young woman was murdered in that cottage."

"Whoa, that's harsh." He asked no more questions.

Truth was, Vertesi could have told him pretty much everything, but he wanted to stay focused on what he was doing, even if he wasn't entirely sure what that was. "Do you know anything about that cottage, Book?"

"I think it's an investment property, but I've never seen anyone in or around it, ever."

"Where's your cottage from here?"

"We're way down the other end of the lake, past the second marina. Our place is part of another grandfather clause. It was an asparagus farm my great-granddad had in the 1920s before the crash. He had four vegetable markets in the city, and while he lost three to the market collapse, he managed to keep one— the big one—and the land up here as well."

"And the asparagus?"

"Naw. He died in the late forties, and the kids—my dad and his three brothers—decided they'd build cottages here instead, so now we go to the store for asparagus like everyone else."

"Why don't you moor your boat at the second marina? It's closer to your place."

"Yeah, it's closer, but Gibbs, the owner, is a pain in the butt and a cheat. I'm not the only one who thinks so. I come here to get away from the hassles, not to run into them."

"How's the fishing?" Vertesi looked over the side, as if expecting to see a fish swim by.

"It goes up and down. I think this year will be good, but the kids at the Ingram place are hell-bent on destroying it."

"How's that?" Vertesi looked through the binoculars at the dock.

"They've got at least three, maybe more, jet boats. That mast you're lookin' at? That was Old Man Ingram's pride and joy. I mean, that's what he called it—*Pride and Joy*. Since he had a mild stroke a couple of seasons ago, *Pride and Joy* is just for show."

"That's a shame."

"No shit. They tear around here in the jet boats and a couple of Sea-Doos for the younger kids, and there's no way a fish can find a minnow for all the racket." Bookner gave up on the line again and put the whole rig back in its slot.

"I should let you get back home . . . to face the music."

"She'll be fine when she hears I was out on police business. Do you have a card so I can show her it's for real?"

"No problem." Vertesi put the binoculars on the blue bench, reached into his jacket pocket and pulled out a thin aluminum cardholder that worked like a Pez dispenser. He slid his thumb across the surface and a card came out. He offered it to Bookner and put the holder away.

"Slick."

"Yeah, my sister got it for me as a joke but I love it. Used to be my cards would come out all crumpled. One last question: if you were over there"—he pointed to the police-taped cottage—"would you necessarily hear the cedar-strip's motor if it was in the middle of the lake?"

"Full out, you would. But if he was trollin', probably not."

"Why's that?"

"The wind usually comes across the lake from behind that ridge of trees. We're in the lee of it here, which is why the fishing's good, but with the ridge that runs behind that cottage"—he nodded across the lake—"the sound bounces around. It's tricky and you might not hear it at all."

"Thanks, Book, you've been great. Let's go home."

Vertesi sat down in the second chair of the wheelhouse. As Bookner swung the Limestone about, he got a better look at the Ingram dock. He could see two low-riding boats, one green and one red, which he took to be the jet boats feared by the fish. Vertesi stood up and steadied himself, saying, "Tim, do ya mind . . . . Let's just swing slowly by the Ingram place and then the murder cottage before we head back. I just wanna get a better sense of the distances." He stepped outside the wheelhouse and leaned against the door frame.

Bookner nodded, swung the big stainless wheel to the left

and powered up so the port side dipped down towards the water. Once he had come within a hundred yards of the dock, he reduced speed and turned in a slow, wide arc to the right. Vertesi staggered back to the blue bench and looked out at the huge summer home. A screened veranda ran along its entire width. At the lake's edge, a pole bore an unfamiliar flag that flapped lazily in the breeze. He trained the binoculars on it and saw a vertical red I-beam with a horizontal band of black railroad tracks running from edge to edge.

The wake from the Limestone hit the dock, and the lines rattled down the length of *Pride and Joy*'s mast as it rocked awkwardly back and forth. Vertesi turned to see if there was a sightline to the yellow-taped cottage, but a heavily treed spit of land obscured it completely. "Smart piece of planning, Mr. Ingram," he said.

He turned the glasses back on the summer house just as a young woman in a yellow bikini came out of the screen door carrying what looked like a large plate of burgers in one hand and a barbecue spatula in the other. She raised her hand to shade her eyes from the sun and looked out at the Limestone before waving the spatula. Without hesitation Vertesi waved back, then made his way forward and tapped the window of the wheelhouse. "It's lunchtime, Book. Let's get back."

Bookner drove the red ball down and swung the craft in a graceful arc to head back down the lake towards the marina. Vertesi watched the Ingram estate shrink into the distance. He watched the head of the spit appear and fade, then the cottage with the yellow tape, some of it already broken and flapping freely in the breeze. He watched the foaming wake and listened to the deep hum of the engine and the rapid *rat-a-tat-tat* of small waves being cut by the bow. Wondering what the fish were thinking, he leaned back and let the wind mess his hair and the sun warm his face. For a moment he closed his eyes and allowed himself to picture the girl in the yellow bikini.

NINE

—

THE YOUNG WOMAN WAS WEARING a housecoat, or maybe it was a bathrobe. It was cream-coloured, or maybe tan. She was cleaning, slowly, a counter or a table, perhaps in a kitchen. She and the place were unfamiliar to him. The light was tinged with yellow—lemon yellow, not sunshine. He didn't know why he was there. Her hair was long and dark; it was morning hair, not all shiny and styled. As he walked by the doorway she turned to him, and she was naked under the housecoat. He saw the outline of her hip, the soft skin of her belly, the black tuft and puffy lips below. She made no move to cover herself or turn away. Neither of them spoke. He stepped slowly through the doorway, and somewhere a phone rang. As he reached out to touch her, the phone rang again. He put his hand inside the housecoat and let it slide along her hip to the top of her thigh. The phone rang again. He let his palm glide over the thigh and up to her navel, where he gently circled its hollow and bump with his thumb.

The phone rang yet again, and MacNeice woke up. Turning quickly, he grabbed it, using his elbow to raise himself slightly. "MacNeice."

"I was worried you weren't there." It was Aziz.

"What've you got?" MacNeice rolled over to the edge of the bed and sat up.

"Two things. The address for Antonin Petrescu. He's apparently a widower, with one son and one daughter—Lydia. The IT director wanted to personally apologize to you for the delay, but I said that it wouldn't be necessary." Aziz paused, not for effect but because she suspected from the sound of MacNeice's voice that he had just woken up. It was, after all, 7:46 on a Saturday morning.

"Right. Well, let's go there together, say for nine. I'll pick you up?"

"That'd be great, Mac. It's 1102 Aberdeen Park—very posh, up by the escarpment. While I'd be happy to cycle up there, I'd have to leave soon, and I just woke up."

"Me too. I'll pick you up at 8:45—is that all right?"

"Yes, sir, that's fine. I'll jump into the shower, grab some toast and be ready." She was about to put the phone down when she heard his voice again. "Aziz, Aziz . . . Fiza?"

"Sorry. Yes, Mac?"

"Where do you live?"

"Right, right—so we're both sleepy. I'm at 354 Princess Boulevard, out by the university, apartment 312. I'll be downstairs waiting for you."

"See you soon."

MacNeice hung up and sat for a moment, haunted by the woman in his dream. It wasn't Kate. He didn't know who it was, but he wished Fiza's phone call had come later—much later.

The dreams he had of Kate were never erotic in an obvious way, like this one had been. But then, this woman wasn't Kate. Frantic searching was the through-line of every Kate dream, and most often he never found her. It was as if love— the act of love—was what he was pursuing and never finding. And, just like this morning, something always interrupted those dreams, leaving him spiritually restless for the whole day, wondering what would have happened. Would he have seen her, made love to her, or would he find her in the arms of someone else—or dead in their bed, as he had three years ago when he got out of the shower.

That morning he'd eased gently out of bed; her breathing had been shallow, interrupted by long pauses, as it had been for a week or more. When he returned, wrapped in a towel, she was gone, a tear resting like a drop of rain in the hollow below her right eye. He kissed it, then stood up to look at her. Stunned for a moment by the finality of her death, he realized that the tear, still wet on his lips, was the last thing he'd receive from her body, and he collapsed.

DRIVING THROUGH THE WINDING STREETS to Aziz's apartment, MacNeice was struck by how little he knew about her. The fifties apartment block was well maintained and the landscaping showed signs of recent care. He pulled the Chevy into the lay-by directly in front of the walkway.

Aziz threw open the glass door, briefcase in one hand and shaking her hair with the other—the way women do when they've not had time to dry it completely—combing it with her fingers and fluffing it so it wouldn't dry flat. She was walking quickly, looking down, and it wasn't till she reached the end of the walkway that she realized MacNeice was already there, watching her approach. She smiled, embarrassed, as she opened the car door. "Sorry, I didn't see you."

He turned on the ignition, but left the car in park. "Are you ready for this?"

"Yes, I think so."

"We'll have to ask him to identify the body, and let him know, as tactfully as possible, that it's not going to be easy."

"Well, I have worked hard on building a thick skin."

He eased the Chevy onto the street and proceeded well below the speed limit, as if he too was dreading this meeting. Turning right at the next intersection, he glanced at Aziz. She was wearing a charcoal grey suit with thin dark green pin-stripes, and a green silk blouse with a scalloped collar. Aware that MacNeice was scrutinizing her, and curious as to why, she met his eyes.

"Everything okay, boss?"

"Very okay."

"I had already gotten dressed like a cop, and then I realized that it might be inappropriate, so I changed."

"Yes, indeed. One cop suit in the room is more than enough."

They drove on in silence, back down Main and then right on Aberdeen Street to the leafy lanes and boulevards where Saturday papers had been tossed onto porches, waiting to be retrieved, where tricycles sat abandoned on front lawns, colourful Japanese carp banners fluttered among tinkling wind chimes, and wicker chairs on front verandas signalled family comfort.

He thought about turning on the police radio, but he didn't. He thought about slipping some Johnny Hartman and Coltrane into the CD player, but he didn't. He was getting more and more uncomfortable the closer they got to Petrescu's home. He turned off Aberdeen Street onto Aberdeen Park Boulevard, so called, he imagined, because the homes and lots could more accurately be defined as estates.

Outside the iron gate of a stately grey stone house, MacNeice parked and turned off the ignition. He didn't get out of the car.

"You see, the strange thing about the killing is the symbolism of it," he said. "A syringe loaded with acid would have been effective injected pretty much anywhere. Her heart, for example, would have exploded like a birthday balloon. Last night I did some reading on the medial temporal lobe and the hippocampus. The needle and its contents effectively disappeared her memory and her brain imaging—the ability to form thought. It had nothing and everything to do with her. I think it was a message to someone who loved her."

"When I was working on my thesis," Aziz said, "there was a stat that stuck in my head: there are fifty to a hundred billion neurons and a hundred trillion synaptic connections in the brain. In short, there's an unlimited capacity to do harm . . . and good."

"I think we are about to deliver the killer's message. In a way, we are about to become accomplices." He turned to see her face. There was no sadness there, perhaps only acceptance of their role. He found it slightly unsettling.

In his mirror every morning he'd noticed the slight downturn of his mouth and the weakness of his smile as he tried to correct it. The bags that had appeared under his eyes never went away, no matter how long he slept. Was it age or the residue of grief? Whatever it was, Aziz seemed free of it.

"Okay, let's do it."

Two square stone columns stood on either side of the locked iron gate. On one, a small stainless steel speaker and a silver button were mounted below the brushed chrome street numbers—1102—which looked like they would light up at night with a blue neon glow. MacNeice pressed the button and glanced through the gate. Two stone planters stood on either side of the columned entrance to the house. Petrescu liked symmetry and order.

A curt voice emerged from the box. "Who is it?"

"Detective Superintendent MacNeice and Detective Inspector Aziz here to speak to Antonin Petrescu." There was a pause, marked by static that indicated the line was still active.

"Come in."

An electronic trigger in the locking mechanism swung the gate open slowly. MacNeice motioned for Aziz to enter ahead of him. At the front door, he was about to use the enormous knocker when it swung open. An older woman in a white blouse and grey calf-length skirt looked at them both before speaking.

"Monsieur Petrescu is in the garden. Please come to the library and he'll be with you shortly."

She ushered them into a large room to the left of the main entrance. It was lit by the front bay window, and the walls were panelled in dark oak, with built-in bookcases. In the middle of the room was an ancient oak table with four matching chairs, two to a side. A low white ceramic bowl sat in the centre of it, elegant but empty. At the far end of the room were four upholstered chairs, a low table and another bay window, looking out to the garden. On one wall the books gave way to a floor-to-ceiling fireplace, the mantel clad in stone. The ceiling was vaulted, with fanciful plaster moulding that seemed to have no set pattern, and the floor had a shiny dark oak finish and the widest planking MacNeice had ever seen.

"What's that smell?" Aziz said.

"Money."

"I think it's the wood, and maybe the books."

"I think you're right . . . along with the money."

The door opened to reveal a trim, aristocratic man in his early sixties. His hair was grey and coarse, the kind MacNeice thought would make a good brush cut. He was wearing tan summer-weight corduroy pants, brown suede shoes and a white shirt open at the neck and rolled up at the sleeves. He entered without hesitation, looked first at Aziz and offered her his hand.

"Antonin Petrescu. And you are . . . ?"

"Detective Inspector Aziz, sir, and this is Detective Superintendent MacNeice." Both of them held out their badges but Petrescu only glanced at them.

He shook hands with MacNeice and motioned them to the chairs near the garden window. "Please sit down. How can I help you?" His voice was clipped, his English perfect, and he showed no signs of fear or concern. "I'll order tea or refreshments?"

"That's very kind, but it won't be necessary, Mr. Petrescu," MacNeice said as he sat down next to Aziz.

"Then tell me, how can I help you?"

"Can you confirm that your daughter, Lydia, just graduated from the professional program at the Conservatory?"

"Yes, I can, but—"

"And you have not seen your daughter in the past forty-eight hours?"

"No. She was supposed to come for the weekend on Saturday, but her graduation . . ."

"I'm afraid, sir, that I have the difficult task of informing you that we believe your daughter, Lydia Petrescu, has been killed."

Petrescu leaned forward as if he was hard of hearing, then fell back in his chair, his hands clasping at the upholstered arms. "I don't understand you. . . . I'm sorry, I don't know what you're saying."

Aziz gently reinforced the news. "Sir, your daughter, Lydia, has died. She was killed last night."

"Not my daughter . . . No. Lydia is not dead. You've made a mistake." He stood up and waved his hand as if showing them the door. Neither moved. "What do you mean, you— you— What do you know of my daughter?"

"Sir, is this your daughter?" MacNeice held out the snapshot.

The older man rocked back on his heels and then forward. His mouth was half-open but he said nothing, just sank slowly into his chair.

"Please, Mr. Petrescu, we will need you to identify the body, sir, but—"

"Was it . . . an accident? A car crash? How can you be certain? I mean, you don't know my daughter. How . . . ?" He looked down at the snapshot again, and he knew it was true. He sat up straight, bracing himself with his arms.

"It was not an accident, sir. Your daughter was murdered." MacNeice's voice was low and calm. His eyes stayed on the older man's face. He hoped, although he couldn't know for sure, that his own conveyed some compassion, but he was also observing Petrescu. A sad part of his job was that this wouldn't be the first time a father had killed a daughter.

"Who would have any reason to kill my Lydia? No one. Everyone loves her." His eyes welled and a tear dropped to his thigh. "You've seen her? She's beautiful . . . so talented . . ." Petrescu held out the snapshot and looked at it again before placing it gently on the table. His voice trailed off, but his eyes still wanted answers to his questions. He made no move to wipe the tears tracking down his cheeks.

"We know some of the details of her death, enough to know with some certainty that she didn't suffer. But we have no idea at the moment who could have killed her, or why."

Petrescu's head fell back against the chair, his mouth opened, and a cry that sounded at first like it was far away came from somewhere deep inside him. His hands turned to fists and slammed several times into his face before he began to sob uncontrollably. The library door flew open and the woman who'd let them in rushed to his side.

"What has happened? What have you done?" She stared at MacNeice and Aziz accusingly.

MacNeice stood up, followed by Aziz. Neither responded to the woman's questions as she held Petrescu's shoulders. MacNeice could feel his right leg shaking at the knee; he hoped it wasn't visible to anyone. After several minutes passed, the older man removed his trembling hands from his face and looked up at them. He knew there were no more answers, and it did not look as if he had the courage to ask any more questions.

Glancing up at the woman, he said, "It's Lydia—she's dead." The woman threw her hands to her mouth, her eyes opened wide and she shook her head several times in disbelief. Then she again moved close to Petrescu and placed a hand gently on his shoulder, her eyes filling with tears.

"We do need you to identify her, sir," Aziz said.

"How do I do that?"

The woman handed him a tissue from the sleeve of her blouse. He wiped his eyes and cheeks.

"Detective Aziz will come back to pick you up when you're ready, Mr. Petrescu, to take you to the morgue. It will not be easy, and I'd recommend that you bring your son or someone else close to you."

"My son? No, that won't be possible. He's a colonel in the Romanian army, stationed in Bucharest." He looked up at the woman beside him. "Perhaps, Madeleine, you would accompany me?"

"Of course, Monsieur Petrescu."

"You will no doubt have many more questions, sir, as we will," MacNeice said. "We'll do our best to answer, but this investigation is unfolding as we speak—"

"How did she die?" Petrescu's hands were now in his lap, slowly twisting the tissue.

"She was drugged and unconscious when she was injected with a lethal substance."

Petrescu groaned deeply and dropped his head to his chest, once more covering his face with his hands. Madeleine inhaled sharply and looked as if she'd gone weak at the knees; the fingers of her right hand dug into the man's shoulder.

"Here is my card, Mr. Petrescu. I will be available to you at any time and I can be here within fifteen minutes of your call." Aziz handed him her card. Then she bowed slightly and said, "I am very sorry for your loss, Mr. Petrescu."

The older man nodded. "I will call you. Madeleine, please show the detectives out." He turned to face the garden as MacNeice and Aziz were led to the door.

They walked silently to the car and MacNeice pulled away slowly. After several silent blocks he pushed the button on the car stereo. Miles took over.

WHEN HE PULLED UP in front of Aziz's apartment building, MacNeice turned off the ignition and handed her the keys.

"What are you doing?"

"Don't bother going downtown to get a car. Take mine."

"What are you going to do?"

"I need some air. I'll walk, and think. You can keep the car for Petrescu. I'll have my cell if you need me."

"Why did you set me up to take him for the viewing?"

"Because I think you're the right one to do this. He needs an open spirit, not necessarily to speak to, but to be with . . . and I'm just not. Let him know we'll both be back at his house this evening, say eight p.m., to learn more about Lydia's life. I'll take a cab if necessary." MacNeice nodded to her and got out of the car.

He was across the street, headed towards the highway and home, before Aziz got out of the car. Calling over the roof to him, she asked, "What if he wants to know about the case, our progress?"

"You tell him that we will find the person or persons who did this, so help us God." And with that MacNeice rounded the corner and was gone from view.

Whose god would that be? Aziz asked herself as she shut the door, pushed the button on the key fob and turned towards her building. The car answered with a cheery *tweet, tweet.*

HE WALKED TO END OF the next street, which sloped down to the Royal Reserve, a 2,700-acre wildlife sanctuary of rolling

hills on either side of a wide marsh, which doubled, when necessary, as a storm-runoff reservoir for Aziz's residential community and the university. The area was crisscrossed with bike
and walking paths and dotted with picnic tables. MacNeice
knew the Royal well because it was the best place in the city
to cycle and think; it had been years since he'd walked it.

For a Saturday in June, there was surprisingly little activity.
He passed by a large family gathered on blankets on the grass
near the lilac; people of all ages were sitting, standing, talking,
laughing as kids played badminton with imaginary nets while
others picked through the assortment of food and juices that
covered the picnic table.

As the sounds of King Street and the happy family faded,
MacNeice listened for birdsong and the metallic whirring of
bikes coming up behind him. Feeling the heat of the day, he
took off his jacket, put his cellphone in his pants pocket,
rolled up both shirtsleeves and settled into a loping stride,
one that would raise his heart rate but hopefully not sweat
up his shirt.

MacNeice wondered how many steps it would take to cover
the mile or so that he would walk before cutting across to the
far side of the reserve; he gave up counting when his mind wandered. Focusing on a young couple sitting by themselves at a
picnic table well off the path, he noticed the wary look they
gave him as he passed. It suggested that one of them or both
were cheating, and that this semi-public rendezvous was their
one opportunity for intimacy. A flash of orange and black flew
by just above his head—a Baltimore oriole settled on the branch
of a maple and hopped about to watch him.

Crossing the bridge over the stream, he sat down on the
bench that ran its length. A few hundred feet upstream and

high above where he was sitting, a train trestle, built in the 1930s, stood grey and stern against the blue sky, a circling crow the only movement. This was Kate's favourite place in the reserve, and it was where they had come to sit and talk after the doctor's appointment that changed everything.

MacNeice closed his eyes. He could hear the water falling lazily over rocks that had been there since the ice age; he could hear the call and response of chickadees and cruising crows, and a songbird he didn't recognize. They sang out along the creek bed and in the birch, maple and oak woods of the hills on either side. He opened his eyes only when he heard the rhythmic thumping of a cyclist riding across the wooden boards at the far end of the bridge.

A young woman, helmeted and wearing reflective orange sunglasses, beaming from exertion, approached on a sleek red road bike. He pulled in his feet to let her pass and she smiled, nodded and said a breathless "Thanks." He inhaled deeply as she passed, hoping to catch a sense of her. He knew nothing about perfume but enjoyed breathing in the subtle scent that followed a beautiful woman. There was a faint, almost citrus current in the air; had he been exhaling at that moment, he'd have missed it.

He looked down at the stream and let his thoughts drift back to Lydia Petrescu. Her death was a crime so lacking in passion that he had already ruled out former lovers and jealous rivals. He supposed her death could be a message to a lover they didn't yet know about, but if her killing was meant for her father, who would hate that gracious man enough to destroy her?

His cellphone rang. "Hi, boss. Mr. Petrescu wants to go over for the viewing now. I hear birdsong—where are you?"

"I'm sitting on a bridge overlooking a creek in the Royal, just south of the train trestle. Do you need me to come with you?"

"No, sir. I called Mary Richardson, and she'll be there herself, not that creepy dweeb. She'll answer his questions and I know she'll be considerate. He's also agreed to meet with us again tonight. Said he tried to reach his son but there was no answer."

"Okay, then. I'll leave my cell on."

"What you saw at the morgue—do you think he'll be able to handle it?"

"No. Well . . . actually, I never looked at her."

"Shall I pick you up at home tonight?"

"That would be great. Do you know how to get to me?"

"I'll find you. And by the way, I love that bridge; it's my favourite spot in the reserve."

"Good luck, Aziz." He put the cellphone back in his pocket.

His thoughts took him back to the cottage on the lake, to the beautiful girl and the music, and he found himself humming the opening bars of the Schubert. Why had the killer—it had to be the killer—thrown the record jacket onto the beach?

He got up and began walking again. As he stepped off the bridge, turning up the gravel trail towards the roadway, he recalled a time, many years before, when he had seen an LP cover slicing through the air, and the ultimate thrill of throwing the vinyl itself.

The record, Johnny Mathis's *Johnny's Greatest Hits*, had come from David White's house. Davey hated his mother, so far as anyone could tell, and he particularly hated the music his mother loved. Abducting her Mathis record was in his mind some sort of sweet revenge. On the deserted school grounds he took the cover with the impossibly happy Mathis face, handed MacNeice the LP to hold, and wound himself up like a cartoon pitcher. With a violent whirl he unwound, sending the jacket on a line drive towards the gym exit doors. It flew beautifully for the first twenty yards, but then the drag of the open pocket came into play, and it descended, skipped and skidded harmlessly before coming to a stop just shy of the building.

In the dim light of that dreary grey place—dreary grey even in the daytime—they could see Johnny smiling up at the night sky, happy as a clam to lie there on the cold concrete of Stinton High. "Okay, Mac, let 'er rip." Lacking all that built-up hatred, MacNeice nonetheless did his best—and learned something about aerodynamics.

Caught in the prison-yard lighting of the perimeter poles that washed the fenced-in yard to discourage the kind of hanky-panky they were up to, the shiny black disc climbed swiftly in a sinister arc before banking menacingly towards the school. It shattered against the second-floor brick wall, inches from the window of Room 10A, his and David's homeroom. "*Ho-ly shit, that was great!*"

They took off running, Davey laughing himself silly and threatening to bring his mother's whole collection out there and let them fly. MacNeice felt nothing but lucky, though seeing the LP exploding like dried tar hit with a hammer—well, that was pretty cool. He'd done stupid things before and he would again—mostly getting caught for them—but he decided he'd forgo any more flying vinyl with Davey.

Davey had ended up forgoing it too. At the Stone Road slate quarry a week later, on a dare, he took a short run and went head first into the UNSAFE end of the NO TRESPASSING local swimming hole, right where, local lore had it, a tractor lay submerged some ten feet under the slate black water. Davey found the tractor. His head split like a cantaloupe fallen off a truck, and he floated up, all done for this trip.

TEN

—

RICHARDSON WAS WAITING FOR THEM in the upper
lobby, wearing a grey suit and without her usual white
lab coat. The drive to the morgue had been tense, and
Aziz could feel the fear mounting inside her as she introduced
Petrescu and Madeleine to the pathologist. Petrescu's face was
frozen. He said nothing but accepted Richardson's hand with
a nod.

"Before we go on, may I speak to you a moment, Detective
Aziz?" Richardson didn't wait for an answer but walked several
feet away.

"What is it, Doctor?" Aziz said, following her. Petrescu's
back was towards them, but she noticed that Madeleine was
watching them closely.

"As you can imagine, the acid caused considerable damage.
We've covered her skull, and I don't recommend he look at it,
but to make the identification he'll need to see her face—which

has turned black. We flushed out the brain pan so it won't erode further, but there was nothing else we could do."

"My God."

"Yes, though that wasn't what I wanted to tell you. After we finished the autopsy I did a further check of her abdomen. Her blood and many of her organs had been so compromised that the usual tests we run would not have worked. However, her womb remained intact, and when I dissected it I discovered that this young woman was three to three and a half months pregnant."

"Are you certain?"

"I'll let that pass, Detective. And I'll leave it to you to tell her father."

"Would she have known?"

"Most certainly. Let's not keep them waiting any longer."

As the pathologist led the way, Aziz had to wonder whether she was up to the task after all. She took a slow, deep breath and caught up as they entered the hallway to the morgue.

Outside the swinging metal doors, Richardson turned to Petrescu and said, "Sir, this will be difficult for you, beyond anything you can imagine. Do you have any questions before we go in?"

"I want only to see my daughter." He stared at the metal doors in front of him.

"As you wish." Richardson reached out and pushed open the door to the viewing room.

The first thing Aziz noticed was how cold it was inside, a frigid, sterile space with a stainless steel wall of drawers and white ceramic tiles under fluorescent lights.

Petrescu stood next to the covered gurney with Madeleine, grim and pale, to his left and Aziz to his right. His daughter's body lay waiting under the crisp white sheet.

Richardson asked, "Are you ready, sir?"

"Yes," he said, a slight shiver in his voice.

The pathologist pulled the sheet back to reveal Lydia's face. Petrescu screamed and fell sideways into Aziz, who struggled to support him. The full horror of the girl's face had taken her breath away, but she concentrated on keeping the man from falling. Madeleine had turned sharply away and stood there with her head in her hands. Petrescu wailed again, the sound echoing off the hard surfaces of the room.

"Shall we leave, sir?" Aziz said with difficulty.

Several seconds passed before he was able to answer. "Leave me alone with her, please." He pulled away from Aziz, repeating his request. "I want to be alone with Lydia."

Madeleine averted her eyes from the gurney but put her arms around him. "Monsieur Petrescu, I don't—"

"Leave me." He shook himself free of her too.

Aziz looked over at Richardson, who nodded. The pathologist folded the sheet just below Lydia's neck and said, "I'm sorry, Mr. Petrescu. Though we can step aside, we cannot leave the room."

He ignored her, reaching out tentatively towards his daughter's shoulder.

Aziz and Madeleine went to stand near the door and Richardson joined them. Madeleine took out several tissues and wiped the tears from her face. Aziz looked again at Lydia. Her face was almost blue-black. She could make out, even from ten feet away, the veins that traced her cheeks and forehead; as dark as her face was, they were darker still, a network of black lines.

Petrescu supported himself with one hand on the edge of the gurney and rested the other for a moment on his daughter's shoulder. When he reached for the cloth that covered her skull, Madeleine drew a sharp breath.

Richardson said, "Do not touch that, sir. I'm sorry, but I cannot let you remove it."

He took his hand away quickly and rested it again on her shoulder, patting it gently several times.

"Sleep, my daughter. Sleep." He leaned over and kissed her cheek. He was crying openly, his anguish so raw that he was shivering. He turned towards them, then back for one last look at his daughter before he stumbled towards the door.

"Thank you, Dr. Richardson," Aziz said, as she followed Petrescu and Madeleine out of the room.

PETRESCU SAT IN THE FRONT SEAT on the way home, staring out the side window as he quietly wept. From the back seat Madeleine leaned forward to rest her hand on his shoulder, but he simply patted it twice, as he had patted his dead daughter, and removed it. No one spoke.

As they came to a stop outside the house, Aziz said, "If there is anything we can do for you, Mr. Petrescu, please don't hesitate—"

"Find who did this."

He met her eyes briefly, then got out of the car and walked to the gate. Aziz watched as Madeleine opened it, and then the door to the house. They disappeared inside as if in slow motion, but when the door closed firmly behind them, the finality of it all rang like a gunshot. Aziz took a long, deep breath and eased the Chevy away from the curb.

ELEVEN

—

TURNING ONTO THE SIDE ROAD to Gibbs Marina, Vertesi could see the mechanic working on the underside of a boat hanging in a cradle outside his workshop. He parked in front, crossed the road to the tuck shop and went inside. It sold just what he'd expected it to sell: tackle and bait, fish buckets, life jackets and milk, bread and ice cream.

Gibbs was behind the counter taking cash for two buckets of worms from a teenager in flip-flops who had put down a twenty-dollar bill. As Gibbs handed back the change by dropping it onto the counter, he gave Vertesi the once-over without meeting his eyes. The kid looked at his change and said, "Ah, sorry, Mr. Gibbs, but I think you owe me another four dollars. I gave you a twenty."

"I don't think so." Gibbs frowned at the teen and looked in his cash drawer.

"Yes, he did give you a twenty," Vertesi said, smiling.

The teen nodded. He hadn't picked up the change, as if doing so would somehow complicate the issue further.

"Okay. Yeah, sorry. So I owe you four bucks." Gibbs took out two coins and slapped them onto the counter.

The teen thanked him, picked up the toonies and the buckets and left the shop.

"Mr. Gibbs, I'm Detective Inspector Michael Vertesi." He offered his hand but Gibbs leaned back against the cigarette rack with his arms folded and said nothing. "I'm here on an investigation and have a few questions."

"What questions?"

"You rented out a boat, the one that was hauled up from the bottom of the lake. . . ."

"What's that got to do with you?"

"Well, to begin with, there was a body in that boat. That makes it homicide—and I'm a homicide detective, so it has a lot to do with me. For starters, I need to see your register."

"You mean my cash register?"

"No, I mean the book you keep to record who you rent your boats to, with their names and addresses."

"You got a warrant?"

"No, I don't. Would you like me to get one, or could I just see the register?"

"I don't have one." Gibbs busied himself with arranging the stack of newspapers on the counter.

"Then how do you keep track of your rentals for tax purposes?"

"I know who rents my boats and I pay my taxes."

"Fine. Who rented the boat that was pulled up from the lake?"

"Ruvola. An old customer."

"Did he pay with cash?"

"Credit card." He picked up a toothpick from the little dispenser on the counter next to the beef jerky and stuck it in his mouth with a sly smile.

"Can I see the receipt, please?" Vertesi knew that Ruvola wasn't the name on the credit card slip, and he was working hard to keep his temper.

"You get yourself a warrant first."

"Mr. Gibbs, you are aware that Ruvola's body was found in your boat and that he was a known drug dealer, aren't you?"

"You accusing me of something?" He rolled the toothpick with his tongue to the side of his mouth.

"You'll know when I'm accusing you of something serious. Right now all I'm accusing you of is being a jerk."

"Get the fuck off my property." Gibbs stepped to the side of the counter and pointed to the door, his face reddening.

"I'll be back, with the paperwork," Vertesi said. "And even more questions, like what is it that cranks you up? And what on earth are you hiding?"

Gibbs glared at the young detective before throwing the toothpick on the floor. It was clear that the interview was over. Vertesi smiled and walked out of the shop.

THE MECHANIC, WHO WAS WEARING a well-worn undershirt, cut-off jeans and unlaced construction boots, didn't turn around till he heard the screen door slap shut.

"You heard what happened to our cedar-strip, eh?" he said as Vertesi approached.

"Yes, I did, and I just wanted to check a couple of things before writing up my report. We met earlier—the name's Thompson, isn't it?"

"Yessir, Dennis Thompson, with a P."

"With a P . . . thanks. Dennis, have you seen it?" The mechanic had turned away from him and was staring at the underside of the boat again.

"Yessir. Good for shit now."

"You mean the hole?"

"Yeah. It's done that boat." He reached up to turn the propeller, its edges menacingly serrated from coming into contact with the shoals.

"What kind of drill would do a job like that?"

"Not a drill, chief. No, that was an auger—ya know, like an ice auger." He watched as Vertesi wrote down *auger*, then he said, "C'mere, I'll show you. We got a half-dozen of 'em for when the guys go ice fishing."

He led Vertesi to a smaller corrugated steel building the size of a double garage. Swallows swung out from under the eaves as they went inside. As Vertesi's eyes adjusted slowly to the dimness, Thompson marched on into the gloom where the sweet smell of oil hung in the air. Outboard motors of various sizes lined the racks on one wall, and on the other were fibreglass canoes and plastic kayaks, all stencilled with GIBBS MARINA, stacked three high. At the end of the shed was another rack; from it Thompson lifted a three-foot drill with a circular bit that looked like a cake tin.

"This is your basic ice auger, chief. It'll go through a couple feet of ice in February quicker 'n stink through a pig."

"You said you have six of them. I count five."

"What? Yeah, we got six." Thompson turned around, put the one he was holding back in the rack and counted them quietly to himself. Scratching the *Miami Vice* stubble on his chin, he looked around the garage, then back at the rack.

"Is this open all day?" Vertesi looked back out the open doorway and across the road to the tuck shop.

"Yessir." Thompson was still looking around for the missing auger.

"If you're in your workshop you can't see the entrance to this building, am I right?"

"Well, yeah. But up here we don't lock the doors till night, eh? It's not like the city. . . ."

"That's true. But what if the guy who took the auger wasn't from up here?"

"I see where you're going with this, chief. You think it was our auger that did the boat, eh?"

"Don't you?" Vertesi glanced over at the mechanic, who was kneeling down at the dark end of garage looking at the augers.

"Whad'dya say the diameter of the hole was?"

"I didn't. Ten inches." He could hear Thompson mumbling something as he checked out the business ends of the remaining augers.

"We got three eights and three ten-inchers. The one that's missing is a ten. I better tell Gibbs. He won't be too happy— the tens were all new last October. D'ya think you'll find her?"

Everything's female to guys like Thompson—except females, Vertesi thought. Motors: "she's a bitch to get the head off 'er." Cars: "she'll climb trees with that hemi in 'er." Boats and bikes: "she'll go like a banshee, that one!" But when it comes to flesh and blood late on a Saturday night, the romance has all been spent on machines.

"I doubt we'll find her, unless we dredge the lake." Vertesi stepped into the sun and sat on a crate between the two buildings to finish his notes. "This must be your favourite spot for a coffee break."

"Why d'ya say that?"

"It's surrounded by butts, Dennis, and the grass is worn away."

"Yeah, well. Yeah, I sit here a lot. I'm the only marine mechanic for miles. I ain't got a union but I got coffee breaks." He headed for the tuck shop. "I'm gonna tell Gibbs. If I'm not out in ten minutes, chief, pull out that pistol and come and get me."

"Are you really worried?" Though, having just spent ten minutes with Gibbs, he knew what Thompson meant.

"He's got a temper—always had one. He's what you'd call a first-class badass." The mechanic chuckled to himself as if he'd cracked a line in a cop show. "The place used to be run by his wife and she was a gem. But when she died, Gibbs took over, and he just seems angry all the time."

As Thompson went to tell Gibbs about the auger, Vertesi opened his notebook and made his summary:

Gibbs aggressive, uncooperative—will definitely require warrants.
Gibbs likely knows much more than he'll be willing to say.
Check the house too. Gibbs may be on something nasty.
Ruvola was "an old customer"—maybe it wasn't all about boats!
10 in. hole in the cedar strip was probably done with an ice auger.
A 10 in. ice auger is missing from Gibbs Marina, purchased in
    October of last year.
Gibbs may have a serial number and registration for it.
Probability: this auger's augured into the bottom of the lake.

Enjoying his small joke, he put his notebook away, stamped the dust off his shoes and got into his car. He took his cell-phone off the dashboard, heard the screen door slap angrily and saw Gibbs walking quickly in his direction, Thompson following like an old mutt some distance behind. Gibbs's head was down and he had the look of someone who's just about had enough. Vertesi rolled the window down. "Can I help you, Mr. Gibbs?"

"You tell Denny here that my auger is likely in the lake, Officer?"

"Detective, Mr. Gibbs. Yes, I did."

Gibbs put his hands on the roof of the sedan and leaned closer to make his point. "Detective, I'm out a cedar-strip, a damn fine motor, a five-gallon gas tank and a couple of oars. Now I find out I'm out a brand new auger too. I don't need a smartass slick-suit wop from the city making wisecracks about my missing property—I need someone who's gonna find out where my property is at." He slammed the roof of the car with both palms.

"Well, Mr. Gibbs, I was ready to slap the cuffs on you when you got to *smartass*—but *wop*? Step away from the car, sir."

Reluctantly Gibbs moved back a few feet, clenched his hands and tucked his thumbs into the aging belt that held up his baggy fatigues. Vertesi opened the door and stepped out. Thompson's eyes were popping.

"Dennis," Vertesi said, "don't you love it when a cop says 'step away from the car'? I know I do." With one hand he was reaching into his inside jacket pocket for his badge and with the other for the weapon in the belt holster. He produced both and showed them to Gibbs. He then tossed them onto the driver's seat and turned to face the older man.

"Mr. Gibbs, I have no idea what happened to your auger, but I am getting a good sense of what happened to your boat. Still, the one thing that has seriously messed me up today is being called a wop." Vertesi took off his jacket and tossed that into the car as well. Gibbs unhooked his thumbs from his belt and let his hands hang down. Vertesi rolled up the sleeves of his shirt and took a step towards the man, who shifted slightly as if he was expecting a blow.

"I've got a witness here." Gibbs nodded in Thompson's direction.

"Same witness I have, Mr. Gibbs, and he heard you calling me a wop. What you're going to do, Mr. Gibbs, is you're going to apologize for uttering a slur against me, my father and my ancestors, or I'm going to smack you about—as a citizen, not as a smartass detective." He took another step towards Gibbs.

"You'd hit an older man?" Gibbs kept looking over to Thompson for support. The mechanic had taken a rag out of his jeans pocket and was wiping his forehead nervously, smearing grease across his brow.

"As a citizen, ordinarily, no. As a cop, never. Honestly, I can take lots of abuse, and I think you can tell that I'm not even angry. I'm just one of those guys who has an invisible trigger, and you just pulled it."

As Vertesi took his next step forward both his hands came up, and Gibbs knew there was no more talk to be talked.

"Denny, go inside and call the cops. Now!"

Thompson looked back and forth between Gibbs and Vertesi. "Mr. Gibbs, he is a cop." He stepped back to make it clear this wasn't his fight.

With no ally watching his back, Gibbs finally made the only move that would keep him from a beating. "I— I was upset, you know, about what the— about the boat and auger, and what you said. I'm sorry, Detective, sorry I insulted you." Gibbs had his hands raised in surrender.

Vertesi dropped his own slowly, looking straight at Gibbs, who was breathing as if he was going to have a heart attack or a stroke or something like that. "You'd risk a beating for an ice auger, Mr. Gibbs?" Deliberately he began rolling his sleeves down and then buttoned each cuff.

"It's been rough— well, losing the boat, now the auger. And I don't know if Denny told you, but I also lost the missus a while back. I'm pretty strung out, I guess, is all I can say."

"I accept your apology, Mr. Gibbs. Now this wop's going back to police work. *Ciao*, gentlemen." He opened the door to the Chevy, put on his jacket, and tucked the weapon into its holster and fastened it before clipping it onto his belt. He put the badge back into his inside pocket. Gibbs and Thompson were still frozen to the spot as he eased the car into reverse and backed out of his parking spot, then pulled away slowly without kicking up any gravel. He looked back through the rear-view mirror before he turned out of the marina lot; they were still standing there but Gibbs was now yapping at Thompson and waving his arms about. He caught his own eyes in the mirror and said, "That was for you, Pop."

During the drive back, Vertesi wondered what Gibbs was trying to hide. He seemed too old to be acquainted with a bad actor like Ruvola, who didn't strike him as a sport fisherman. Maybe Ruvola had been supplying him with dope, and now that source was gone. . . . He was less than a half-hour from the city when his cellphone rang.

"Vertesi."

"Michael. Mac. Give me an update."

"I'm just coming back from Gibbs Marina. That guy has some serious anger issues, boss, and I'll have to get a warrant to look at his records and receipts. Anyway, the drill that went through that boat is called an auger; they use it for ice fishing. It's likely that it came from Gibbs's place, since he had six and one of them is gone." Vertesi pulled off the road so he could concentrate.

"Killing Ruvola would have been easy. Why would they do it in such an elaborate fashion? Anything else?"

"Well, you may have to cover for me if Mr. Gibbs lodges a complaint. He was pissed off enough about losing the boat and the auger to make a discriminatory remark."

"What, he called you a wop?"

"Exactly, sir."

"But everybody calls you a wop."

"Yeah, but they know me. We can call each other names and it's not an insult. Anyway, I didn't touch him. I would have touched him—a smack or two—if he hadn't apologized, but he did."

"You threatened him?"

"Yeah, but I'd taken off my badge and removed my weapon—they were both in the car. You know, the guy is seriously wound up and just generally pissed off." There was what seemed like a long pause, with only static on the line. "Sir?"

"I'm here; I'm just buckling up. If they ask me I'll have to say, 'We're here to serve and protect,' but I do take your point."

"Thanks, sir. What's been happening at your end?"

"Have you had dinner?"

"No, I was going to go back to the office and see if anything's come in on the guy who owns the cottage."

"Let's eat. There's a lot to talk about before Aziz and I go over to Petrescu's house."

"Who's Petrescu?"

"Exactly. Meet us at Marcello's."

"I'm there." Vertesi ended the call, tucked his cellphone into his jacket and, pulling back onto the highway, powered onto the three-lane leading into the city.

TWELVE

—

MacNeice looked across the table at Aziz sitting very erect next to Vertesi, who was rounding up crumbs on the table with his middle finger.

"Lydia Petrescu was pregnant," he said to Vertesi. "Mary Richardson told Aziz when they went to view the body. I doubt that her father knew, or he would have said something."

"Or he knew and he was purposefully saying nothing. What if he was hoping it wouldn't be discovered?" Aziz said, looking down at the tiny circle of crumbs in front of her colleague.

"Meaning what? That he's a suspect? No way, not after the way you say he reacted to her death. No way, Aziz," Vertesi said.

"No, meaning that he possibly knew she was pregnant and possibly knows who the father is." Her delivery was flat; it was difficult to tell if she believed this or not.

"We don't know anything about this woman and we don't know anything about her father's circle. Are they assimilated, or do they stay close to their own?" MacNeice glanced up at Marcello, watching from the bar, who nodded—a shorthand way of asking, *You need something?* MacNeice shook his head. "I'd also like to know more about how Antonin Petrescu makes his money."

"I can look into that," Vertesi said.

"I called the Conservatory," Aziz offered. "No one's in the offices till Monday morning. But I thought maybe we should speak to some of her fellow students and the professors." She looked at MacNeice. "If someone there—another musician, or maybe a professor—was her lover, and her father found out . . ."

"Are we talking honour killing here?" Vertesi shoved his crumb circle off the end of the table. "Because I don't get honour killing with this one. Why the needle, why buddy in the boat, the music in the cottage? None of it fits what we know about that shit."

"No, it doesn't. But it might fit what we don't know about that 'shit'." MacNeice waited to see if they understood him. They did. They both remembered him telling them the Miles Davis anecdote, the one where he was auditioning a new musician and stopped him while he was playing with, "Don't play what you know—I don't care what you know. Play what you don't know."

"Well, here's all I got. The only person anyone saw at the marina was Ruvola. He was on the bottom in a boat about thirty yards off the nearest shore, so I think we're looking for another boat—one that Gibbs hasn't mentioned." Vertesi drew a boat with a sail, little choppy waves and a shark's fin on the paper table cover.

"Who's the shark?" Aziz asked.

"I don't know. But using the boss's play-what-you-don't-know method, I'd still say we're dealing with foreigners." Vertesi drew a happy face on the sail of the boat with crossed bones beneath it. MacNeice and Aziz exchanged glances and smiled.

"Right. Well, on that note—and I'm not necessarily disagreeing with you, Michael—Fiza and I have to go and see Mr. Petrescu."

Vertesi put his notebook and pen away. "Do we still have tomorrow off?"

"I don't expect either of you to give up your day off." MacNeice meant it, but when he looked up from signing for dinner, he caught the two younger detectives playing hairy eyeball.

Aziz was sheepish at being caught. "I can work it," she said.

"Me too." Vertesi was less convincing.

"Take the day off, both of you. I wasn't kidding. The people who did this are either long gone or they're still here. They're not worried about whether the three of us are working Sunday, and I'm certainly not."

They could see it was a genuine offer—he never said things he didn't mean—but MacNeice qualified the thought. "Sad fact is," he said, "no matter what you do on your day off, this won't be far from your thoughts."

"Make yourselves comfortable. I know this cannot be a pleasant task for you. Madeleine has already made tea; she will not join us unless you feel it important that she does." Though his face was pale and his eyes red-rimmed, Antonin Petrescu was composed and dignified. "Milk or sugar, Detective?"

"No, thank you. Just black." Aziz sat nearest the window in the library, where she could see the garden.

"And you, Detective MacNeice?"

"Milk please, no sugar."

Petrescu poured and offered the tea, then poured a cup for himself and eased down into the chair opposite Aziz.

"Sir, while our questions will be difficult for you, I know you understand their importance." MacNeice opened his note-book to signal the start of the interview; Aziz's pen was already poised above her page.

"I am desperate to discover what happened, or rather, who did this to my daughter." Petrescu picked up his cup and saucer, perhaps just to occupy his hands, as he didn't take a sip.

"The pathologist has discovered that your daughter was three months pregnant. Were you aware of that?"

Petrescu's cup shivered in its saucer. He quickly put it down on the table and looked out to the garden. Aziz could see that his eyes, already swollen with grief, were spilling more tears down his cheeks. She nodded at MacNeice; it was clear that the man was hearing this news for the first time. MacNeice waited. Petrescu's chest rose slowly and sank with a shudder, but in a few moments he'd composed himself enough to turn back to them. He used a floral paper napkin to wipe his eyes, then folded it slowly into a neat rectangle and laid it beside the saucer. He shook his head—*no*—at MacNeice.

"Did Lydia have a boyfriend?"

"Lydia, my daughter, is a good girl. She is— I— I'm sorry— was . . ." His faced flushed as he held his breath in an effort to keep his composure. His eyes filled again, and he turned towards Aziz as if pleading for something only a female could provide. Aziz lowered her eyes and bowed her head in what

MacNeice took to be a sign of respect and compassion. The tears rushed down Petrescu's cheeks.

"Sir," said MacNeice softly, "we can come back another time. . . ."

Petrescu raised his hand, seeking a pause, not an end to the meeting. Once again he took the napkin and wiped his eyes and face. "You see . . . I loved her very much. She— Lydia was a brilliant musician . . . poised and confident. Her life, in so many ways, was just beginning." He looked out to the garden before continuing, "She grew up without a mother. . . . I never remarried after her mother died. I put Lydia ahead of everything else in my life . . . she's such a beautiful daughter—" He waved his hand just above the table as if erasing the mistaken tense of his statement.

"Did she bring her friends home?"

"Not often, no. In her final year at the Conservatory she wanted to have a place of her own downtown. I understood that. Her bedroom"—he looked up to the ceiling—"is just above us. She had this beautiful garden to look out at . . . but I understood." He stared again at the garden, and after another deep sigh he said, "I rented an apartment for her, in a safe neighbourhood, not far from the Conservatory."

"Is this the key, sir?" MacNeice held out his snapshot of the key from Lydia's bag.

"Yes, that's it. *LP.*"

Aziz looked up from her notebook for a moment. "Can you give me the address, Mr. Petrescu?"

"Yes, of course. It's the big new condominium building on Strathearn Avenue, number eighty-eight. Her flat is on the sixteenth floor—1604. It faces south, very bright. Lydia loved light." He sat up straight in the chair and looked at MacNeice.

"Do you know who she was seeing—?"

"Yes, you wanted to know who her boyfriend was. I don't know, but I was to meet someone she said was 'special' this weekend. She said, 'It's a surprise, Daddy.'"

"You were very close to her," MacNeice said. He found it odd that her father hadn't known how close she was to someone else.

"Yes, terribly. But you know, Detective—do you have children?"

"No."

"Alexandrina, my wife, was thirty-two when she died of pancreatic cancer. Lydia was only four. She grew up feeling, I think, that she was both a daughter and a mother to me, as I was also without my son." MacNeice noticed his jaw tighten for a moment. "I encouraged both roles." Tears again filled his eyes. "When she began studying at the Conservatory, I could see she wanted something more from life, and I encouraged that also."

"Does your son know what has happened?" Aziz asked.

"Not yet. I've called Bucharest and left messages with his adjutant to have him call at any hour."

"What is your son's role in the military?" MacNeice asked the question idly, as if he were just mildly curious.

"Gregori is a microbiologist. Romania is a poor country, and many people leave to work elsewhere in the European Union. Some, like my son, go into the military, where they can get paid for their skills while they protect the country."

"What is his interest in microbiology, Mr. Petrescu?" Aziz asked.

He turned to her. "His doctorate is in plant mutation and his focus is what you would call infectious disease control.

Where are you from, Detective?"

If Aziz was offended by the question, she didn't show it. "Why do you ask, sir?"

"I mean no disrespect, but your name intrigues me." Petrescu seemed as detached as Aziz. MacNeice felt like he was observing a dance between ancient peoples, and he was curious to see where it would go. He sipped his tea and scrutinized the library shelves as if he weren't paying attention.

"I see. Although I grew up in the U.K., my family is from Lebanon." Her smile, he thought, was enigmatic but benign.

"Then you have an understanding for what I'll loosely call our part of the world. It is dangerous and largely poor, and there are many ancient quarrels that determine the destinies of millions today. My son has chosen to remain part of that world."

"Well put, sir. Yes, I understand." Aziz turned to MacNeice, who read her opaque look as his cue to take over.

"Would it be appropriate if, while you and I continue speaking, Madeleine could show Detective Aziz your daughter's bedroom?"

"Yes, certainly. While it is as she left it, there is of course her flat." He pushed a button and in a moment the door opened and Madeleine appeared. "Please show Detective Aziz Lydia's room."

"As you wish." Madeleine gave a slight nod and led Aziz out of the library.

"More tea?" Petrescu gestured towards the pot.

"No, thank you, I'm fine. Is there anyone you can think of who might want to harm your daughter as a way of harming you?"

"I don't follow you."

"The manner in which your daughter died was so elaborate that it could be interpreted as a message." MacNeice spoke with an authority that made it clear he was not speculating.

"If you mean that her death is a message to me, I'm afraid I don't understand."

"The business you have is successful." It was an observation to which MacNeice added what he hoped would be taken as a complimentary glance about the library.

"Yes, in that regard I'm very fortunate."

"And there are no associates or competitors who would wish you harm?" He kept his questions flat, as if completing a checklist.

"I have no competitors here, which is why I have done so well." Petrescu was beginning to bristle, but MacNeice pursued his point.

"And those abroad—in Europe—no one who would qualify as—"

"Detective, I know you're doing your best to discover who did this to my daughter, but I deal with fine furniture and old papers." Petrescu crossed his legs and rested his hands, one on top of the other, on his thigh. "I live a quiet life, as you can see."

"When was the last time you saw Lydia?"

"At her graduation ceremony Wednesday afternoon. She played beautifully."

"And afterwards, did you go to dinner?"

"No, Lydia wanted to celebrate with the other graduates and then spend the weekend here." His eyes began to well up again and MacNeice knew he should wrap up the session.

"Are there any questions you have for me at the moment, sir?"

"I know I have questions—many of them—beyond the obvious one, but at the moment I cannot continue." Petrescu unfolded his legs, put his hands flat on both thighs and slowly stood up.

"One small detail, sir. Did your daughter own a Seabreeze portable record player?"

"Yes, she bought one two months ago so she could listen to a record—the Schubert piano trios. It was, she felt, the finest recording of the pieces. The second trio was to be her professional debut, as part of a graduating ensemble. She listened to it constantly."

As if on cue, the door opened and Aziz came through, followed by Madeleine.

"Was it helpful, Detective?" Petrescu asked.

"Yes, sir, it was, and I'm grateful to you."

MacNeice said, "Mr. Petrescu, you have our office and cell numbers. Please don't hesitate to call either me or Detective Aziz." He reached over and shook Petrescu's hand, registering again the older man's strong grip. Aziz offered hers and Petrescu held it gently, for perhaps a second too long. MacNeice wondered if it was a form of apology.

They didn't speak until the Chevy had moved away from the curb.

"What was that about?" MacNeice asked.

"I'm not quite sure, sir, but to suggest that Lebanon is a neighbour of Romania is a new one on me. I can only think that he's talking geopolitically, maybe referring to the divide between Christianity and Islam."

"How so?"

"Well, the son is a microbiologist. The Black Sea borders both Muslim and Christian countries and Turkey spans the whole southern coast. Turkey borders Syria and Iraq on the south and Russia on the east. I suppose it's safe to say that being a colonel in an infectious disease unit is a strategic alternative to being a colonel in charge of Soviet nuclear weapons."

"Meaning?"

"Meaning he could argue that—assuming they're not weaponized—research on infectious diseases is doing good for humanity."

"I guess paranoia, real or imagined, is very real to the paranoiac," MacNeice offered.

"I am intrigued nonetheless . . . curious that Petrescu put it on the table." Aziz adjusted her position in the seat.

"I thought you were the one who put it on the table." MacNeice stopped for a light and waited for her to respond.

"I asked about his son. I asked what he did in microbiology. It was a reasonable question and Petrescu took it from there. The question is, why? It should have been a simple inquiry about the brother of a murdered girl, but it became something else. I didn't do that—he did."

"What did you find in the girl's room?"

"It had a beautiful view of the garden, as Petrescu said. A couple of teddy bears were placed neatly against the pillows on the bed. There's a photograph on the dresser of, I assume, Lydia in her mother's arms—she looks less than a year old. The mother is beaming and proud. A boy, maybe four or five, is rushing to get out of the picture—he's blurry. The background is a garden wall, very high, made of stone and covered with clematis. The image looks European; there are rooftops just above the wall with chimneys in a style I've never seen before."

"That's it?"

"There was a desk in the garden window, but other than silver toilet articles with *LP* engraved on them, a desk pad and a pen-and-pencil set, it was very neat. It looked like a movie set. Madeleine said nothing, just stood by the door as I looked about the room. I think we'd need permission to go through the drawers and closet."

"That's fine. I'll have downtown secure her apartment and go over in the morning to check it out." MacNeice pulled up to the curb in front of Aziz's place. It was just past nine but it felt like midnight. When he had gotten up from his chair at Petrescu's, he was surprised how stiff his legs were, and realized that he'd been holding his body tense throughout the entire meeting. Petrescu stood up more easily than he had. As they left the library MacNeice noticed an entire shelf of books dedicated to microbiology, most of which bore English titles.

After she'd stepped out of the car, Aziz leaned back in. "I'd like to go with you tomorrow, boss, if it's okay. You're right—I'd just be sitting at home wondering what was up."

"Your call. Pick you up at eight thirty?"

"Actually, I'm okay. It's a good twenty-minute walk, and that'll make up for my lack of exercise today. Good night, sir. Get some rest."

THIRTEEN

—

THE HOUSE LOOKED VAGUELY familiar. The door opened easily and he walked in without knowing why he was there. He could sense her presence but she didn't answer when he called out. The silence of the place soon filled him with dread and he began searching the rooms frantically; if he went faster and looked harder—didn't even take the time to blink—he'd find her. A curtain would move as he opened another door, tantalizing him. Finally, in the second-storey bedroom, he looked out the window just in time to see the backyard gate close.

Tearing down the stairs, he used the newel post to whip himself around towards the back door. But in the hall he was confronted by a woman who blocked his way.

"Do I know you?" he said.

"I know you. Look, MacNeice, she doesn't want to see you. It would be best for all concerned if you forget her."

"Get the fuck out of my way."

"You won't find her. She doesn't want to see you again, ever. Please, for your own sake, stop looking."

MacNeice shoved her aside and ran out the back door. The garden seemed much longer and wider than it had through the window, and when he reached the gate, it wouldn't open. He rattled the metal handle, kicked at the frame where the latch connected. Frustrated and out of breath, he yelled, "Kate, Kate! Let me see you, Kate. Please, Kate!"

He woke up, his T-shirt soaked with sweat. The room was still dark, though a sliver of daylight was bleeding through at the top of the curtains. He breathed deeply to slow the panic in his chest and looked over at the clock—7:47 a.m.

"Christ!"

MacNeice tucked his camera into his jacket pocket, locked his car and took a deep breath before walking across the driveway to the door of the building. Aziz was waiting for him in the lobby, talking to one of the uniforms who had been there overnight. "Good morning, sir," she said. "This is Officer Scales. His partner is outside the flat."

"Good to meet you, sir. I've heard a lot about you." Scales was taller than MacNeice by at least four inches. His handshake was earnest—too earnest for how fragile MacNeice was feeling. When he'd extricated his hand, he asked, "Has anyone come by asking about the place, or why you're here?"

"A few of the other condo owners. There's a young couple—they live two doors down the hall from the deceased woman—who were very upset to hear that she'd died. We haven't interviewed anyone, but you see that camera up there . . ."

Scales pointed to the security camera looking back at them

from the corner of the lobby. "There's another one by the elevators. There's also one in the drive-by just outside and one on
every floor. There's a whole security room setup just through
that door on the left. The guard is willing to review the digital
files with us, but they erase them every seven days."

"Thank you, Scales. We'll take him up on that after Aziz
and I look at the apartment. Did you get the key from the
super?"

"I have it, boss," Aziz said. "Though they don't have a
super here—he's a *concierge*."

THEY STOOD ON THE THRESHOLD, staring into light. A wall
of windows took up the whole south side of the apartment; it
was covered with what looked like white parachute silk. There
was a faint but not unpleasant odour, like sugar.

"What's that smell, Aziz?"

"Gardenia, I'd say, but I'm not certain."

MacNeice moved farther into the room as Aziz softly closed
the door. To the left was the kitchen, with a small dining area
by the window wall, and to the right the bedroom and a large
hall closet system with frosted glass sliders. The furniture was
for the most part modern, accented by a few older pieces—a
table, a mirror, a reclining chair with a zebra-skin cushion—
that had surely come from home, or from her father's shop.
The carpet was white plush. Aziz took off her shoes at the door.
MacNeice thought about keeping on his black brogues but then
kicked them off and set them beside Aziz's.

The freesias on the table—the possible source of the scent—
still looked fresh. There were green-covered music scores and
magazines on the coffee table, classical music magazines mostly,
but also a *Vogue*. On the end table, next to the deep green and

grey sofa, was a glass with what looked like orange juice in the bottom. A music stand held a closed score—*Schubert Piano Trios*—and on the dining room table was a violin case. MacNeice slipped on his latex gloves and unsnapped the lid—a Guarneri, its surface a deep umber sheen—a beauty. He closed the lid and looked into the kitchen. There were no dishes in the sink, and nothing on the counter that would suggest someone coming back for dinner.

"Mac, I think you should see this." Aziz was calling from the bedroom.

On the bed were a black bra and panties, a white terrycloth robe and an airline ticket wallet, all lying there as if thrown down in a hurry. Aziz put on her gloves, leaned over and picked up the ticket. "One business class round-trip ticket to Istanbul—Lydia Petrescu, seat 6A. Date of departure, this Monday, seven p.m." She put it back down on the bed.

MacNeice stepped into the washroom, an opus of light grey granite, white porcelain and tempered glass. It had a shower stall, a deep tub like those he remembered from France, a bidet and a toilet. On the marble counter of the two-sink chrome vanity was a perfume bottle with the glass stopper sitting beside it.

"What kind of girl leaves the stopper out of her perfume bottle, Aziz?"

"None that I know of, sir, not even the ones with money to burn. Is it gardenia?" Aziz stood in the doorway, admiring the black-and-white print on the wall of a young woman dressed in a bathing suit from the thirties, smiling at the camera as she shielded her eyes from the sun.

"Ah, no, it's jasmine."

"Figures. I've never been good at perfumes."

"Actually, it says it's a body splash, but it smells like perfume to me."

The bath towel had been hurriedly draped over the rail. Below it, on the grey granite floor, were white satin slippers, one upright, the other on its side.

"You tell me, does this look like someone was late for a date?" He turned around and studied the bedroom through the doorway, breathing in the joy and anticipation that hung in the air like a frozen reminder of her life.

"From the look of the place, I'd say yes. . . ." Aziz walked over to the night table and opened the drawer—Aspirin, a new passport, a book of poems, folded letters from her father, a point-and-shoot camera with no images on the memory card, several tubes of lipstick in different shades of deep red edging towards brown, and a small box of condoms. "This suggests she didn't get pregnant the first time she had sex."

MacNeice looked down at the contents of the drawer. "Peeling the onion can be as disheartening as it is revealing. We can see how her father saw her and—for good or bad—we get to see her as she actually was."

He moved over to the closet, four mirrored doors that afforded a perfect reflection of the bed. He swung two of the doors open and the air filled with the faint scent of cedar from the closet lining. A dozen pairs of shoes sat on two racks on the floor, several pairs of boots beside them; her clothing was neatly hung in a progression of colours from bluish pinks to deep greens and blues. Above on a shelf were folded sweaters—more variations of blue—scarves, and several summer hats aligned like soldiers on parade.

MacNeice reached up to feel the depth of the shelf. Realizing that what was on display was well forward of the back wall of

the closet, he lifted out the stacks of sweaters and scarves, placing them neatly on the end of the bed. He took out the tiny
Maglite that never seemed to find its way onto his keychain
and used it to inspect the shelf. Standing at the back was a large
black book.

He retrieved what turned out to be a photo album with a
black leather cover. Carrying it over to the credenza that ran
the length of the window, he set it down and flipped it open to
the first page past the patterned tissue endpapers—a satin-finish
photograph with the Guarneri's backside filling the frame. The
shot revealed the grain and depth of the violin's finish, but also
the wear of almost three centuries of being embraced in the
same fashion. The oil from bodies long gone had sunk into the
surface and created a rich hue that the photographer had
worked hard to capture. "Beauty," said MacNeice.

"Sorry, sir?" Aziz looked up from the night table.

"A photo album—a shot of her violin that's quite extraordinary." MacNeice turned the page, inhaled sharply and said,
"Well. . . ."

Another satin print, this one in black and white. The image
was of a tall woman, naked but for high heels, her back to the
camera, playing the violin in front of the parachute-silk
curtains.

"I think we've found her lover."

There was no indication that she knew the photograph was
being taken—but how could she not? She seemed intent, head
to one side, right arm above her shoulder line, drawing the bow
down across the instrument. The light from the window ate
away at the details, her hair, her legs, her arms, the bow narrowed by its intensity. Her right leg was slightly ahead of the
left, and while the backlight flattened the details, he could see

the lovely diving curve of her behind. "I think he's the photographer . . . and he's good. Very good."

Aziz came over and looked down. "Oh my, yes. So lovely."

MacNeice turned the page. This time Lydia was seated, the violin on her lap, and behind her the same white curtain. Her legs were slightly open and the photographer was at knee height. She was smiling down at him, moving a wisp of hair that had fallen across her face; her breasts, while not large, were beautifully formed, and the nipples were taut.

MacNeice looked at the smile on her face—she was in love. "I don't think this is what her father sent her to the Conservatory for."

"No, not likely." Aziz leaned closer to see the grain and detail of the image.

On the next page Lydia was confronting the camera face on, standing at ease in both the military and sexual senses of the word. Both arms were down, the bow in her right hand, the violin in the left. She smiled at the camera with some mischief. Her stomach was flat, her hips even.

"I don't think we should show these to Vertesi," Aziz said.

MacNeice turned the page, and the page after that—there was no escaping her beauty. The violin and bow were in each shot, but it wasn't until the last image that the location changed to the bedroom. "Here we go," MacNeice said.

Lydia was standing—no bow, no violin—legs apart, her left hip thrust upward and both hands in her hair, her eyes looking directly into the camera. In the mirror behind her there was a reflection. A bushy-haired young man, also naked, sitting on the bed with his legs crossed, looking into the top of a camera. "The boyfriend—he's using either a Rolleiflex or a Hasselblad. Can you make out which?"

Aziz looked closely, then said, "Wait a minute." She left the room and came back a moment later with an empty glass from the kitchen. She flattened the page and laid the heavy tumbler on its side, using the thick base as a magnifying glass. "We have . . . a Hasselblad here . . . and the lab will give us the lens as well. But wait—just under his collarbone there's a tattoo. I can't make it out in the shadow, but the lab will be able to."

MacNeice moved away from the album and looked at the bed, then over to the mirrored doors.

"What do you want to do now?"

"We call the geeks, that's what we do." MacNeice reached inside his jacket and took out his cellphone.

"Put this back, boss?" Aziz had closed the album and was leaning against the credenza.

"No, not just yet. I'd like to take some shots of the boy-friend in the mirror and start asking questions."

"I'll go through the rest of the drawers to check if there's anything else."

"I think we've found the Rosetta Stone, but yes, keep looking."

He walked over to the credenza, opened the album again and smoothed it flat, then shot several close-ups of the boy-friend in the mirror before putting his camera down to call Forensics. Aziz heard him say, "No, we're not going to wait. There's a uniformed officer downstairs—Scales. Check in with him. Aziz and I will be in the security room reviewing the dig-ital files from several cameras. Yes, digital, but only a week's worth. . . ."

MacNeice hung up, remembered to turn his camera off and tuck it back in his pocket, then looked down again at the photograph.

"Do you think he could have done that to her?" Aziz was putting the sweaters back on the shelf.

MacNeice said, "I don't think so. That young man is an artist, and it's not that artists don't occasionally kill their lovers . . . but I couldn't see him doing it that way." He moved aside some of the sweaters and put the album back where he'd found it, then removed his latex gloves.

Riding down in the elevator, Aziz said, "Do we tell the father about this?"

"Not just yet." MacNeice stared up at the floor numbers as the elevator descended.

"Why would a woman with such talent pose like that?"

"Love." MacNeice was still looking at the numbers and she couldn't tell whether he was being serious.

"I don't buy that. Well, not completely."

"A mixture then, of love and lust and trust, and maybe a sense of knowing . . ."

"Knowing what, exactly?"

"That she wouldn't always look like that, that maybe this was her last shot at rebellion, her first time choosing another persona, and another person to love other than her father." MacNeice glanced over at her as the doors opened.

As they walked across the lobby to the security room, he said, "So, no desktop or laptop in the apartment—just that silver unit next to the desk and dozens of CDs."

"But there was a jack beside the desk."

"So who's got her computer? And why?"

FOURTEEN

—

VERTESI HAD FOUND A DIFFERENT WAY to spend his day off, which he rationalized by also qualifying it as police work. It's a funny thing about screened porches, especially the ones that surround old cottages. You can't see a damn thing till you're standing there rapping on the door like a travelling salesman.

"Hi, can I help you?" An older woman in a summer dress opened the door, and Vertesi had to step down to let it swing past. Beyond her the inner door to the cottage was wide open, and to the left he could see an older man asleep on a wicker triple-seater, a newspaper on his lap. There was a glass on the floor next to a pair of sandals.

"Yes, I hope you can. My name is Detective Inspector Michael Vertesi and I'm investigating a crime that was committed around the point from your cottage. I'd like to ask you some questions. Is this a good time?" He glanced towards the sleeper, who hadn't moved.

"Oh, yes, I think so. We've heard about it, of course—a real tragedy." She was nodding her head from side to side, the way some people do when what they're saying calls for up and down.

"It is. Very tragic. May I come in?" He already had control of the door and was beginning to step up.

"Oh, certainly, but you know, Detective—"

"Vertesi. It's Italian." He showed her his badge and smiled— charmingly, he hoped.

"Vertesi. Yes, well, I was going to say that we—well, not I, but my husband"—she glanced over to the wicker sofa—"we told a young man named . . . Palmer, I think it was . . . everything we—well, my husband, that is—knew." Again it was a misdirection of sorts, since she was already leading him into the cottage.

"This is more of a follow-up, Mrs. . . . ."

"Ingram, Louise Ingram. But please call me Lou; everyone out here does . . . but not when we're back in the city—do you find that strange? I always have."

The room was huge, with a wooden staircase to the left that led to a balcony surrounding the open space on three sides. At one end, a stone fireplace he could have stood in was full of wild flowers in several pots and tin cans.

"This is a beautiful place, Lou, really beautiful." He realized he was twirling around slowly the way kids do watching the stars at night, and stopped. The light from the lake danced like diamonds through the windows, and offshore he could see roughly where *Book's Boat* had taken him. There were people down on the dock. He turned back to Mrs. Ingram. "Shall we sit here?" He motioned to an old leather couch with a cat curled up sleeping on a flat pillow near the arm.

"Oh no. It's a pretty day in June; we should sit on the porch lakeside. Would you like a lemonade, or perhaps a beer?"

"A lemonade would be great. Can I help?"

"Don't be silly, Detective Vertesi. We make gallons of lemonade up here every day, and by noon it's all gone." She smiled and swung easily towards the kitchen door on the far side of the fireplace.

After half an hour on the lakeside porch, Vertesi had asked Mrs. Ingram all the questions he could think of, and no one had come up from the dock. He closed his notebook and was about to stand up when at last a young woman came running up from the lake. Slapping the screen door open, she said, "Oh, hi. Sorry—be back in a minute," and rushed past them into the cottage. A few minutes later, as Vertesi was standing, notebook in hand, looking out at the lake, she was back. "Sorry, I had to pee," she announced.

"Oh, God, Rachel," Mrs. Ingram said. "Detective Vertesi, this is my youngest, Rachel Ingram." She left the porch to go inside.

"Sweet, isn't she? I'm twenty-five and I can still embarrass my mom."

"Not just your mom." Vertesi held out his hand but pulled it back just before hers touched his. "Did you wash your hands, Rachel?"

He could hear her mother laugh, and after a moment's hesitation, Rachel did too.

"I see," she said. "A comic cop. Well, I guess you're here about the murder." She was wearing a turquoise bikini very much like the yellow one he'd seen her in the day before. Perhaps she bought them by the dozen.

"I am. Do you know the people who own the cottage?" He'd already learned that no one knew Dr. Michael Hadley.

"Ah, actually no. But I do know Book's boat, and I think I waved to you yesterday sitting in the back of it. Am I right, Detective?" She was smiling at him.

"Well, yeah."

"Look, everyone up here waves! I was doing what cottagers do—we wave to passing boats." She stifled a laugh and looked out at the lake. "Did you think it was something else?"

"I'm Italian." He was feeling awkward, but enjoying it.

"Right, like I'm supposed to know what that means."

"It means, Miss—Rachel—that I saw a beautiful girl— sorry, woman—and I thought to myself, *God, I'd love to meet that woman.* And yeah, I hoped that you could see me sitting there in Book's boat, all uncomfortable because I'm not from around here, and that you saw me looking back at you. I was trying to say something to you, like 'I want to walk along the beach or out on the lane and have you tell me what it is that's so special about this place.' That's what I meant, I think. I come from a long line of Sicilian explorers."

"And flirts. Did you practise that?"

"No. Did it work? . . . I mean, I'm serious—I'm not a *saputo.*" He put his hand on his heart and then, realizing how that might look to her, dropped it quickly, but not quickly enough.

"Wow, you're good. Hand on heart . . . No, Detective, I don't think you're a *saputo*. By the way, what the hell is a *saputo*?"

"Well, he'd be the opposite of me."

She looked him over and said, "I'll go change. You're making me look bad in your suit and all."

As he waited, Vertesi picked up an old copy of *National Geographic* and flipped idly through its pages. When he came to several spreads of South American insects in full colour, he put it back on the table next to a mosquito candle that looked as if it had been there for years. All around the wick were dead insects partly submerged in the yellow wax.

Rachel returned in a white cotton tank top and a pair of blue shorts like the ones he used to wear in gym class with the stripes down both sides. "Where do you want to go, Detective Vertesi—for a boat ride?"

"No. To tell you the truth, it made me nauseous yesterday. Let's just walk."

She laughed. "But I thought you were an Italian explorer."

"Yeah, well. I guess we explored Europe, maybe Sweden . . . or Russia."

"Come on, we'll take the beach road down to the point." She nodded in the general direction of the spit of land beyond which, somewhere in the distance, was a cottage surrounded by yellow police tape.

JESSE WILSON, THE SENIOR security manager, was a pale, slim man in his mid-thirties. Easily manoeuvring the joystick, he controlled the speed of the video so that people walked back and forth like Keystone Kops. Each time he came to Lydia he slowed it down to normal speed.

It took just over three hours to review a week's worth of digital video from the drive-by, the lobby, the elevators and the sixteenth-floor cameras. Flickering images of people going and coming, unloading groceries, carrying lapdogs, holding hands, pausing to pick up mail or stealing kisses in front of the elevators—aware or unaware that they were being captured on camera. Daily footage of Lydia Petrescu breezing out, violin over her shoulder, carrying a black backpack, and returning in the evening with her violin case and the same black backpack.

Under his breath MacNeice said, "We'll find the laptop and the entire digital age in that backpack."

"Sir?" Aziz said.

"The backpack. She was into portability; I bet she used a laptop for music class, emails, everything. With the possible exception of the trip to the beach house, she probably never went anywhere without it."

On two occasions—one on the previous Tuesday at 8:10 p.m. and the other on Wednesday morning at 9:42 a.m.—Lydia came in with the tall, bushy-haired young man. MacNeice marked the dates and times in his notebook. "Where did he go afterwards?"

Wilson looked up at him blankly. "What do you mean?"

"Where did he go? He came in—he must have come out. Why aren't we seeing him come out? She comes out two hours later in her gown, but he's not with her."

"Maybe we missed it." Wilson pushed the joystick in the opposite direction and everyone rushed comically backwards, but they couldn't spot the young man leaving the building.

"Do you recall ever seeing him in the lobby?"

"Not me. There are 450 units in this complex. We have a two-man team on day shift, and that means I'm either here in the office scanning the screens or I'm out there shaking hands or opening doors. At night we have just one concierge, and that would be Ted Zazulak. He might have spoken to them. The concierge desk has three screens—one for the drive-by, one for the front doors and the third for the ground-floor elevators—but they all feed through to this room, where we have rotating views of the elevators on each floor. If he breezed on past Zaz, he didn't mention anything in the logbook."

"Is there another way out of the building that isn't covered by your cameras?"

"Yeah, the back exit out of the underground parking. If you took the elevator to the parking level and came out that exit, you'd avoid all of the cameras—except for the one that caught you going into the elevator." He smiled as if that made the system foolproof.

"Is there a camera that covers the stairwell?" MacNeice asked.

"The stairwell?" Wilson looked up at the wall of screens.

"Yes, I noticed that the camera that covers the elevator is facing away from the exit stairwell."

"Well, yeah, but nobody takes the stairs here. We've got four super-fast elevators." Wilson was still looking at the wall as if the strategic placement of the video surveillance cameras was obvious.

MacNeice stepped up to the console and pointed to the screen for the sixteenth-floor elevator camera. "This camera will catch anyone coming out of either elevator, but it's pointed away from the direction of Lydia Petrescu's flat. So if you were someone who didn't want to be seen, wouldn't you just go down the stairs to the parking level and out the exit to the street?"

"That could happen, I guess." Wilson went back to the joystick and pulled it towards him. The images whirred forward.

"Stop the camera." MacNeice had seen something he'd been looking for, something that didn't look like anything else. "Go slowly now . . . stop again." The image froze with a diagonal shiver of static lines. Two men were coming through the door. Both wore black leather jackets that hung straight to just below the waist. "Who are these two? Are they residents?"

"No way they live here. Maybe they're delivery guys."

"Not likely, since they're empty-handed. Okay, line up all the other cameras to this time frame. I want especially to see the drive-by and the sixteenth-floor elevator footage. And when you get them together, let them play in real time."

It took several minutes, but to his credit, Wilson didn't fume or fuss about it. Finally he said, "Okay, here we go. I'm giving it to you in real time, left to right—left being the drive-by." He pushed a button on the console and sat back to watch the screens.

A black Range Rover pulled slowly into the drive-by and stopped at the far edge so that only the wheels and lower body were visible. After several seconds a figure got out of the front passenger seat, closed the door and waited. It was just possible to see the bottom of his black leather jacket. He was wearing jeans and what looked like black hiking boots. In a moment another figure walked into the frame from the right, presumably the driver, and as the two passed under the camera, one glanced up directly into the lens. He smiled briefly. Both wore sunglasses and had short-cropped fair hair.

The next screen showed them coming through the lobby door, where they would have had to use a resident's key fob or punch in a code. They did neither. The one who'd looked up at the drive-by camera turned around and looked up again. His body was shielding the taller man, the driver. In a moment they were both through the door.

"How'd they do that?" Wilson said, suddenly sitting up. He reached for the joystick.

"Let it run," MacNeice said.

At the elevators, both kept their heads down to avoid the more direct stare of the camera. The doors opened and they walked quickly inside.

"Why aren't there cameras in the elevators?" Aziz asked.

"There are, but when the building opened, the residents' association asked that they be turned off to avoid invasion of privacy. I don't know what they get up to in the elevators that's so private, but they were deactivated in the first six months of operation."

The two men appeared briefly on the sixteenth floor. They turned left, in the direction of the Petrescu apartment. Again Wilson moved to stop play.

"Let it run," MacNeice said again.

"Sir, look at the drive-by." Aziz was looking three screens to the left.

The rear door of the Range Rover opened and someone stepped out. He stood by the vehicle, walked slowly forward, kicked the front tire as if checking the air pressure, and walked back. He leaned against the side of the Rover.

"He's havin' a smoke," Wilson said quietly.

"I think you're right. Notice anything else?" MacNeice said.

"Uh . . . well, no. But I'm a smoker and I can spot the walk—that dumb wandering to kill time while you're havin' a butt."

"Black trousers with a very tight crease. His shoes, even with this feed, look as if they've been shined by a professional, and so far as I can tell, he's not wearing a leather jacket. His suit looks expensive."

"Wow, that's impressive." Wilson really did seem impressed, and he rocked back for a moment in his chair.

On the far monitor the two men appeared at the bottom of the screen. As the second elevator opened they walked up-frame and into it, and for a moment it was possible to see both of them clearly.

"I make the lapsed time between exiting and returning to the elevator roughly five and a half minutes," Aziz said.

"Big boys. They look like cops to me," Wilson said.

"They're not cops," MacNeice said flatly.

"How can you tell for sure?" Wilson watched as the two exited the elevators and came into view of the lobby camera.

"Well, for one, cops don't drive Range Rovers with guys with sharp creases sitting in the back seat. But there's something else about them."

"What's that, sir?" Aziz wanted to see what MacNeice was seeing.

"They don't walk like we do. It looks military, but it's not a North American military walk. I'm sure of it."

The two men left the building and joined Shiny Shoes next to the vehicle. A butt descended from the top of the frame, falling parallel to the creases. When it hit the pavement, one of the shoes ground the life out of it. They all got into the Rover and disappeared slowly from the screen.

"Told you he was a smoker." Wilson smiled.

"We'll review all of this footage again to see if these boys show up anywhere else, but we can have our people do it. What's the resolution?"

"Probably in the eight megapixel range, like a still camera. This system is the best I've ever worked with—you could make a billboard out of this stuff. Okay if I give it to you on a DVD?"

"That'll be fine. How long will it take to download it?" MacNeice checked his watch—10:58 a.m.

"About the time it took that guy to have a cigarette. If you want to wait, there's a lounge down the hall with an espresso machine. There's a fridge there too."

"That's perfect. Do you want us to bring a coffee back for you?"

"No, thanks. I've got enough of a buzz on just watching these screens."

Settling into a club chair with her espresso cup, Aziz glanced up at MacNeice, who was looking out at the courtyard garden, a space that looked both idyllic and lonely—intended to be seen and never wandered through. "What was it exactly about the way they walked?"

"Maybe something with the arm swing. North American men generally don't swing their arms like that. And the short steps they took—for big men it seemed strange, foreign."

"I think I get what you mean. The police academy's ju-jitsu coach took short steps when he walked. I assumed it was so he could react quicker than if he was using a long stride. It looked strange though, and a little threatening, because he had long legs."

"That's it. In all the great samurai movies, the samurai always take quick, short steps. And big men over here, even the ones who are violent—cops or otherwise—tend to saunter as if nothing could threaten them, as if they have lots of time. These guys walked as they were trained to walk."

"But how did you notice them in the first place?"

"Because they looked so out of place. Everybody coming and going—including Petrescu and her boyfriend—looked like they belonged here . . . but not those boys."

MacNeice put down his espresso cup on the counter. "Here's an exercise for you. Next time you look at that footage, try to convince yourself that those two men grew up here, went to college, got jobs and maybe have wives and kids, a house with a lawn sprinkler going and bikes in the driveway."

"Is this a new technique, sir?" Aziz smiled as she stood up and carried her cup over to the counter.

"Years ago, an artist I knew told me that he would take his drawings—you know, just when he felt they were really good— and turn them upside down to look at them. Invariably he'd spot things that didn't work, didn't fit, that he couldn't see looking right side up. His theory was that the true form of the drawing was revealed only when he turned it upside down. Well, this is a bit like that. I wasn't looking at what they were doing or even so much where they were going. There was something upside down about the way they looked and walked— even the shoes."

"What about the shoes?"

"Two heavies wearing the same footgear makes me think standard issue military."

Wilson appeared at the door with an envelope in his hand. "Here you go—it's all there." He handed it to MacNeice. "Let me know if there's anything else you need."

"Well, we'll need to know who the concierge was when these boys came through, and whether he noticed how they gained access. How many shifts do you use to cover this place?" MacNeice asked.

"Six of us on rotating shifts—two weeks of nights, two of days, two of afternoons, and we also rotate weekends. It's a good gig. A bit quiet, normally, but good."

"Why do they call you a concierge?" Aziz asked.

"Just bullshit, really. I mean, I answer the phone if someone calls and I can order cabs, take in dry cleaning, book restaurants and that kind of thing, but really my background is digital surveillance. The guys on the desk are more like concierges, if that's the word. I come here, I wear this Italian suit and a black tie, but for the most part I'm watching that console. . . . Speaking of which, I should get back."

"Thanks for your help." MacNeice picked up his notebook and took one last look at the garden. *A plant prison*, he thought.

He and Aziz shook hands with Wilson and walked ahead of him towards the entrance, passing the concierge, who was reading a magazine. As Wilson reached the door to his security room he turned back. "Oh, one thing I thought of, concerning the boyfriend . . ."

"What's that?" MacNeice asked

"Well, if the guy had a bicycle, there's a bike rack in the basement. Maybe he went down the stairs to the basement and rode out on his bike." He shrugged to cover himself in case it wasn't much of a theory.

"That's good—very good." MacNeice smiled at him, and Wilson smiled back before he returned to his darkened room.

Walking across the drive-by to the car, MacNeice said, "You see, just when I begin to think highly of my powers of observation, along comes hi-tech Jesse Wilson with a credible theory about the boyfriend that hadn't occurred to me. It sure does keep you humble. And he doesn't look like he's seen the light—well, sunlight, at least—for days."

"Years." Aziz opened the passenger door of the Chevy.

FIFTEEN

—

As MacNeice pulled up in front of her apartment, Aziz unfastened her seatbelt but didn't reach for the door handle. "What do you want me to focus on tomorrow?"

"Well, the plates on that Range Rover had plastic shields, but the number might be readable in spite of the glare. Could you get the lab guys on that?"

"Right. Anything else?"

"We don't know much about Antonin Petrescu other than that he owns a shop that trades in expensive furniture and old papers. I want to know if he's connected to the two heavies in leather jackets." MacNeice turned off the ignition and sat back. "We know his son is in the Romanian military, doing biomedical work of some kind. I want to know what kind, and where he is now."

"I have an idea. A good friend of mine in my doctoral

graduating class ended up working for the U.N. as a security analyst. She did that for a few years and then last year she took a job with Interpol—again in security. She might know who we can speak to about the brother. I'll Skype her when I get upstairs. She's six hours ahead, so I might not reach her, but she'll know I'm trying."

"Call me when you've spoken to her. She might be able to find out more about the father too."

"Why don't you come up? I'll make some tea and we can see if she's online now."

"That would be nice, but Fiza . . . I don't want to intrude."

"You're not intruding, sir, and besides, I'd like to keep chasing this."

THE APARTMENT WAS MUCH SMALLER than Lydia Petrescu's but with no less light. The view was somewhat obscured by a lower building next door, but looking over its roof MacNeice could see the Carolinian forest of the Royal Reserve rolling beyond the rooftops. "It's a beautiful view."

From the kitchen she said, "Thanks, I love it." He could hear the electric kettle coming to life. "I'm just going to change. Make yourself comfortable."

He looked at the paintings on the wall, mostly abstract and very colourful. On a bookcase shelf, sitting proud of the dozens of novels and fat volumes on criminology and psychology, was a photograph of Aziz standing at attention with her parents in London. She must have been fourteen or so, and she wore black trousers, a tweed jacket and a headscarf. She wasn't smiling, but neither did she appear unhappy—a look MacNeice had come to know. Her parents were smiling broadly, and he noted that her mother hadn't covered her hair, and was using a hand to keep it from flying into her face in the breeze. Behind them was one of the bridges that stretch over the Thames.

"I had just won a scholarship to a very exclusive school. They were very proud and I was very nervous."

He turned to look at Aziz, who was now in a T-shirt and sweatpants. "Nervous? You don't show it. What bridge is that?"

"Waterloo. Have you been to London?" She headed back to the kitchen.

"Yes, though not for some time. When we were there, it rained so much we were always running from cabs to hotels, cabs to restaurants, cabs to museums and concert halls. I got to know and love the London taxis." He moved to the dining room table, which was positioned somewhat tightly next to the kitchen. He sat down to watch her making tea.

"You must be hungry—I certainly am. I have some beautiful cured ham that the Mennonites make, and I've also got a baguette." Without waiting for his response, she sliced the baguette in half and then sliced the two pieces lengthwise.

The small kitchen had by necessity been designed ergonomically, and like a dancer she pivoted tidily from counter to refrigerator and took out the ham, some cheese and prepared mustard. In a couple of minutes she was in front of him with a plate. "I've got the tea cozy over the pot so the tea can steep. How about some water, though?"

"Water'd be great, thank you. I remember how the English complained about the damp and cold and how people seemed to be freezing all the time, but everyone had a tea cozy to keep their tea warm."

Aziz smiled but made no comment.

They made small talk about the neighbourhood as they ate,

and when they'd finished their sandwiches, MacNeice said, "I thought Muslims didn't eat pork."

"That's true. And Catholics don't eat meat on Fridays."

"I hope I'm not being rude."

"You aren't, and I'm not sensitive about it. Nor was I earlier with Mr. Petrescu, though I was happy you thought I was and got me out of the room."

"I'm embarrassed to say that I know little about your religion beyond what I read in the newspapers. I hope my curiosity isn't offensive to you."

"It isn't. I just happen to be fairly private about my beliefs, in part because I know that my religion is a cause of great suspicion and fear around the world."

"Not for me it isn't."

"Perhaps not. . . . Yes, I can see that it isn't."

"Seeing the photo in London, though, I did wonder about the headscarf, and why you don't wear one now."

"I'm still devout but, paradoxically, I've chosen to ignore many of the outward signs of that belief—such as not eating pork, such as that headscarf. My family has an aversion to any kind of fundamentalism." She looked over at the picture on the bookshelf and changed the subject. "Let's look and see if my friend is online. Her name is Bozana Pietrowska; she's got two passports, and one is Polish."

The computer was on a small desk by the living room window. He pulled up one of the dining room chairs to sit next to her. Aziz logged on and fired off a message that showed up onscreen as a grey silhouette. With an electronic burp, a blonde woman with high cheekbones and a flashing smile replaced the silhouette. She was wearing a deep blue sweater that looked electric in the low-res image.

"What a lovely surprise, and how typically you, Fiz. I was just finishing notes from a meeting today and getting ready to shut down. How are you? And who's that next to you? Ask him to slide into view."

"It's my boss, Bo. Meet Detective Superintendent MacNeice. Mac, this is my former roommate, Bozana Pietrowska." To MacNeice she said, "You see this little window on the screen? You've got to get closer to see yourself and be seen."

MacNeice shoved his chair over so it was touching hers. Suddenly he appeared beside her in the small frame above Bozana Pietrowska's head. She smiled, smoothed her hair back with both hands and said, "Is this a business call?" Something in her voice suggested she was hoping it was otherwise.

"Yes, Bo. We're dealing with the murder of a young woman here and there's a connection to Romania."

"Arggh—all roads these days are leading to Romania for me." Bozana turned away for a moment, then came back into frame. "What is it?"

"A microbiologist specializing in infectious diseases. He's a colonel in the Romanian army named Gregori Petrescu, stationed in Bucharest."

Bozana had opened her laptop computer and was tapping in the information.

"He's the brother of the deceased," Aziz continued. "We're interested in knowing his whereabouts and what exactly he's working on."

MacNeice moved slightly closer to Aziz and centred himself in the window on the screen before he spoke. "We also want to know anything about the father, who lives here but has ties there as well. His name is Antonin Petrescu. He deals in antique furniture and papers, documents and letters, and he too appears to have a background in microbiology."

"Why don't you just ask him?" Bozana kept typing, though she did look up at the screen for his response.

"A good question. My only answer at the moment is that this killing seems to be some form of message to the father."

"Fair enough. Anything else?"

After a quick nod from MacNeice, Aziz said, "That's it for now. Sleep well, Bo, and thanks. I'll call you tomorrow."

"You too, Fiz—you look tired. It's Sunday over there; what are you doing working my friend on a Sunday, Detective MacNeice?"

Aziz jumped in before he could answer. "Totally my choice."

"Lighten up, Fiz. Listen, I'll have something for you when you wake up. Like I said, I've been a bit inundated with Romania, so you've lucked out—I've got three people dedicated to it on my team. *Dobranoc*, Fiza, and goodnight, Detective MacNeice." The window went blank with another burp, and their images disappeared with it.

"What's *dobranoc*?" MacNeice said, moving his chair away from her.

"It's Polish for goodnight." Aziz shut down the computer. "Right, let's have our tea."

MacNeice helped clear the lunch dishes, then she led him over to one of the two upholstered chairs adjacent to the sofa and sat on the sofa facing him. "I want to know more about what influences your work, Mac."

"Influences . . . . It sounds so lofty. Almost everything, I guess."

She could see that he was struggling to provide more of an answer, and waited patiently.

"I think what we do is intuitive, but it's also essentially

about observation." He was looking down at his cup as if he was reading the tea leaves. "If your work is about observation, then it seems only natural—to me at least—that you never stop observing. You observe obsessively . . . and minutely. You train yourself to look inside, outside, peripherally. You study art and music, the way people dance, walk, lie—and tell the truth. You record your dreams and you're willing to learn from them." He put the cup down on top of the circular end table next to him. "Am I making any sense?"

"I think so. Go on." She looked at him over the rim of her cup.

"Sadly, I can't. I only know that much. Everything influences my observation—absolutely everything." He moved slightly, as if he was uncomfortable or about to stand up, but he didn't. "Sitting at the computer just now, I noticed the wear on the desk where you put your hands every day. I noticed the imprint from a ballpoint pen where you've written letters and signed cheques on the soft wood—white pine, I think. Some keys on your computer are more worn than others, and there's a slight whitening on the edge of the desk where I suspect you rub your right hand when it's itchy or numb from working at the keyboard—but not your left, because you're right-handed."

Aziz looked nonplussed but said, "Anything else?"

"The stains on the right where you put your teacup—they're all within an inch of each other, like a series of quarter-moons on the pine. Your attention is usually on the computer when you set the cup down—conveniently within reach, so you can pick it up without looking. I also noticed a bookmark in your criminology text that I think is a boarding pass—Lufthansa, 2006."

He paused as if considering whether he should go on. "I noticed a scent about you that wasn't there till you changed clothes—lavender, I think." Until then he'd been looking at her feet, but now he met her gaze. "There's a crumb on the left side of your mouth that's been there since you took the second-to-last bite of your sandwich." He smiled awkwardly and looked away. "All this while we were talking to someone who could really help in the case."

Aziz set her cup down on the end table and wiped her mouth.

When MacNeice spoke next, he sounded apologetic. "It's probably a clinical obsession. It's not something I can turn off and it's not necessarily something I think you should learn how to do."

"My mother makes sachets of lavender from her garden. I have one in every drawer. I don't notice it anymore."

"I like it." He stood up. She sat watching him as he moved towards the window and looked out over the rooftops to the forest. "I should go."

"Okay. I'll see you off then." She stood up and went over to the door.

MacNeice came away from the window, walked over to her and shook her hand. "Thank you, Fiza, for the sandwich and tea, and also for the call to Bozana. I'll see you tomorrow." He was gone before she could say goodbye.

BOZANA WAS PEERING THROUGH both distance and time. For her it was one in the afternoon, for Fiza Aziz it was six a.m.

"Sorry, Bo, I stayed up late . . . ." She yawned and roughed up her sleep-flattened hair.

"Good for you! I thought there might be something between you two." Bozana wagged a finger at the screen and laughed.

"What? No! It's not like that. He's my bloody boss— I mean, my superior officer. Can you hold on while I get a glass of water?" She didn't wait for a reply but heard Bozana's voice say, "Sure."

As she slid back into the chair and into frame, Bozana said, "Okay, okay. Though you two do look good together."

"Thank you, I think. What do you have?"

Aziz wiped the sleep from her eyes and tried to focus on what Bozana was saying, but her mind kept going back to MacNeice. After realizing she'd missed several seconds of what her friend was telling her, she held up a hand. "Sorry, Bo, I spaced out for a second. Could you tell me again? I promise I'll pay attention." She picked up a pad and made a show of being ready to write everything down.

"Okay, so listen this time. I've tracked down your Gregori Petrescu—well, at least to where he was a few days ago. I can also tell you that he is running the infectious diseases unit of the Romanian army." She reached over, brought a folder into frame and opened it on her desk. "I haven't found out exactly what he does, but I think he's a spook. My suspicion is that his unit is developing infectious diseases, not ways to guard against them, though probably he's doing that too."

"Who have they got to use them against?"

"It's hard to say. It might just be insurance. But when you consider that it's Romania . . . Under that repressive, paranoid Stalinist Nicolae Ceausescu, who was extremely suspicious of Moscow, they probably got up to a lot of skulduggery. Then *pffft*, Ceausescu is deposed and the government falls. But old habits die hard. Most of these guys, including your Gregori— who was just a kid at the time—learned their trade in the Soviet bloc era."

"But who are they afraid of now?"

"Well, they're not Slavic and they're virtually surrounded by Slavs they distrust. Adding to that, less than one percent of Romania is Muslim—"

"Thank goodness for that," Aziz said wryly and took another sip of water.

"Well, sure, but right next to them, Bulgaria has a twelve percent Muslim population, and below them is Turkey, which is ninety-eight percent Muslim. And all around the Black Sea are people itching for a fight. Meanwhile, seventy percent of Romanians are Orthodox Christians."

"I don't get it. Are you talking the old orthodoxy rag?"

"Partly. But there's an exodus of young people going to work in Italy and Germany and so on, and the folks who remain in Romania may be feeling threatened enough to shore up their borders and their defences . . . . But what all this geo-politicking has to do with a murdered girl from Dundurn is anybody's guess."

"The father? Anything turn up on him?"

"Your superior officer"—she paused cheekily for effect, which Fiza registered but ignored—"said he deals in papers and antiques."

"Yes, he has a very exclusive shop full of beautiful odds and sods and he has a lovely house with a terrific garden."

"Well, your MacNeice has a very refined nose. Antonin Petrescu was a minister in the Ceausescu government, and he is indeed—or was—a microbiologist. And can you guess what his area of interest was?" She crossed her arms and looked at her friend.

"Infectious diseases."

"It's a family affair. No information here about what Petrescu senior was doing, but it's safe to say that Soviet-era

Romania had no shortage of enemies and none of the moralistic posturing of the West about engaging in bio-warfare. It's cheap and effective—if you're upwind. Petrescu got out just before the government fell. How did MacNeice pick up on that?"

"He's an observationist, Bo. That may not be a word, but it does describe him. He spotted a row of microbiology books in Petrescu's library."

"Didn't you?"

"No, I'm an observationist-in-training. When MacNeice was here yesterday, he gave me a tutorial on observation that was incredible—and a bit terrifying."

"How so?"

"Well, I don't know. But if everything that you see, feel, hear, touch, sense, imagine and even dream doesn't just pass you by, but is observed and considered in some way before you move on—"

"It sounds exhausting."

"Exactly."

"But it also sounds like you're training with the right boss. I mean, I wouldn't want to be like that—or even particularly close to someone who is like that—but I'd want such a man investigating my murder. How was the girl killed?"

"By a needle through the left ear and into her brain. The syringe was loaded with battery acid. She was dissolved from the inside out."

Bozana winced and instinctively cupped her ear. "Christ, I wish you hadn't told me that!"

"It has us a bit freaked too, though each of us seems to deal with it differently. She was an up-and-coming violinist who had just graduated from the Conservatory. She was looking forward to a wonderful career in which she would play her music dressed in beautiful gowns, taking bows and giving encores."

"Fuck. Okay, I don't know what else I can do from here, but if you make a request—not too many, mind you—I'll do whatever I can. But if it goes too far, this will have to be a formal affair, and trust me, you don't want to go there." Bozana closed the file folder and shoved back her chair.

SIXTEEN

—

MacNeice eased himself behind the wheel of the Chevy at 7:34 a.m. He'd had too much grappa the night before, initially to help him sleep. When the second shot didn't work, he went for a third. The room swam as he lay in bed, and when he finally did drop off, he was set upon by dreams he now couldn't recall. He woke with a headache and the distinct impression that they had all been bad.

He'd felt deeply embarrassed by his ramblings to Aziz. He'd even felt some shame, as if he'd been caught showing off or looking through her underwear drawer. Her desk was just a desk, after all. Where she placed her coffee cup, whether her right palm was itchy . . . He considered the explanations or apologies he might offer and almost settled on "I have nothing to teach you that you cannot discover on your own." But in the end he decided he'd said enough.

He reached over to the car's CD player, hit the On button and immediately regretted it. Frank Zappa was into a second verse of brilliant lunacy: "Movin' to Montana soon / Gonna be a dental floss tycoon . . . ." Zappa was the greatest thing for clearing his head but the worst thing for a massive headache. MacNeice turned him off and didn't bother scanning the CDs for something more mellow.

He powered the Chevy down the hill and onto Mountain Road. The light slashed through the windshield and he saw flashing dots everywhere. He pulled over to the shoulder, found his sunglasses and put them on. Driving in the slow lane, MacNeice tried his deep-breathing exercises and before long was feeling light-headed. He turned west on King Street, determined not to think about anything else till he reached division headquarters.

The two-way radio was off, but his cellphone suddenly buzzed to life. MacNeice pushed the button on the phone, and over the in-car speaker he heard Wallace's voice: "MacNeice, you there?"

"Yes, sir."

"Give me an update. Your desk sergeant told me you worked the weekend. What have you got for me?"

"The girl was pregnant, sir. The father is grief-stricken, as you'd expect. The brother is a colonel in the Romanian army. There's a young man we're looking for—we have a digital security capture of him and we'll be going to the Conservatory to find out if anyone can identify him. He was her boyfriend."

"A strong suspect, then?"

"A suspect? Not in my opinion, sir, but he is a person of interest."

"Word's out about the relationship with the boyfriend, MacNeice. I know it wasn't your crew that leaked it, but the media are building a sensational story about how this beautiful girl came to be found dead in a beach house." He stopped there, clearly hoping that his detective would have a sense of how uncomfortable this was going to get.

"I'm sorry to hear that, sir, but I guess it was inevitable. Has how she died been leaked?"

"Not yet. I've been saying that the manner of her death is still under investigation. I hope that will give you some more time. How much do you think you need?"

"I have no idea, sir. We're making headway, I think, but I can't give you a time frame." By this point MacNeice's hand was cupping his head, his elbow resting on the window frame as he cruised slowly down the road.

"Right. Keep me in the loop. I've got a policing conference in Toronto that I have to attend and I know our chief will be grinding me all the way there. I'm counting on you."

The surround-sound of his voice disappeared and MacNeice heaved a huge sigh. About a mile later, the cellphone buzzed again.

He signalled his intention to pull off onto the shoulder so he wouldn't have to listen and drive. As he came to a stop, he pushed the button. "Yes, sir?"

"Is that you, MacNeice?" The cheerful English accent was a welcome relief from the suppressed anxiety in the deputy chief's voice.

"Yes, I'm here."

"Let's speak on a land line. Call this number. . . ."

Judging by the ambient noise, Donald Ferguson was calling from a phone booth, probably downtown. MacNeice pulled off King next to a booth outside Betty's Burgers.

"While I don't want to alarm you," Ferguson said when he picked up, "I think we can't be too careful."

"Sure."

"Splendid. Look, I thought I should let you know what I have on your stainless steel syringe. No one in Canada or the U.S. fits the bill, but there are two men—one wonders why it's always men who specialize in such things—and they're both Bulgarian."

"Bulgarian, not Romanian?"

"Right. These two were trained in Moscow but they are most definitely Bulgarian."

"How can you be so sure of that, Ferguson?" MacNeice was reaching for his notebook.

"There was an East German candidate, but he has been inactive since the Wall came down. Now I'm told he's dead of lung cancer. So I'm very certain—or rather my source is certain—but as to which Bulgarian it is . . . Well, that, I'm afraid, is your problem."

"I take it I cannot speak to your source?" MacNeice already knew the answer.

"That would be imprudent, Detective, and it would render me useless to you in the future. It would also put me at serious risk." Ferguson hadn't lost the brightness in his voice, though MacNeice could detect a shadow of surprise that MacNeice had put such a question to him.

"Can you give me the names of the men?"

"Gheorghi—George, I suppose, with a couple of H's—Borisov; he's from Sofia and is the younger of the two, possibly in his early forties. The other is Hrista—H-R-I-S-T-A—Popov, just as it sounds. He's from Stara Zagora, again like it sounds."

"Thank you for this. Is there anything I can do for you?" MacNeice put his notebook and pen away.

"No, of course not; I'm happy to help. These are both nasty customers but they don't operate independently. They're for hire, I'm told, and very accomplished."

"What do you mean exactly?"

"They're engineers—very refined tool-and-die makers like me—and they build what they're paid to build. Should anyone ask, Detective, I'll deny knowing anything about this. Cheerio."

The line went dead, leaving only the sound of traffic streaming by and his shallow breathing. MacNeice hung up the phone, took a deep breath and instantly regretted it as his nostrils filled with the smell of stale grease from the burger joint. On the bright side, he realized that his headache had abated, but it was soon replaced by the thought that he might be in over his head, and way outside his territory.

ARRIVING AT DIVISION, HE PARKED in the space closest to a small clump of evergreens and birch trees at the edge of the lot. Like a radio signal that flips from old-time rock to classical music without warning, his mind reeled between Lydia Petrescu and the potentially ever-expanding cast of Eastern Europeans.

A slam on the car roof sent an electric shock of fear through him. He looked up to see Swetsky's wide face grinning at him through the driver's-side window. "You okay, Mac?"

MacNeice nodded and took the key out of the ignition. Getting out of the car, he said, "You scared the shit out me."

"I figured if you were having a heart attack, a good smack on the roof would work as well as a defibrillator." He slapped MacNeice on the back. "Actually, I thought you'd see me comin' in your mirror—you drove past me as you came into the lot."

MacNeice locked the Chevy and together they walked to the side entrance. "What are you doing here?" MacNeice asked. "You're not on today."

"The DC called. He wants me to pitch in full-time with you guys. I guess the mayor and the media are climbin' up his backside. You're the lead—give me somethin' to do." Swetsky knew how this would appear to someone of MacNeice's experience. "I'll play it anyway you want, Mac. This fucker's going to move on, but you and I will still be here. Your call."

"I'm glad, Swets. But it would've been great if he'd told me when he called this morning, before you scared the bejesus out of me."

Inside, Swetsky turned to MacNeice. "Wanna coffee from the caff? I'll grab you one."

"No thanks, I'm coffee'd out already. I'll see you upstairs."

Leaving Swetsky in the lobby, MacNeice pushed open the stairwell door, looked at his watch, waited for the second hand to reach three, then took off. This morning he needed to grab at the railing to haul himself up the stairs. At his floor, his chest heaving and feeling slightly nauseous, he looked at his watch. "Sixteen seconds. Ah well, considering . . ."

Aziz was already online and Vertesi, with his feet propped up on the edge of his desk, was holding forth about something.

"I didn't mean to interrupt, Vertesi. Go on," MacNeice said, as he dropped his notebook on his desk and switched on his computer.

Aziz turned around, smiling. "Vertesi was just telling me about his date, sir."

"How did it go?" MacNeice swung his chair around to face him.

"Aw, well. . . . Well, it was great, actually." Vertesi took his bottle of water in hand but didn't drink.

"He's being coy, sir. He told me he may be in love with a girl he met at the lake." Aziz turned back to her computer.

"Jesus, Aziz!" Vertesi raised his hands in a what-the-fuck gesture that both his colleagues were familiar with.

MacNeice waited for the moment to pass. "Perhaps *shy* is a better word, Aziz."

"You're right, sir, *shy*." Aziz was keying something in and didn't turn around.

"Hey, you two, any second Swetsky's gonna show up. He's been put on our team full-time by the deputy chief. He'll probably use his own desk, but we should give him a full briefing here."

"What the hell is that about?" Vertesi said. "Wallace doesn't think we can crack this?"

"He's taking heat. What's the headline this morning—"Cops Stumped on Beach House Killing"? So you're probably right. This will signal that he's doing something more proactive. But Swetsky's one of us, and I'm happy to have him in our corner."

Vertesi didn't look so sure.

Soon Swetsky arrived, carrying four paper cups of coffee, a small stack of sugar packets, milk and cream cuplets and brown plastic stirrers. "I don't know how you guys take it, but for future reference, I'm double-double." He smiled, put the coffee tray down on the counter between Aziz and Vertesi and looked around for a chair.

"Michael, grab a chair for Swets."

Vertesi nodded and got up.

Swets took a look at the younger man's face and said, "Guys, I know this isn't what you would have chosen. I'm not that happy about it either. Apart from getting to work days—which is nice—I'd rather each of us work our own cases."

"Thanks for the coffee, Swets." Vertesi went to get the chair.

"Yes, thank you," Aziz said. "I'm coffee'd out, though."

"That's what your boss said. Yeah, well, it's there if you feel like it later. You can stick it in the microwave—it's not half bad, but not like that expresso Mac makes."

"That's *espresso*, with an S." MacNeice stood up, clapped him on both shoulders and gestured for the big man to take his chair. "Take a load off and let's get started."

He took out his notebook and, glancing at the page for the spellings, wrote on the board in red marker: *Gheorghi Borisov and Hrista Popov, Bulgarians—potential syringe connection.*

Vertesi slid a new chair into the space beside the whiteboard as MacNeice looked back at Swetsky sipping slowly from his cup. "A lot's happened since the beach house, so we'll bring you up to speed and then determine next steps."

It was after eleven a.m. before the three detectives had finished briefing their new colleague and—as each was party to new information—each other. Then MacNeice divided the day's efforts equally between them, giving Swetsky the job of tracking down the doctor who owned the beach house. When he finally put the marker back in its tray, it was 11:48 a.m.

"I'm hungry. I'm going over to Marcello's—who's coming?"

"I'm off to the doctor's office. I figure the best time to nose around is over the lunch hour, so I'll catch a sandwich on the way back." Swetsky hauled himself out of the chair and, in a move more graceful than MacNeice thought possible for such a big man, he was out of the cubicle and gone.

"I've kind of got a date. I've got some more questions to ask the Ingram girl." Vertesi stood, sheepish, avoiding their eyes.

MacNeice looked down at Aziz, who said, "I'm going to let Bozana know about the two Bulgarians, which will take a few minutes, but then I'd be happy to join you."

"Perfect. I'll go down to the lab to see if there's anything on the Range Rover. Be back in ten."

THEY TOOK THE LAST BOOTH, nearest the kitchen. While it was the busiest area of the restaurant, it was also the most private, since the only people going by were wait staff.

The special was Marcello's mother's handmade sage-and-goat-cheese ravioli. The food arrived as Aziz was telling MacNeice more about Vertesi's new girlfriend.

"He apparently walked right up to the cottage—or as he describes it, the family resort—and asked her to go out with him." She stopped for her first bite of ravioli and hummed approvingly. "They went for a walk—this is so good—and they sat out on a point and talked for two and a half hours."

"About the case?" A stupid question, MacNeice thought, too late.

"Initially it seemed like no, that this was Vertesi responding to the male urge to mate in springtime, but in the end they did. She actually remembered seeing the boat—two boats, in fact. The second one arrived later, anchored offshore a few hundred yards and just sat there."

"Two boats. From the same marina?" MacNeice had barely touched his ravioli.

"Mac"—she stopped eating and looked up at him—"I thought you were starved."

"You're right. Of course, sorry, go on." He took a bite.

"She couldn't tell for sure, because it was dusk and she wasn't paying that much attention. But she remembered seeing a girl in the bow, her hand over the side, trailing in the water, and a man at the tiller of the outboard. She was fishing off the end of the dock and saw them land at the beach. As you thought, he jumped out and carried her up towards the cottage, which is hidden behind the point—she can't see it from the dock."

She had managed to finish the ravioli between sentences, and now she picked up a piece of bread, broke off a bite-size chunk and swirled it around in the leftover sauce. Just before putting it in her mouth, she added, "Vertesi says she thought the girl was wearing a gown, because it looked so billowy and out of place. She assumed it was a honeymoon, except—and get this—the guy was in cut-off jeans or shorts." She smiled and popped the bread into her mouth. "She couldn't remember anything about the second boat other than there were four guys in it."

MacNeice had stopped eating again. Aziz dropped her hands to the table edge and said, "Are you okay?"

"I was just wondering where this takes us. Why didn't Vertesi mention this in the briefing with Swetsky? Was there anything else?"

"He wanted to tell you. If I hadn't teased him he probably would have, but you know Vertesi—he's a big team player and Swetsky coming on probably threw him. He's having lunch with her today. She's a teacher. He took a shot of Ruvola with him to see if she'd recognize him."

"Romance and police work usually don't mix well, but maybe Vertesi will prove that theory wrong," MacNeice said, finally digging into his ravioli.

SEVENTEEN

—

"**W**HY DIDN'T YOU TELL THE POLICE what you saw?" Vertesi was sitting in the park opposite Rachel's school. They had just finished sandwiches and orange sodas and some breezy conversation about life in high school.

"When I heard that my parents had talked with the cops—that was the first time I thought what I had seen could mean something. I was out on the dock fishing when I saw the boat land, and it wasn't till the next day that I heard the girl had been murdered." She waved away some flies that had landed on the sandwich wrappers.

"Still, why not call the police once you'd figured it out?" Vertesi wasn't being aggressive; he was simply determined to find out the answer to something that had been bothering him.

"To be honest, Michael, I didn't want to get involved. My mother and father and especially my brothers didn't want me to get involved. Just before you showed up, I'd made up my mind to call when I got back to the city." She scrunched the wrappers into a tight ball and tossed it into the trash bin five feet away. It didn't touch the rim.

"Three points." He met her eyes. "So is that why you agreed to go for a walk with me?"

"No. Well, yes, I realized if I went for a walk with you I could handle it right then and there. . . ." She smiled to soften it.

"I'll need you to make a formal statement. I hope you don't mind."

"I don't mind. Will you be there?"

"I can be there if you want me to—or not." He was roughing up the gravel in front of the bench, playing soccer with the ring from a pop can.

"I do want you there." She said it so firmly that he rocked her slightly with his shoulder, and she pushed back.

"Where'd the second boat go?"

"I don't know. It was getting dark and I hadn't caught anything, so I walked back to see if I could get some leftover dinner. I knew that my brothers and their wives would be finished eating and off doing something else. I didn't feel like making nice-nice." She was staring at one of her students, who was walking with his arm around a girl.

"You didn't hear it, or the other one leaving the beach in front of the cottage?"

"No, I ate something, and since Mom and Dad were upstairs in their room watching television, I turned on the stereo, poured a glass of wine and started marking the last of my end-of-term exams on the couch."

"How soon can you come in?"

"After school today. Will you meet me?"

"Meet you? I'll come back and get you!" He stood up and offered her his hand.

The teenager and his girlfriend walked by just in time to catch it. "Whoa, Miss Ingram, get a load of you," he teased. The girlfriend smacked him but giggled as they passed.

"Now you've done it, Detective Vertesi. How am I going to live this one down? By one thirty this will be all over the school."

"Let me walk you to the door, teach." Remembering the photo of Ruvola, he pulled it out of his inside pocket. "Ever see this guy around the lake or the marina? There's a kiss in it for you if you have."

Rachel cocked an eyebrow at him but studied the mug shot, then shook her head. "No, I've never seen him."

"My mother would tell you—will tell you—that I'm actually very shy, and mostly I am," Vertesi said, to mitigate the line about the kiss. "I'll be here when, at three thirty?"

"You can be here then, but I won't be out until four fifteen. I'll meet you on the steps over there."

"Oh, and one last question—what do you make of Old Man Gibbs? The guy snapped when I started asking questions."

"He's always snapping. Since Florence died he's apparently been weirder than ever. My brothers think he's off his meds, but I honestly don't know. Most of us just avoid his place."

"Thanks. That's it—no more questions."

They shook hands at the door. The gesture was greeted by loud catcalls and whistles and someone yelling, "Don't be stingy, Miss Ingram. Kiss the man!" followed by more shouts and laughter.

She grinned at him, then turned and climbed the stairs without looking back.

HEADING OFF TO GIBBS MARINA, Vertesi forced himself to switch focus from Rachel to the second boat. He needed to find out whether Thompson or Gibbs had just forgotten to mention it or if there was a reason they hadn't. Did the two boats go out separately and the second one return on its own? If that was the case, there was nothing to report; they were separate contracts. Though his warrant wouldn't be issued before Tuesday morning, Vertesi thought it wouldn't hurt to ask the mechanic about the marina's rental logs and how thorough they were.

As he rounded the bend to the marina, a Canada goose led her four comical goslings into his path. He slowed, then stopped and waited for them to clear. As the geese were crossing the road, Gibbs came out of the tuck shop, looked towards Vertesi's car and then headed for his mechanic's workshop. "So much for being discreet," Vertesi said to himself.

Parking in front of the workshop's open doors, he shut down the engine and grabbed his notebook. For no reason that he could later put a finger on, he checked that his service revolver was on his hip with the restraining strap unsnapped.

"Mr. Gibbs, can I have a word with you?" he called as he came around the side of his vehicle. There was a flash of white inside the dark garage and he was blown back against the fender, landing face up on the hood. Struggling to get up, he rolled over onto his side and slid down the front of the car, ending up face down in the dirt. Cigarette butts and gravel stuck to his clothes as he rolled over on his back, to find Gibbs standing over him with a sixteen-gauge shotgun cracked open.

The man was reaching into the thigh pocket of his fatigues for another shell.

"Smartass little fucker. Ain't so smart now, are ya?" Gibbs spat at him but missed.

Vertesi felt a sticky mess on the left side of his abdomen and lifted his hand to find it drenched. He held it up towards Gibbs in an attempt to ward off the next round, and Gibbs laughed. "Fucking wop wop wop. Who's the smart fucker now?"

Vertesi tried to get enough leverage to sit up, to get away, but his legs slid helplessly beneath him. His right hand was pinned under his body; he struggled to pull it out, gasping for every breath. He reached for his weapon.

"You take shit all day for fuckin' years and then—*bang*—you hit a fuckin' wall and it's over!" Gibbs was screaming now, spewing saliva as he rushed to get the words out. "This morning, fucker, I hit the wall!" The shell was sliding into the chamber when he realized what Vertesi was doing. He quickly snapped the barrel shut.

Vertesi fired upwards. The round tore into the old man's neck and swung him sideways. Wide-eyed with shock, Gibbs lowered his weapon and clutched at the gaping wound, now gurgling with blood. He stumbled backwards, regained his balance and, his finger still on the trigger, tried to raise the barrel of the shotgun. Vertesi fired again, blowing off Gibbs's Caterpillar cap and most of the top of his head. The man dropped to the ground, still clinging to the shotgun. Vertesi rolled slightly to his left to see Gibbs choking on blood as if he was gargling.

Realizing he was going to pass out, Vertesi held up his weapon once more and fired the remaining rounds in the air, hoping Dennis or someone would come. Then he lay back, tried to breathe slowly, and looked at the soft white clouds above. "Beautiful," he managed to say before he sank into darkness.

IT WAS JUST PAST FOUR P.M. when Swetsky met them outside the surgical unit. Several uniformed officers were standing nearby in a cluster, and off to the side was a woman in her thirties with her arm around an older woman; MacNeice took them to be Vertesi's mother and sister. The father, a tall, elegant man with a thick moustache, was at the water cooler filling a tiny paper cup.

Swetsky took MacNeice aside as Aziz went over to the family. "He's lost a lot of blood—that isn't good—but the round tore through the flesh on the left side of his stomach. There's no kidney or spleen damage and the ribs weren't shattered, so the lungs are fine. But they need to stabilize him before they operate."

"What the hell happened, Swets?" MacNeice looked over his shoulder at Aziz; she had her arms around Vertesi's sister, whose shoulders were heaving. The mother stood sobbing quietly next to her husband, who was looking down at the two paper cups of water he was holding.

"Dennis Thompson—he's the mechanic—had gone to get something in the back of the shop when he heard the blast and the place lit up. He had been cleaning the shotguns, said Gibbs complained that they hadn't been cleaned properly at the end of hunting season the year before. Thompson had finished the single-barrel that was Gibbs's wife's. If he'd done one of the others first—the ten- or the twelve-gauge double-barrel—Vertesi would've been finished. When he went down, Gibbs had one in the chamber and two more in his pocket. The guy had flipped; he would have used them all if Vertesi hadn't taken him out."

"Was it the mechanic who called it in?"

"Yeah, and the kid is lucky for another reason. Out on one of the docks was a . . ." Swetsky pulled out his notebook to check. ". . . a Dr. Van der Hilst—he's an oncologist over at St. Joe's. He was just about to set out for an afternoon's sailing when it happened. The call went in to Search and Rescue out on Kendal Island, and within eleven minutes the medivac helicopter had landed on the road. Twenty-seven minutes later he was here."

"Christ almighty, and bleeding all the time."

"Yeah, but Van der Hilst had plugged pretty much all the wadding from the marina's first aid kit into the wound, and then he got some more from his boat. He'd packed and wrapped it so well the medivac guys just put in a plasma drip and got him the hell out of there."

"What about Gibbs?"

"Vertesi fired two rounds—one took out his neck and the other the top of his head. Then he pumped the rest into the sky to get some attention. Hell, they must have thought a war had broken out on that road." Swetsky seemed impressed.

"But what went wrong?" MacNeice saw the doors swing open. A young woman rushed through, her face contorted by fear as she looked around frantically.

"Van der Hilst said Gibbs was a time bomb, and nobody wanted to be around when he went off. He'd lost half his boat storage and moorage business—and all of his profit—because he would flip out and tear into his customers. The doc once suggested to Gibbs that he see a neurologist about his headaches and mood swings. Gibbs told him to go fuck himself and walked away. His wife had been sick with cancer for three years. When she died last winter, he just got weirder. I asked him if Gibbs was medicated and he said maybe, and then he added, 'Maybe not legally.' He figures Vertesi was just the last straw."

"Can you send someone out there to get the rental diary or logbook? I don't want that going south on us while we deal with all this." MacNeice put his hand on the big man's shoulder.

"Yep, but don't worry. The place is shut down tighter than a loan shark's heart." Swetsky pulled out his cellphone and moved over to the windows.

MacNeice studied the agitated young woman waiting at the reception desk, went over to her and held out his hand. "Rachel? Rachel Ingram?"

She turned to him, wide-eyed, and took his hand. "Yes. I'm here for—about—Michael Vertesi. He's a police detective. He's been hurt."

"The surgical team is trying to stabilize him before they operate." MacNeice let go of her hand.

"Is he going to be okay?"

"I've been told he's lost a lot of blood but that this is a very good team, so his chances are better than even."

"Who are you?" She met his eyes for the first time.

"I'm Detective Superintendent MacNeice, Michael's commanding officer."

"He's told me about you. He worships you, I think." She was doing her best to hold back tears. "What on earth was he doing out there?"

"He was gathering information for an investigation. It was expected to be a routine call. How did you hear about it?"

"My mother called me at school. The news was all over the lake. I guess Dennis Thompson was talking and then . . ." Her voice trailed off. "Michael was supposed to come and get me after school. I wanted to make a formal statement about what I saw the other night—when the girl died." She looked around the waiting room, past the clutch of police officers that had now grown to seven, in and out of uniform, to where Aziz was standing next to the Vertesis. "Are those his parents?"

"Yes. And his sister. Next to them is Detective Inspector Fiza Aziz, another colleague of Michael's. Would you like to meet them?"

"Oh God, I don't know. I hardly know Michael. I mean, it feels like I've known him all my life, though we only just met, but . . ."

"But what?"

"Do you think it's appropriate? I mean, I don't want to offend them."

"I don't think that's likely, Rachel. Come on, we'll meet them together." She nodded, and as he took her by the arm, a trail of tissues dropped from her jacket pocket onto the floor. MacNeice picked them up and put them in his pocket.

Aziz came towards them as they approached. "They're very upset, obviously, but they're dealing with it."

"Fiza Aziz, this is Rachel Ingram. I thought Rachel should meet Michael's parents and sister."

The two shook hands and Aziz said, "Michael told me about you. I'm glad you came." She put her arm around Rachel just as MacNeice's cellphone buzzed in his pocket. He wheeled away towards the windows.

"MacNeice."

"Yes, sir."

"What in the world is going on? I mean, we've got serious heat coming down and one of your people gets taken out by some cracker in the woods?" With each phrase the deputy chief's volume rose.

"At a marina, sir."

"I want to know what's going on with your crew. Are you in control over there?"

"Vertesi was at that marina for more information about the—"

"Are you saying you sent him there alone?"

"It was routine, sir. He just found himself in the wrong place when the old man snapped."

"Right out of the blue? The guy just snaps when he sees your man? Don't bullshit me! What went on?"

"There was a slight altercation on his last visit, but nothing to indicate—"

"Indicate what? That the next time he was going to haul out a shotgun and blast away at Vertesi without warning? I'm sorry about your soldier, MacNeice, but this is a sideshow you've got us into. You've seen the headlines, heard the news. I want the killer of that girl, and you're back down to three people. Get it done!"

"Understood, sir."

The phone went dead. MacNeice slid it back into his pocket as Swetsky came to stand beside him. They both looked out the window, MacNeice following the flight line of several crows that were pedalling against the wind over the trees beyond the parking lot.

"You know, I've always thought crows were the biker gangs of bird land," he said.

"Is Wallace thinking this was your fuck-up? Did he even ask how Vertesi was doing?" Swetsky didn't seem the least bit interested in crows.

"Well, it is my fuck-up. No doubt about it—I own it. And in a moment I'm going to have to own it with his family."

"How so?"

"I knew the old man and Vertesi had had a go-round the last time he was out there. Gibbs called him a wop and Vertesi dumped his weapon and badge and was going to beat the prejudiced shit out of him until he apologized. He apologized."

"So what? Let's say, for instance, I'd gone with him today. He gets out of the car, the old man pops him and maybe me, and we're here and they're working on both of us. The old man snapped. It would'na mattered a sweet goddamn if we had the Fifth fuckin' Cavalry there. I've said it before and I'll say it again—people get weird when they spend too much time at the lake."

"Nice try, Swets, but you know the rules as well as I do. I didn't even know he was headed out there today. He's keen— too keen."

Swetsky was looking out at several birds that had settled along the eaves of a building next to the parking lot. "What about those guys?" He nodded in their direction.

"Starlings—the mimics of the bird world. They want to be bad but they only end up comical." He turned away from the view, resting his hand briefly on Swetsky's shoulder before walking over to the family. Aziz introduced him.

"Mr. and Mrs. Vertesi, Lisa, this is Superintendent Detective MacNeice, our commanding officer." They all shook his hand, but the mother and father barely looked at him.

"I'm terribly sorry that we are meeting for the first time under these circumstances. Michael is a wonderful man, as no doubt you know better than I, and I can tell you he's an equally wonderful detective."

The father nodded, the mother looked away and only the sister watched MacNeice as he was speaking. It was difficult for him to decipher whether it was with contempt or rage or both.

In heavily accented English, the old man spoke. "That man, he called my son a wop. Did you know that, Mr. MacNeice?" There was the fury of a lifetime in the question.

"I did, sir. And frankly, though I regret it now, I was proud of what your son did in response. He is a very courageous man, and I have tremendous respect for courage—and family."

"Maybe a bit too much courage, maybe. I think so."

"I'm proud of your son, Mr. Vertesi, and I'm confident he'll come through this, in part because of his courage."

MacNeice nodded again and retreated, pushing through the waiting room doors to the exit stairwell. He didn't check his watch as he tore down the stairs two at a time. Stepping outside, he leaned up against the wall facing the parking lot and tried breathing deeply. The sun was warm on his face and he closed his eyes.

The door opened slowly beside him and Aziz appeared. "What are you doing, Mac?"

"I'll be right up. I needed some air." He stood away from the wall with his hands in his pockets, looking out on the sea of shiny metal.

"Mac, this is not your fault. And Vertesi is going to come out of this a smarter cop." She put a hand on his shoulder and looked up into his eyes.

"I know. I couldn't say that to his parents, but I know."

"And you couldn't have known, any more than Vertesi did, that this guy was going to go ballistic."

"Funny thing, that. Do you remember, Aziz, we used to call it 'going postal'? Someone shows up one day at work with an assault rifle and runs amok. . . . Well, in every case, without exception, when you track back through the story, there is always immense human wreckage. No, the problem with Gibbs going postal is there's never enough attention given when the signs are presenting themselves."

"But we can't do that job."

"No, we can only become better at noticing those signs. I promise you, Michael will see more intensely, more . . . finely, from here on. At least, I hope so."

"I hope so too. Come on, let's go back up." She made a move for the door.

"I'll want Rachel Ingram to give her statement before she leaves, and I'd like you to take it."

"No problem, boss."

"She's already very attached to Michael. They may be a perfect match—assuming he comes out of this with a healthy frame of mind."

"Yes, it's been a real Sidney Carton day."

MacNeice found himself smiling. "Now, when's the last time two cops got together and made a reference to Charles Dickens? Let's go and see how he's doing." He reached over and opened the door.

"I'll race you upstairs," Aziz said. "You want to time us?" She didn't wait for his answer but hit the stairs running. She opened the door at their floor a second ahead of him, breathless and grinning.

"How'd you know that about me?" He moved beside her.

"I get paid for being observant, sir."

IT WAS 8:46 A.M. LYING ON THE stone tiles, a ginger cat with white front paws rolled back and forth in the sun, kicking its legs about, playing with a piece of copper wire. MacNeice sipped his espresso and watched, happy to be distracted. He,

Aziz and Swetsky were sitting on a bench outside the entrance to division headquarters. None of them could remember ever sitting there before, but the combination of sun and stress over Michael's shooting had made the office cubicles unappealing.

After a long silence during which they watched the cat roll about, MacNeice said, "Aziz, get down to the Conservatory with a photo of the boyfriend. Let's see if anyone knows him."

She nodded. MacNeice looked over to Swetsky, who was sipping a large double-double. "Now that we have Rachel Ingram's statement, can you find out what happened to the second boat? It'll either be booked in back at the marina or it's still missing. And get back onto the doctor who owns the cottage."

Swetsky stood up with his coffee in hand. "Yeah, that got dropped yesterday. Okay, where can I find you?"

"I'm going over to see Petrescu." Both Aziz and Swetsky looked at MacNeice. "I want to check in on him, ask him more about his son, and maybe, if the time is right, why he failed to mention that he is also a microbiologist." He stood up and tossed his paper espresso cup into the bin next to the door.

"That's it?" Aziz squinted up through the sun at MacNeice.

"I want to know if he thinks his past has come to claim his daughter . . . and if it has, why it happened." He smiled, offered a hand to Aziz and hoisted her up.

Swetsky noticed the gesture, subtly raised an eyebrow and dropped what remained of his double-double into the bin.

"Do you want a lift?" MacNeice asked her as he walked towards his car.

"Nope, I'm going to take my bike. I could use the exercise." Aziz walked away, pulling her shoulders back and swaying from side to side with each step like an exaggerated tough guy, knowing they were both watching her. She smiled back at them when she reached the rack where her tall black Amsterdam bike was locked.

HE SAW IT THE MOMENT he turned the corner—a black Range Rover parked outside Petrescu's grey mansion. MacNeice pulled over and tucked the Chevy in behind a parked car so he could check it out. One of the sturdy black-jacketed blonds from the surveillance video stood beside the vehicle, his hands in front of him like a soccer player lining up for a penalty shot. MacNeice shut off his engine and took out his cellphone to call it in, but then thought the better of it. What was he calling in? He got out of the car to walk the short distance to the house and regi-stered exactly when the blond became aware of him. The heavy reached into his right pocket—the one closest to MacNeice—and took out cigarettes and a lighter. Most people's attention would shift to his hands. MacNeice stayed focused on his face.

Stopping shy of the rear of the Range Rover, MacNeice took out his notebook and pen and wrote down the plate number. The blond came slowly towards him. "What you doing?"

"And you are?" MacNeice said, putting the notebook away and looking up at him.

"What business you have with the truck?"

MacNeice pulled out his shield, showed it to him and said, "I asked you who you are."

"Fuck off." The blond smiled, put the cigarette in his mouth and turned back to take up position at the rear door of the vehicle.

Looking at the bulk of the man, MacNeice didn't think he'd fare well in a fair fight, and he doubted that fair fights were the man's style. His thoughts turned to Vertesi and he suddenly felt naked without his service weapon. He decided to ignore the insult and head for the gate.

As he reached for the ornate metal handle, a heavy hand slammed down hard on his right shoulder. Instinctively he dropped with the weight of it, spun low to the right and drove his fist up and into the man's groin. The blond let out a deep howl, bending into the pain. MacNeice grabbed him by the shoulders of his leather jacket and jerked his face down to meet his right knee coming up. The man's nose blew apart on impact, and as MacNeice released him, he sagged sideways to the ground, groaning and clutching at his crotch, sputtering something foreign through the blood streaming from his nose into his mouth.

MacNeice walked quickly back to the Chevy, where he retrieved his service weapon from the glove compartment. When he returned, the blond was struggling to get up, still spitting blood onto the sidewalk. MacNeice took the weapon out of its holster and levelled it at the man's head as he clipped the holster into his belt.

"I'm asking again—who are you?"

"His name is Uri Bavorich. He's my bodyguard." MacNeice turned to see a young man on the other side of the gate; he was wearing a black suit with a tight burgundy T-shirt and shiny black shoes. Next to him was the second blond, whose right hand was behind him, presumably resting on a weapon.

"And you are—?" MacNeice kept his gun on the man sitting on the sidewalk, wiping his nose on his sleeve.

"I am Colonel Petrescu. This is my father's house." He nodded towards the grey mansion. His father stood in the doorway, looking very pale.

"Why would you need a bodyguard, Mr. Petrescu?" MacNeice moved aside so he could cover the man on the ground and be ready for anything from blond number two. His right leg was shaking slightly inside his pant leg. This sometimes happened to him, though it was rare these days that he found himself in a physical confrontation. He wondered whether it was fear or simply an animal nerve instinct, like the twitching tail of a cat just before it pounces on a sparrow. He hoped it was the latter, but he wasn't sure.

The *whurp whurp* of approaching squad car sirens interrupted the discussion. Within seconds four patrolmen with their weapons drawn approached the Range Rover, two from the front and two from the rear. MacNeice recognized the older of the two at the back.

"MacNeice. You okay?" Patrolman Bolton asked.

"I am. Check these two for weapons and get their identification."

"Will do. Stephens, you check buddy on the ground. I'll take the one behind the gate. Hutchings, you cover me. Poznansky, cover Stephens."

"You're making a mistake, Officer." The colonel pushed the gate open and stepped through.

"Detective. Your man made the mistake, Mr. Petrescu." To Bolton he said, "When you're done with him, check Mr. Petrescu."

"I am a colonel in the Romanian army, Detective, and I demand the respect due to my rank." Petrescu stood in front of MacNeice, apparently unperturbed.

"I know who you are, and I don't believe I'm compelled to call you anything but mister. I asked why you needed a bodyguard."

"I'm not compelled to answer you, detective." Petrescu smiled, took a cigarette out of a silver case, tapped it against the top of the case and slipped it into his mouth. From his jacket pocket he took out a lighter and, without taking his eyes off MacNeice, lit the cigarette and inhaled deeply.

"Some kind of stick." Bolton held up a foot-long hardwood dowel he'd retrieved from the back pocket of the bodyguard standing near Petrescu. It was roughly an inch and a half in diameter. "His name's Petrov, Nicolai Petrov, a Romanian national."

Kneeling next to the bodyguard on the ground, Stephens said, "Same here, sir. A stick—that's it." He tucked it under his arm before looking through the downed man's wallet. "This guy's called Uri Bavorich, also Romanian."

"Help him up, Stephens. Give him this." MacNeice handed a handkerchief to the officer, who in turn passed it to Bavorich, who clasped it to his nose.

Stephens turned his attention to Petrescu, who raised his arms, cigarette in mouth, as the patrolman patted him down. "Nothing here, sir. Want me to check his ID too?"

"That won't be necessary. Give them both back their sticks and IDs." MacNeice slid his handgun into its holster. "When did you arrive in the country?" he asked Petrescu.

"Last night. Bucharest-Rome-New York . . . here."

"Where are you staying and for how long?"

"Chelsea Manor." He inhaled, and on the exhale said, "I'm here for the funeral of my sister, however long it takes to get her body released. Now if you have no further questions, we will be leaving." He turned towards the Range Rover, dropped the cigarette onto the sidewalk and ground it twice with his shiny shoe.

MacNeice stood aside as the bloodied Bavorich opened the rear door and Petrescu climbed in. His nose angry and swollen, he turned to smile broadly at MacNeice, revealing the blood rimming his teeth, before he climbed into the front seat and shut the door. MacNeice had always admired the pampered, insulated sound of a luxury-car door closing. Petrov, the driver, walked quickly past the officers without making eye contact, opened his door and climbed in. In a moment the Range Rover had powered off, leaving the four patrolmen looking at MacNeice.

"Why didn't we arrest them, sir?" Bolton asked.

"Well, other than telling me to fuck off and putting a hand on my shoulder and carrying sticks, there wasn't much we could book them for."

"Your call. But I imagine those boys know how to use those sticks, and I wouldn't want to be on the receiving end when they do." Bolton adjusted his vest and signalled his partner to head back to the car.

"Who called you in?" MacNeice asked as he made to leave.

"Someone inside—a woman, I think. It's funny, we were having a coffee at Sacred Grounds two blocks away and shootin' the shit about Vertesi when we got the call."

"I'm glad you showed up when you did."

MacNeice looked up at the house and saw Madeleine's face behind the sheers. It had been ten minutes since he'd seen the old man at the door—now shut—but presumably he too was somewhere inside watching. He shook Bolton's hand and said goodbye, then turned towards the mansion.

ONCE AGAIN HE FOUND HIMSELF in the library. Nothing had changed, but there was an ache to the place he'd not noticed before, as if all the life had been sucked out of it. He had been in museums that felt more alive.

He stood by the window and waited, looking out to the garden, where a robin was busy searching for worms. The door opened behind him and Antonin Petrescu stepped in. "Detective MacNeice. Please, sit."

MacNeice took the chair by the window where Aziz had sat last time, and Petrescu sat opposite him. "As you know, I met your son and his colleagues outside," MacNeice said.

"Unpleasant. I trust you were not without justification in your actions." Petrescu's hands rested on his thighs, his eyes riveted on MacNeice's.

"Yes, I was justified. Mr. Petrescu, is there anything I should know about your son?"

"In what regard, Detective?"

"Why does he need bodyguards?"

"His work is sensitive in nature and he would be a prize catch for several . . . competing interests."

"What was his relationship to your daughter? While I understand that he has spent most of his time in Romania with the military, I found him less than—"

"Grief-stricken." The older man looked away from MacNeice then, studying the garden.

"Cold is how I would describe him. I can only think that this is difficult for you, sir." MacNeice watched as Petrescu's left hand began folding over the crease of his grey trousers.

"They weren't close, it's true. And while it's painful to admit, neither are we."

"Your son said that he arrived last night. Was that because you called him, or was it a coincidence?"

"I had called and left a message, yes. But he was already en route."

"A scheduled visit, sir?"

"Not exactly. From time to time Gregori is called to join the Romanian delegation at the United Nations. When that happens, he'll often come here first. But you're not here to talk about my son. What can you tell me about the investigation?"

"I believe that someone killed your daughter to deliver a message to you. It was a passionless act that had nothing to do with Lydia other than her being your daughter. Do you have any idea who that might be?"

Petrescu simply stared at him. "That's very cruel speculation on your part, Detective." He put both hands on the arms of the chair, preparing to stand. "If you have no more information or real questions for me, I think you should go. I'm extremely tired."

"I did have one last question, sir. What did you do before coming to this country?"

Petrescu's chest deflated as if he'd been punched, and his hands dropped back onto his thighs. He gestured weakly towards MacNeice. "No more, no more. I must ask you to leave, Detective. I will answer your question, but not now."

"I understand." MacNeice put away his notebook and got up. "Thank you for seeing me, Mr. Petrescu. I'll find my own way out."

As he opened the gate, he noticed his handkerchief on the ground, covered in the bodyguard's blood. He picked it up and put it in the waste bin at the corner before returning to his car.

EIGHTEEN

—

AZIZ WAS ALONE IN THEIR CUBICLE. Vertesi's chair was shoved under his desktop where the cleaning staff had left it. Other than when he was on vacation, MacNeice couldn't recall ever seeing it like that. He swung it out and sat down next to Aziz.

"His name is Marcus Johnson," she said. "He's an on-again, off-again student at the art college down the street from the Conservatory." MacNeice swivelled the chair towards her. "Several of the Conservatory staff recalled seeing him around, but even better, one of Lydia's classmates told me who he is and where he lives."

"Strange that he hasn't come forward. Any word from the hospital?" MacNeice took out his notebook and put it on the desk.

"Yes. Good news. They've gotten all the buckshot out of Vertesi and they've managed to sew up the wound. His blood count is back to where it should be and the only concern now is infection. In time they'll do a skin graft and they feel the muscle that was torn can be repaired. They think he'll be fine." She turned in his direction, her knees only inches from his.

"Good to hear."

"What happened at Petrescu's?"

"I met the son. He's Shiny Shoes from the condominium security video. I met his bodyguards too—had a run-in with one of them."

"Define run-in." She moved her chair back slightly.

"He slammed my shoulder from behind and—I don't know, I guess some long-ago training I thought I'd forgotten kicked in."

"Uh-huh." She moved her chair another inch or two away.

"I applied blunt force to his testicles and then broke his nose. You want an espresso?"

"No."

MacNeice got up and left the cubicle. When he returned, espresso in hand, she said, "Did you arrest him?"

"No. I even gave him my hanky. If I had arrested him, he might have had a good case for being assaulted by a police officer." He leaned against the desk.

"You know, I had a funny feeling about your going there alone." Aziz seemed angry.

"I'm okay. Really." MacNeice put his cup down.

"One cowboy on this team is already in the hospital." Aziz's voice was steely. "Let's do this thing together from now on—seriously."

"I wasn't— Okay, you're right. No more going solo. Actually, I lucked out. Madeleine called it in and there were two cruisers there before it got really weird. Shall we go over to Marcus Johnson's place?"

"Yes. And Petrescu senior, did you see him?"

"I did. It was fairly brief, as he was exhausted."

Aziz grabbed her jacket off the back of the chair and stood to leave. As MacNeice stepped aside to let her pass, she looked down at his hip. "That's the first time I've seen you carrying your weapon."

"Well, pilgrim, I felt naked without it." It was bad John Wayne, intended to break the tension.

"Right. Very funny, Clint Eastwood."

"John Wayne."

"Who's he?"

"Right."

THE HOUSE WHERE LYDIA'S BOYFRIEND lived was a wide, stately brick Victorian, not especially attractive but beautifully maintained. A translucent curtain backed the tall oval cut-glass door with dark oak trim, and beside it were individual doorbells to four apartments. Marcus Johnson's name wasn't listed beside any of them. Through the curtain they could vaguely make out a figure coming down the hall towards the door.

"Mrs. Hausser?" Aziz asked, when the woman opened the door.

"Just Miss. How can I help you?" She wasn't unpleasant, just precise.

"We're police detectives. This is Detective Superintendent MacNeice and I'm Detective Inspector Aziz. We're looking for Marcus Johnson. Does he live here?"

"He did. Come in, come in."

"When did he leave, Miss Hausser?" MacNeice asked as they stepped inside.

"Yesterday—rather abruptly, though his month was paid up, so I cannot complain. He said he was going home because his mother was dying."

"Did he leave anything behind?" Aziz asked.

"He didn't have much, but what he had, he took—except for his bicycle, which is in the garage, and a knapsack he said belonged to a friend. He asked me to keep it until he could come back for it and the bike."

"We are currently investigating the death of a young woman, a close friend of his. Have you looked inside the knapsack to see whose it is?"

"No, it's not my place to do so. I can tell you there's a cellphone inside, though. It has gone off several times in the last couple of days."

Aziz reached into her bag and took out a photograph of Lydia Petrescu. "Did you ever see him in the company of this woman?"

"No."

"Did he say where his mother lived, or when he'd be back?"

"No, though once I saw a letter addressed to him and it was postmarked . . . what was it . . . Wawa? Yes, Wawa. I thought it was such an interesting word—*Wawa,* like a baby crying— that I remembered it. I believe it is somewhere up north."

"Did he have a phone in his apartment?"

"There is a phone, but you know these young people don't use land lines. They're always texting and talking on cellphones. He never activated the line."

"Do you mind if we look at his apartment, Miss Hausser?" MacNeice asked.

"I don't, but I have already cleaned it, Detective, and I have a young woman coming to see it. I thought it was she when the doorbell rang. What has Marcus done? Is he in trouble?"

"No, we just need to speak with him. Can we take a look? We won't be long," MacNeice said. "And we'll take the knapsack when we leave. It will help with the investigation."

"Come along, then." She opened the door to her apartment and a smell of flowers wafted out into the hall. "Wait here. I'll get the key."

"What is that lovely smell?" MacNeice asked.

As she walked towards the fireplace mantel, Miss Hausser turned and smiled at him, revealing a gold tooth on the left side of her mouth. She disappeared behind a dark oak door. In a moment she came back with the key and the backpack, handing it to MacNeice. "That's lily of the valley from my garden," she said. "I'm so happy you noticed. I have the key, so come, come."

They followed her upstairs and into the small front apartment. She had indeed cleaned it. There was a bay window, and on each of its three sections, an accordion-fold blind was lowered exactly to the crosspiece of the bottom pane. In the bedroom, leaning on the mantel of a disused fireplace, were two photographs: one a close-up of a bouquet of white lilacs, and the other the back of a violin with its mirrored and complex grain and delicate shadows. Both were framed in cheap black wood.

"These are his images," MacNeice said.

"Yes, they are. So you know his work. I think he's very talented, yes. When he was leaving, he said to me, 'Keep these— they belong here.' I have a large stand of lilacs in the garden and he was always out there when they bloomed. Pointing his camera so close, it looked funny, but he's good. Good."

"Yes, he is. He has a wonderful eye for light and form. Are you going to leave them here for the next tenant?"

"No, no. Goodness, no, I will take them downstairs to my apartment. But they do look so pretty here, yes?" She looked at the prints and then up at MacNeice, who nodded.

The doorbell rang and Miss Hausser turned away from the fireplace.

"Thank you, Miss Hausser, for showing us the apartment," MacNeice said. "Here's my card. If Marcus Johnson gets back in touch, please tell him we're interested in hearing from him."

"Yes, certainly," said the landlady. Then she volunteered, with a worried frown, "He looks rough, but he's a good boy, Marcus."

NINETEEN

—

ON THE WAY BACK TO DIVISION, Aziz tried to start Lydia's laptop but found it needed a password, so she closed it up and put it back in the knapsack. They dropped off the computer for Ryan, the new IT kid, to figure out and arrived at their cubicle just as MacNeice's telephone rang.

"I've spoken to Dr. Hadley, the guy who owns the beach house." It was clear from the background noise that Swetsky was walking along a busy street. "You're gonna love this. The reason he didn't come forward earlier? He hasn't been declaring the revenue he makes from renting the cottage—it's all been cash."

"But from the pristine shape the cottage was in, it looks like he hasn't even been renting it." MacNeice was at his desk looking through the backpack; he handed the cellphone he found to Aziz. "Hang on, Swets." He cupped his hand over the phone.

Cellphone in hand, Aziz was leaving the cubicle. "I'm going to ask Ryan to download all the messages on the cell, in and out," she said, "so we can review its contents along with all the laptop files and emails."

MacNeice nodded and went back to his call. "Go ahead."

"Exactly right, Mac. When I pushed him on that, he said he's only rented it five times—four for what he calls rendezvous, between his stockbroker and a girlfriend, and once to a guy. . . ." The sound of music blaring in the background obscured his voice.

"I missed that last one. He rented it to whom?" MacNeice picked up his pen and turned to an open page in his notebook.

"A kid who wanted to treat his girlfriend to a real romantic night on the lake after her graduation from college. He said he didn't remember the kid's name but he was a tall, lanky, good-looking kid with a big mop of hair. He paid fifteen hundred cash and offered a premium of five hundred dollars for the short stay, which the good dentist accepted." The street noise on Swetsky's side of the conversation ended with the *thunk* of a car door closing.

"Did he know how the kid found out about the beach house?"

"Yeah, the kid told him that the stockbroker's girl was a friend of his. I've made two calls and I've got her number. Her name's Sarah Vachon—she's a bartender at the Boogie Bin on James Street. Got a pen handy?"

MacNeice wrote down the number. "Thanks, Swets. See you later."

Aziz swung around in her chair, but he was already dialling. "Who are you calling, boss?"

"A bartender," he said. It rang several times before he heard a sleepy voice say, "Hullo?"

"Sarah Vachon? This is Detective Superintendent MacNeice of Metro Homicide."

"No shit?" She sounded as if she thought it might be a prank call, but then she asked, "What do you want with me, Detective?"

"You know Dr. Michael Hadley?"

"Ah, no, I don't."

"Right. But you do know a friend of his and you did have several sleepovers at Dr. Hadley's beach house, am I correct?"

"So what?"

"Sarah, we can do this over the phone and be pleasant to each other, or I can have you picked up and brought downtown and we can be rude to each other. Which would you prefer?"

"Let's be nice. What do you want to know? Did I fuck his friend? Yes, I fucked his friend."

"Sarah, I don't care what you did at the beach house. I want to know what you know about Marcus Johnson, an art student and photographer."

She fell silent. As MacNeice waited her out, he looked over at Aziz and raised his eyebrows. She in turn raised hers and held up several notebooks and music scores from the backpack, whispering to him, "All music, all the time."

"He's not in trouble, is he?"

"Johnson?"

"Yeah. And what's he told you about me?"

"Nothing, Sarah. We just found out that you knew him and we'd like to know more about him."

"Why's that?"

"Because we believe he knows someone who was killed Friday in that very same beach house."

"Fuck! I wondered about that the minute I heard someone was offed at the lake. It's all over the TV."

"Can you tell us about Johnson? We understand he's a student at the art college, and we've seen several of his images that suggest he's quite talented."

"He showed you the nudes of me?"

"No, Sarah, none of you."

"I don't give a shit if he did, ya know. He's an artist—maybe a fucked-up artist—but I'm proud of those photos."

"Why is he fucked up?"

"Oh, shit. . . . He comes from up north—Wawa. He's a rough piece of work—oh boy, is he ever—not violent, just . . . What's that great phrase I heard on *Oprah* the other day? . . . Oh, shit." The line was reduced to static as Sarah tried to remember. "Right—Marcus has no moral compass. Does that mean anything to you?"

"I think so, Sarah—he's a bit reckless and adrift?"

"Yeah, adrift. A talented fucker who's adrift—yeah, that's Marcus. He was beaten as a kid or something, and then his mother left and he was dumped with a grandmother. I grew up about a mile from him. He ran away at fourteen, lived on the streets here and was doing dope and graffiti and stuff when some youth worker from downtown started tracking his tags."

"That's his signature, right?"

"Yeah, and he was great. So this guy takes a liking to him and before long Marcus is presenting a portfolio of drawings and photographs—some of me, but not the nudes—at the art college. He gets accepted! Man, we drank ourselves silly that night. I was training to be a bartender and I mixed up a wicked jug of margaritas."

"Did he ever mention someone named Ruvola?"

"Well, sure. Ronnie supplies weed to most of the north end. I never met the guy but Marcus is tight with him. You see Marcus, unlike me, was never really heavy into alcohol; he prefers the buzz he gets from weed, says it helps him creatively. Like, each to his own, eh?"

"Did he ever tell you about a girl named Lydia Petrescu?"

"Did he ever! She's the violinist from uptown, right? He said he was in love with her, that he'd done the best work ever with her." There was a pause in which MacNeice could almost hear Sarah make the connection. "So it was her at the lake, right?"

"Yes."

"There's no fuckin' way Marcus would have killed her. He's a lover, not a fighter. I know that firsthand."

"We don't believe he killed Lydia, but we are trying to find him. Can you help us?"

"All I know is that big old house he stays in—nice place, with a front room and fireplace."

"He's moved out. Do you have a cellphone number for him? We were told he went back to Wawa to be with his dying mother."

"Ha! That's rich. Marcus's mother died about eight years ago, and anyway, he hadn't seen her in years."

"I'm not surprised to hear that. And his cellphone?"

"Dead. I tried it yesterday."

"Sarah, if there's anything else that occurs to you, anything at all, I'd appreciate a call. Will you promise to do that?"

"Absolutely. What'd you say your name was anyways?"

"MacNeice." He asked her to write down his cellphone number, and once he was satisfied that she had, he said good-bye. Then he gave Aziz a rundown of the call.

"So was he in on it, do you think?" he wondered. "Why did Ruvola and not Johnson rent the boat? Was Gibbs in on it? How much did he get paid?" MacNeice went to the white-board and added Johnson's name next to Gibbs's and Ronnie Ruvola's. Two dead men, MacNeice thought.

"If he paid the doctor, why didn't he rent the boat?" Aziz looked up at MacNeice, who was drawing a line between Ruvola and Johnson.

"Maybe because the money he was spending wasn't his own. Even though this kid's an art student with no moral com-pass, he's smart enough to insist on a division of labour—he rents the beach house and provides the girl and Ruvola rents the boat and handles the logistics."

He wrote down *Gregori Petrescu* with two happy faces beside the name—the bodyguards—and added a dotted line back to Johnson.

"Lydia would have trusted her boyfriend to take her out on the lake—a romantic conclusion to a wonderful day."

Behind her, Skype came to life on Aziz's computer and Bozana appeared in the rectangle on the screen. She was in front of a large window; beyond it was nighttime in Europe. "Dahlink!" she said in a mock Schwarzenegger accent. "What have you gotten me into? Although I must admit your case is a welcome distraction from what we're doing at the moment, which is mostly legal and human rights issues surrounding the Romany—Gypsies, that is, not Romanians. I want to know where you are with this before I tell you where I am."

Aziz moved to one side so MacNeice could take centre

frame. "Hello, Bozana. Well, I've met the son, Gregori Petrescu—he's here for his sister's funeral in the company of two bodyguards."

"One of whom is nursing a broken nose and tender gonads," Aziz added.

"Ouch," said Bozana.

"We've also discovered that her boyfriend, who is likely the father of her unborn child, was the one who took her to the cottage, though whether he was involved in her murder or not, we don't know. The girl's father dodged a question about his past but left the door open to answer it tomorrow."

MacNeice watched as Bozana stood up from her desk and disappeared from the frame. Her voice carried on. "Okay, I'm not going to burden you with geopolitics, but there were constant tensions between Romania and Bulgaria during the Soviet era. The Bulgarians were pro-Moscow and the Romanians were testy, barely manageable by the Kremlin. Though they sit across the Danube looking at each other, they have nothing in common and have always been suspicious of one another." She came back into frame carrying stacks of reports bound in dark covers. "Christ, these are heavy."

"I want you to know that we deeply appreciate your help with this." Without thinking, MacNeice had placed his right hand on his heart as he spoke.

"At some point—and thank you for that—we'll have to get official. There are avenues, protocols and intergovernmental agencies who, if they knew about our little chats, would be very upset." When she sat down, only her face was visible above the stack. "But for now, and even if this is the last thing I can do, let me give you an overview of what Mr.—or rather Dr.— Petrescu senior was up to under the totalitarian government of Ceausescu." Looking up from the pile of paper she said, "You might want to make yourselves comfortable—it's a bit of a slog."

MacNeice rolled back to get his notebook and, returning, nudged closer to Aziz to be in camera range. Bozana looked up, smiled and picked up the first of the documents.

"In the 1980s the foreign policy of Romania was opposed to perestroika while the Bulgarians, under Zhivkov, were all for it. Zhivkov, however, was more concerned about what he called chemical pollution of the Danube by Romania. He didn't know the half of it. Dr. Petrescu was the leading microbiologist in the ministry responsible for chemical plants along the Danube."

"He wasn't military?" Aziz asked.

"No, but his wife was a childhood sweetheart of Nicolae Ceausescu. Petrescu was promoted right out of university to a ministerial position, the rumour goes, so that Ceausescu could be closer to his wife. It was also said at the time that the only reason Petrescu left Romania"—she looked up at the camera— "was that Ceausescu had impregnated his wife. The timing of the child's birth suggests that your victim was Ceausescu's daughter, not Antonin Petrescu's."

"Sweet Jesus," MacNeice said.

"Exactly. They left in a hurry, and shortly thereafter the Soviet regime crumbled and Ceausescu and his wife were executed. Antonin's son, Gregori, who was a kid in military school at the time, had been left behind by his fleeing parents and was declared a ward of the state. Over the next two decades he flourished and became a star, in spite of his parents. That's a testimony to his intelligence and drive." She looked up from her pages. "MacNeice, this is not a man to be fucked with."

"I think I have a sense of that already."

"So leave his gonads, and those of his bodyguards, alone. But more about him later." Bozana put the first report aside and opened the next. "Historically, the Danube has been a cesspool for a long time, with several countries spewing raw sewage into it. But the worst of the worst by far has been Romania, particularly during the Soviet era. And your man had a brilliant, if diabolical, plan."

"Our man meaning Petrescu senior?" Aziz asked.

"Yes. It was in commercial fertilizers that he had his real breakthrough. Then he looked at the steel and paper mills and cranked up the release of effluent—seriously toxic shit. The effluent was supposed to be an industrial spill—a major spill, but in the grand scheme of things, forgivable. The fact was, it was a cover."

"You're beginning to scare the hell out of me, Bo. This guy works in an antique shop. He trades in old papers and fine furniture. He gardens and grows the most beautiful flowers."

"Fair enough." Bozana stood up and reached across her desk for yet another file. "Is this the guy?" She held up to the camera a grainy colour print of a man in a white lab coat, hands in his pockets, standing beside a row of stainless steel vats. The strong cheekbones and the hair, though dark in the photo, were unmistakable—it was Antonin Petrescu. "The caption below identifies him as Minister of the Environment Antonin Petrescu."

"Okay, so keep going." Aziz glanced over to MacNeice, who nodded.

"The fertilizer he'd developed to increase the yield of any type of crop was too lethal for commercial application. He dumped it along with the effluent so that no one detected it.

Petrescu senior had ratcheted up the toxicity of the original effluent so that what travelled downstream—and ended up on beaches all the way to the delta and the Black Sea—was the meanest and most dangerous of pollutants, undetectable to anyone who might be fishing, walking their dog, working on their tan or building sandcastles on the beach. Within a year or so, an extraordinary number of cases of cancer and morbidity showed up—with tumours similar to these."

She held up a book so they could see a girl with a huge growth on the side of her face, then turned the page to reveal a man whose bare chest had lesions that looked as if he'd been swarmed by leeches. "Imagine this occurring on the Danube, and along all the tributaries associated with it and east into the Black Sea. Now imagine the possibility of its getting into the Bosporus, where you're on the doorstep of the Mediterranean. As evil goes, it was pretty impressive stuff."

"Why wasn't he charged when the Romanian government fell?" MacNeice asked.

"He was. He had anticipated it and hired a lawyer from Germany—where the headwaters of the Danube are—who pleaded his case in Bucharest. Petrescu was smart; he knew that once he fled, Ceausescu would try to blame him for the damage, and if Ceausescu didn't survive—which he didn't—those who came after him would as well. He took all the documents that proved he was acting on Ceausescu's orders—his explicit orders—to increase the toxicity of the effluent going into the Danube in order to deal with what his wife's lover saw as increasing Muslim and Soviet threats. Petrescu had a letter proving that he had protested, and attached to it, the response from Ceausescu—a man never open to resistance—who told him in a handwritten note that if he didn't do it, he would have him and his entire family erased. The last bit was underlined and followed by his signature."

"But what was in this for Romania?" MacNeice asked. "Surely the first to suffer would be Romanians downstream from the plants."

"Wrong question, Detective. Imagine a dog or a rat or a leopard caught in a leg trap. What do they do? They eat their leg off to escape the trap. So what would pressure this regime into such a dangerous game? They were surrounded by Soviet satellites and, on the other side of the Black Sea, Mother Russia herself. They saw Islamist states downstream that were becoming more and more fundamentalist; Turkey ruled the entire southern coast of the Black Sea. This kind of struggle had been going on for hundreds, maybe thousands of years. Ceausescu was cornered. He didn't care if every form of life on the Danube disappeared, and if that cost a few thousand Romanian lives? Well, he was a self-professed 'great lover'—he would make the supreme sacrifice of impregnating every woman of childbearing age left in the country, if necessary." Bozana leaned back in her chair.

"You're making that up, Bo." Aziz waved at her dismissively.

"Well, maybe the last bit. But the essence of it is true."

"Why didn't this become an international issue?" MacNeice asked.

"Because the Romanians and even the Bulgarians wanted to keep it quiet. In the wake of the collapse of the Soviet Union, a lot of things got swept under the carpet. This was just one of them. Remember what a happy time it was. Almost a year before Ceausescu was assassinated, Petrescu was accepted into Germany as a refugee who risked being killed if he returned to

Romania. He had the letter to prove it." Bozana removed the remaining pile of documents and sat forward with her hands crossed.

"Are we certain that he actually did release the toxins into the Danube?" Aziz asked.

"No. We know it was his lab that prepared the fertilizer toxins and we know that it was only following the exchange with Ceausescu—when his life was threatened—that he left the country. We also know that the rumours about Ceausescu's fathering the child were true. He left a diary in which he spoke of Mrs. Petrescu as 'the true love of his life' and of the 'bitter disappointment' of not being able to hold his own daughter."

"So Gregori was essentially abandoned?" MacNeice asked.

"It appears so. I don't know why. It may have been that he couldn't get away from the military school in time, but why he didn't escape afterwards is a mystery. He's a stylish shadow—Interpol knows of him only through his published scientific work—but the prevailing thought is that he was engaged in developing chemical warfare materials. Again, I cannot emphasize two things enough, Mac—can I call you Mac?" She stopped to wait for his response.

MacNeice nodded.

"This guy is lethal. He comes out of a sophisticated military school and an even more sophisticated college that dates back to medieval times and uses paranoia as oxygen—they breathe the stuff. He may be Lydia's half-brother, but I can't imagine that they had a relationship of any kind."

"In her apartment we found a round-trip ticket to Istanbul. Any thoughts on that?" Aziz asked.

"No . . . though, given her special status, I'm not sure that she'd willingly go anywhere near Romania, but I don't know."

"And are there now friendly relations between Romania and Bulgaria?" MacNeice asked.

"Lip service, some bilateral agreements. The European Union has changed everything, of course. It's like young actors wanting to move to Hollywood. Everybody wants in, and Interpol is constantly dealing with bad actors from both countries." She looked at her watch. "Okay, kids, gotta go. I've got a big meeting at six tomorrow morning."

"You've been a great help to us, Bozana, and I don't know how to thank you." MacNeice closed his notebook and was about to push back from the desk.

"Thank me by finding out who did it. *Dobranoc*." And with that Bozana smiled and reached out to the keyboard. The screen went dark grey as the connection ended.

A moment later, Ryan, the young intern from the IT department, appeared at the opening of the cubicle and knocked on the partition.

"What is it?" Aziz asked.

"Uh, I got the hard copy of the emails from the laptop." He was holding a stack of paper two inches deep. "I also brought the last week of phone calls and text messages from her cellphone. They're the ones on top, listed backwards from Friday at noon."

"Great. Just put them on my desk. And thank you."

"Do you want all the stuff about music too? It takes up ninety percent of the memory."

"No, just the emails will be fine."

"Then you got 'em. See ya." With that he was gone, back to the windowless room a floor below that was recognizable only by the green glow that oozed out under the door.

"I'll take these home and read them tonight, if that's okay with you," Aziz said.

MacNeice, staring at the whiteboard, said a distracted yes under his breath. He was thinking about adding Antonin Petrescu's name to the list, but he couldn't quite believe that he belonged there.

"The victims of that toxic soup," he said, "were either Romanian or Bulgarian. The syringe was potentially designed by a former KGB agent, a Bulgarian engineer—" MacNeice's cellphone went off. Aziz swung around as he answered, his head down, staring at the carpet. "Yes, this is MacNeice. Yes . . . yes . . . uh-huh," and finally, "We'll be right there— Room 2111, under Clark Terry."

"Who's Clark Terry?" Aziz asked.

"He's a great jazz player. That wasn't him. That was Marcus Johnson. He didn't go to Wawa—that was a ruse. He's terrified." MacNeice was already out of his chair as Swetsky came around the corner of the cubicle.

"I'm coming, boss," Aziz said.

"Swetsky, what about the second boat?" MacNeice asked as they passed him.

"Do you want me out at the marina or with you?" Swetsky's armpits were stained with sweat.

"We're okay, I think. This is the kid—the girl's boyfriend. Check on that boat."

"No problem." He slid over to the telephone on Vertesi's desk. They could hear him as they hit the exit staircase. "Yeah, get me Gibbs's Marina. Yeah, that one."

TWENTY

—

AS THEY GOT OUT OF THE ELEVATOR and turned
right, towards Room 2111, Aziz asked, "How could
Marcus Johnson afford to stay in this place?"

"It's a good question. And since he's obviously not running
from us, who is he running from?"

They stood outside the door for a moment. A DO NOT DIS-
TURB sign was looped over the handle. The television was on,
the volume high enough that they could hear him channel surfing in the hall. MacNeice knocked twice, hard enough to be
heard over the din. The door opened to the length of the security chain and a dishevelled mop of hair and pale face appeared.
"You MacNeice?"

"Detective Superintendent MacNeice and Detective
Inspector Aziz. Open the door, Marcus." The door shut and
reopened, but the young man was already back on the bed
before they could close it behind them.

The room was smoky and dark, and the drapes were drawn. The TV was turned to the food channel, where someone was rapid-fire-cutting leeks. The table lamp was on and Marcus Johnson sat propped up against pillows on the unmade bed— which wouldn't be made till the DO NOT DISTURB sign was taken off the door. He was wearing jeans and a wrinkled T-shirt but no socks.

"Do you mind?" MacNeice said as he walked over to open the patio doors.

"Fuckin' A, I mind. I'm scared shitless here. *Yes, I do fucking mind.*" He buried his hands in his hair and scratched violently back and forth as if he had a massive itch.

"I'll keep the drapes closed, Marcus, but if we don't get some air, Detective Aziz and I will expire, and then you'll have some more explaining to do." MacNeice opened the slider completely and looked out over the railing of the interior balcony to the glass roof of the lobby nineteen storeys below. He closed the brocade drapes, which billowed a bit in the breeze but not enough to reveal the room. When he wasn't glancing at the TV, Johnson shot looks their way as he chewed on a nail.

"Right." MacNeice went over and turned off the television. "We're going to have some order here, Marcus."

"That chef's a hack anyway. I don't care." He rearranged the pillows behind him and sat up straighter.

"Ronnie Ruvola is a friend of yours, I believe?" MacNeice asked.

"Ruvola was my dealer—just for pot, though. I don't do anything stronger."

"Are you aware that he was found tied to a boat at the bottom of Lake Charles?"

"Why do you think I'm here? I knew when the TV said an

unidentified body had been pulled out of the lake that it was probably him."

"He paid for the boat; you paid for the cottage. Why didn't you pay for the boat too?"

MacNeice sat down by the telephone table. Aziz took the only other seat, a club chair by the television set upholstered in salmon and green. She was silent, notebook in hand, watching the young man on the bed.

"Ruvola gave me the cash. He got it from them. I had a couple of bottles of Champagne, some dope and a girlfriend." Tears spilled out of his eyes and tracked down his face. He paid them no mind, just ran a hand through his thick bush of hair and continued. "I was gonna have a romantic fucking sleepover on the lake with the most beautiful woman I've ever met—that was all. We dropped her stuff at my place and headed out. It was the first time I'd ever seen her without a cellphone, and mine was dead, so it was going to be quiet, beautiful, no distractions."

"So who gave Ruvola the cash?" Aziz asked.

"I don't know who it was." Now he was weeping openly, wiping his face with the sleeve of his T-shirt.

"Did you ever wonder why someone would pay you to take her to a cottage?" MacNeice asked.

"Aw, fuck . . . . Look, I'm a photographer. I'm a good photographer. I am." He looked first at MacNeice, then briefly met Aziz's eyes, as if willing them to believe him.

"We know you are, Marcus. We've seen your work." MacNeice's voice was calm.

"No shit? You've seen my work? Where, at the college?"

"You have a wonderful talent, but let's stay focused on why we're here." MacNeice picked up his notebook, indicating that he should continue.

"Okay, so I've taken nude shots of women before—I did the girl who told me about the cottage—but the photos of Lydia were the best, by far the best. She loved them too . . . she loved them." For a moment he looked eager to persuade MacNeice that she did indeed love them, but then he choked up, grabbed a pillow and buried his face in it as he let out a long, agonized groan. When he looked up again, he threw the pillow aside and took out a cigarette. MacNeice just waited, and after Johnson had got his cigarette lit, he shakily carried on.

"When he comes to my place with the weed one night, Ruvola says to me, 'Dude, I've met these guys who'll pay us seventy-five hundred to watch a photo session between you and your girl.' I laughed at him, so he says—like, he spells out each syllable—'That's an even split of se-ven-thou-sand-five-hun-dred-dol-lars, dude, and all you gotta do is do what you do. She won't even know.'"

"You'd shown him your photos of Lydia?" Aziz asked.

"Yeah, well, he came by when I was printing and he saw them. Some of them."

"How was it supposed to work?" MacNeice asked.

"Ruvola would drop off a bag of my gear at the cottage. Lydia and I would go by boat, drinking Champagne on the lake at night. Then I was going to recommend we do some moonlit nude work on the beach, and then some more in the cottage. The men—Ronnie wouldn't say how many—were going be watching from somewhere else. They were supposed to set up hidden cameras inside."

"Were you okay with that, Marcus? Did they actually set up those hidden cameras inside the cottage?" Aziz's voice was steady.

"No, well . . . If she never knew, and somewhere there's a guy jerking off to pictures of her . . . I don't fuckin' know, man. So, was it set up? I don't know that either. We get there and I carry her ashore. She looked amazing, and she was so happy. . . ." He paused for a moment, welling up again. "All I remember is getting there. We finished off a bottle of Champagne on the boat, and we were loosened up, all right. But that's all I remember. I woke up some time later with my face planted in the sand. The boat was gone; there was no one around. I went up the stairs where the music was playing, music that she'd brought with us because it was the piece she was going to do for her first professional concert . . . and there she was—dead. I couldn't believe it. She looked so beautiful, but she was dead. I couldn't find my equipment—my bag was gone. I ran. I figured I'd be blamed if I stayed, so I ran."

"Why did you need the money?" MacNeice asked.

"Shit, man, with that much money I could have my own show. At a serious gallery, I mean, not at the college. A guy in Toronto had already offered me a one-man show, but he said I had to come up with the money for printing and framing, and that shit costs. I could have done it, though. . . . A lot of what I'd be showing was going to be shots of Lydia. She'd be cool with that."

"It's too late to say what she'd be cool with, Marcus," MacNeice said flatly.

"How do you think her father would have felt?" Aziz asked

"Not my problem. Lydia said she'd tell him—this weekend. She was going to be with him Saturday."

"Did you know she was pregnant?"

Johnson just stared at MacNeice as though an insane world had gotten even crazier. Then he realized the detective was waiting for an answer. "Fuck, no. No. Oh God in heaven, I didn't do this, and I don't know why anyone would. I just wanted to make some money. I wouldn't have hurt her. . . . I loved her." Tears spilled down onto his T-shirt, leaving dark stains on the faded grey cotton.

"You hadn't told her what you intended to do at the beach house?" MacNeice asked.

"No, I thought I'd do the gig and then we'd have the rest of the night to make love and celebrate her graduation. Honest to Christ, I wouldn't have done anything to hurt her." He got up off the bed and began to pace in front of the TV. He took a small bottle of whisky from the mini-bar, opened it and drank it down in one long swallow. He put the empty bottle beside several others and then sat on the edge of the bed opposite MacNeice.

"Get dressed, Marcus. I need you to come with us." MacNeice stood up and put his notebook away.

"How'd you pay for the hotel room?" Aziz asked.

"I used a credit card that'll bounce for sure. If I hadn't called Miss Hausser to see if anyone had come looking for me, I'd probably have skipped out on the bill. She gave me your phone number."

"She's a very nice lady. Marcus, let's go. We need to take you in for questioning—and to keep you safe. We don't know if the people who murdered Lydia are coming after you too," MacNeice said.

"Can I just take a shower? I reek, and I haven't changed my clothes for days." He stood up, sniffed at his stained shirt and looked at MacNeice. "I'm okay, though. I'm actually relieved it's over."

"Okay, here's the deal. While I bring the car around to the front entrance, Aziz will pay for the room. You've got ten minutes. If you're not in the lobby in ten, we'll be back up to get you." As he and Aziz headed for the door, Johnson went into the bathroom. They heard the shower start as they stepped into the hall.

At the elevators Aziz said, "Not concerned that he'll bolt, sir?"

"No, I think he's done with running."

In the lobby, a humid two-storey glass-topped greenhouse featuring live palm trees, a water wall with vines growing on either side of it and rainforest birdcalls, Aziz went to the reception desk to check Clark Terry out of his room while MacNeice went out the revolving front door. He was only a few yards into the parking lot when he heard a loud bang followed by several screams. MacNeice burst back through the door. In the lobby, three guests were crouching behind a sofa while Aziz, her weapon drawn, was standing beside the desk clerk, both of them staring straight up.

"Up there," the clerk said. "Oh my God. Call an ambulance!"

Johnson was sprawled face down on top of the glass roof. A splatter of blood around his head, like a burst red-paint balloon, was starting to streak downwards. His arms were above his head as if he were sleeping, or dancing; one leg was straight down, the other tucked awkwardly behind it. His feet were bare. As they looked up, there was a creaking sound. Blood flowed down the glass, puddling at the mullion. Another creak.

"Aziz, are you okay? Look at me." MacNeice reached for her arm. She made no acknowledgment of either his words or his touch. "Aziz, come away. Fiza. Fiza?"

Another creak, and then suddenly a *whoosh*—the entire glass panel, with the young man's body riding it, burst loose and came crashing towards them. MacNeice wrapped his arms around Aziz and threw himself forward as hard as he could. An enormous explosion seemed to envelop them and then half-inch cubes of bloody glass rained down. When the noise stopped, he opened his eyes. Aziz was beneath him, her eyes still screwed shut, tears washing streaks of dust and mascara towards her ears. MacNeice brushed some of the glass out of her hair, then rolled off her and looked around. The glass panel had landed about a foot away from his shoes, and what was left of Marcus Johnson was now bleeding all over the rug. In that strange way that details present themselves in a crisis, MacNeice noticed the small tattoo low on his neck—a blue line drawing of a Hasselblad camera.

"Come on, Fiza, we've got to stand up." MacNeice got to his knees, then pushed himself to his feet, shielding her from the view behind him. "Give me your hand. Come on, that's it." As he lifted her up, she buried her face in his chest and began sobbing convulsively. He held her tight.

The voices around them began to invade—more crying, and people yelling about what to do. The elevator doors opened on a group of guests; seeing the carnage and chaos, they just stood there, hands over mouths, in shock. The doors closed on them again.

He looked around for Aziz's service weapon, a Glock 17, then realized it was still in her hand, hanging down beside her. He patted her back gently and, as her sobbing subsided, reached down and took hold of the weapon, prying her fingers off the grip and away from the trigger.

MacNeice heard sirens approaching as he led her, stiff-legged, to a chair near the lobby entrance. Easing her into it, he smoothed the hair away from her face and took out his handkerchief to wipe away the tears. She looked up at him and said, "I should have stayed with him, Mac. I should have stayed."

"I didn't see anything and you didn't see anything that indicated he was a risk to himself." He could hear the first of the emergency vehicles pulling up to the entrance.

"Observation, Mac. Where was it?" She was crying again.

"It's an imperfect art, Fiza." He removed another cube of glass from her hair.

The first person through the door was a burly black firefighter carrying a large aluminum case. He recognized MacNeice and rushed over. "She okay?" He was looking at Aziz.

"Yes, she is."

"Was he a jumper or was he pushed?" the firefighter asked as he turned towards the body.

The question hit them both like an electric shock. Wide-eyed, Aziz pushed herself out of the chair and started running through the lobby, MacNeice close behind.

"You take the elevator, I'll take the stairs," MacNeice yelled. "But wait— Here, you might need this." He held her weapon out and she grabbed it from him, pressing the Up button as he ran for the exit door to the stairwell.

A second firefighter asked the first, "What'd you say to those two?"

OPENING THE STAIRWAY DOOR, MacNeice stood and listened. He could hear the metallic thumping of someone running up or down the stairs, but before he could identify which it was, it had stopped. So he took off down the stairs, drawing his weapon as he ran. At the first level of the parking garage he threw the door open and listened again. The echo of screeching tires making fast, tight turns sent him running back up. He slammed open the lobby-level door and ran towards the entrance, past the growing mass of police, paramedics and firefighters who were tending to several people who were either in shock or had been cut by the flying chunks of glass. Someone had covered the boy's body with a blanket that was now blotched with large patches of dark blood.

He tore through the front doors and looked up and down the street, but could see nothing. Traffic noise obscured any sound trail. He was certain that they were long gone, but he didn't like the idea of Aziz being on her own. Back in the lobby, he spotted the hotel clerk—"Give me the key to Clark Terry's room, now!"—but the clerk seemed frozen in fear, staring at him as the absurd soundtrack of tropical birdcalls played on. MacNeice took a deep breath and was about to ask again when the clerk snapped out of it and handed him a master key.

He made sure the clerk was making eye contact and said, "Find the cop in charge of the scene. Tell him to rush a forensics unit to 2111. Do you understand me?" He looked down at the plastic identity badge on the man's jacket pocket. "James, do you understand me?"

"Yes, sir. Find the cop in charge. . . . Room 2111."

Turning to head for the elevator, MacNeice said, "Good, and when you're done that, go and check the video feed for the underground parking. I want to know what vehicle left just now."

"Yes, sir." The clerk was in motion by the time the elevator doors had closed on MacNeice.

HE FOUND AZIZ STANDING JUST INSIDE the open door, which showed no signs of being forced. But one glance into the room showed him that Marcus Johnson had put up the fight of his life. Blood was splattered on the carpet near the balcony doors, and the brocade drapes had been torn off their hooks as if he had held onto them in desperation. The coffee table was broken in two, its glass top shattered and scattered about the floor. A Nike duffle bag was open beside the bed, T-shirts, socks and jeans spilling out of it like blue, white and grey guts.

Aziz went over to the balcony. "Boss," she called, "there's blood on the railing and the floor." She looked down. The blanket covering Marcus looked to her like a Rorschach test, black blots on grey. Several people were being treated for cuts in a makeshift triage unit over by the waterfall, next to the long, white snaking sofa. Three uniformed officers were standing beside Johnson's body looking up, trying to imagine the trajectory of his fall.

"They're gone," MacNeice said, holstering his weapon as he stepped onto the balcony and also looked down. "We should get out of here. We know he didn't jump. Aziz, let's go. Forensics will take care of the scene."

"Who did this, Mac?"

A uniformed cop arrived at the door, his weapon drawn.

"Don't allow anyone into this room until Forensics gets here," MacNeice said, leading Aziz past him and out into the hall.

"Do I shut the door, sir?" The cop began reaching for the handle.

"Leave it as it is. Don't touch anything."

"No problem." The cop turned his back to the room, holstered his service weapon and stood at ease for a moment before looking over his shoulder at the room again. "Big job for housekeeping. . . ."

———

AT THE ELEVATORS AZIZ AND MacNeice met the forensics team, two men carrying their kits and a young woman wheeling what looked like a large grey metal suitcase.

"Look for marks from someone swinging something like a baseball bat," MacNeice told them as he held the elevator door open for Aziz. They nodded.

Aziz backed into the corner, against the brass rail, and looked up at the indicator panel as the numbers began descending. "A baseball bat?"

"Well, a little shorter than that. I think I know who was in there. Gregori's bodyguards were both carrying thick hardwood dowels—sticks. Short bats."

"He flew, you know. I mean, he was flying." She turned her gaze to the numbers again.

"Meaning?"

"To land where he did, he had to be at least ten or twelve feet away from the rail, as if he'd been launched off that balcony. Before he went down, he went out."

"So it had to be two—one on either side—to launch him. He couldn't have jumped on his own and one person couldn't have heaved him that far."

The elevator doors opened. As they walked over towards the clutch of police surrounding the body, MacNeice noticed that the deputy chief was there, hands in his pockets, looking up to the open sky through the broken grid.

"MacNeice, a word." Wallace moved over towards the waterfall.

MacNeice handed the keys of the Chevy to Aziz. "Why don't you wait outside in the car. I'll be right there." Then he followed Wallace, who was still standing with his hands in his pockets, now gazing at the tropical splendour.

"Does this kid have anything to do with the dead girl?" The chief pulled a hand out of his pocket and stared down at the screen on his cellphone.

"He was her boyfriend and the father of her child."

"What's the story here?" Wallace looked up from his phone.

"His name was Marcus Johnson."

"He didn't do the girl, though?"

"Marcus was in love with her. . . ." MacNeice was struggling to get a grip on himself, to be specific. He wanted to get out of there, now. "He told us he arranged to take her to the beach house and was paid to take nude pictures of her while someone he didn't know was taking pictures of her too. She didn't know anything about it."

"Christ!" He put his cellphone away, pushed his hands into his pockets and seemed to lift his heels as if to gain a bit more height. "MacNeice, I need to know if we are any closer here."

"I think we are, sir. I don't have a motive yet, but I believe we're very close to making an arrest."

"That's the first thing you've said that has given me hope. I hope you're right. I've got everyone from the mayor to the media climbing up my back for answers."

"There is a but, however."

"Fuck. I hate buts." Wallace glared at him.

"I believe we're going to be dealing with foreign nationals who will claim diplomatic immunity." MacNeice rubbed the back of his neck.

"You do your job, Detective, and I'll deal with the diplomats. For now, am I clear to say that this horrific mess has brought us closer to an arrest?"

"I believe that's accurate, sir."

"Good. Don't prove me wrong." Wallace walked away, passing the body without looking down, and pushed through the revolving door to face the various media already setting up in the parking lot.

MacNeice took one last look at Marcus Johnson and wished he hadn't. The young man's left eye had been dislodged from its socket and was lying like a discarded marble next to his ear. "Jesus," he muttered, not conscious that he'd said it out loud.

The forensics officer glanced up him from his squat. "Yeah, nasty. I don't think it popped out with the first impact, though. The second impact was what shook it loose."

"Please don't go on," MacNeice said, holding up a hand to silence him. "But if you can find them in that awful mess, see if you can spot any initial blows from a wood baton."

"I won't likely be able to figure that out here, sir, but Dr. Richardson might. I'll keep looking, all the same." He turned back to delicately probing the boy's flattened skull.

As MacNeice walked away he was silently apologizing to Marcus Johnson for not keeping him safe, for not even realizing he was at such risk. The young man had had sense enough to hide, but he and Aziz had been complacent. He went out through the revolving door and swung left to avoid the DC, still facing a dozen or so microphones.

When he got to the car, Aziz was staring out the windshield into the middle distance. MacNeice stopped for a moment to phone Mary Richardson before he climbed in. He got her voicemail. "Mary," he said, "you're going to be taking delivery of a young man who was thrown out of a window. I believe he may have been beaten first with a baton, a foot-long dowel roughly an inch and a half in diameter. He's been badly damaged from the fall—well, two falls, actually—but see if you can't find something that suggests he was beaten first."

Putting his cellphone away, he took a deep breath and got into the driver's seat. Aziz was still staring directly ahead. "What's that bird?" she asked.

He followed her gaze to a stand of birch on the opposite side of the lot. Halfway up an almost vertical branch was a black and white bird with a pale yellow breast and a red streak on its head. "It's a yellow-bellied sapsucker, tapping for veins of sap under the bark."

"Funny name," she said.

"It's a beautiful bird, a close relative of the woodpecker."

They sat in silence watching the sapsucker work the upper extremities of the branch, while behind them the deputy chief was busy working the media. Only when MacNeice saw the black van arrive that would take Johnson's body away did he turn the key in the ignition. He eased the Chevy as close as he could to the tree, stopping there so Aziz could watch the bird until it flew off.

"I could use a drink. How about you?" MacNeice said as they drove slowly through streets that for a moment seemed like a parallel universe, one that knew nothing about the violent death of a very talented young man.

"I don't really drink."

"I forgot. Sorry."

"Forgot? No, no, it's nothing to do with my religion. It's just that I have a very low tolerance for it. I end up falling asleep." She shifted, sitting up straight in the seat.

"I could make a case for sleep," he said.

"Okay, let's have a drink. But I'm not up for Marcello's right now." She allowed her head to fall back slowly onto the headrest and looked over at him.

"We'll go to my place. I'll pour you a grappa and we'll look out the window so you can see more birds. I live in a virtual bird sanctuary." He glanced over to see if that was okay with her.

"Right. let's do that. I'd love to try grappa—if only for the name!"

She fell silent, and a few minutes later when he glanced her way, her eyes were closed, but he couldn't tell whether she'd fallen asleep or was closing off the world for a moment. He drove slowly, avoiding sharp turns and sudden acceleration or braking. It wasn't until he came to a stop in front of the gate-house and turned off the engine that she opened her eyes.

TWENTY ONE

—

WALKING INTO MACNEICE'S HOUSE, Aziz was determined to absorb everything about it. She noticed first the dark, wide-planked floor of the hall, then the smell of the place—fresh, as if the windows were always open. The black-and-white photograph on the wall, above the small credenza where he dropped his keys, was of a nude, shot from behind on a stony beach. It immediately, and sadly, brought her mind back to Marcus Johnson's studies of Lydia.

"Who is this?" she asked.

"It's a portrait by Bill Brandt, a gift from a few years ago."

"From whom?"

"From me. It cheers me up. I needed some cheering up. . . . It was an extravagance, but a day never goes by when I don't feel grateful for its being there."

She nodded, then followed MacNeice into the living room,

where he stopped to clear away the only visible clutter, a few books on the sofa. He carried them over to the desk.

"Okay—are you ready?" he said as he walked over to the windows.

"I think so."

He flung open the curtains and the room was immediately flooded with late afternoon light.

"There's oak, maple, birch, cedar and a few serviceberries, but mostly maples as far as you can see. I tapped them for a few years and took the sap to a local farm. I'd come back a week later and there'd be a dozen bottles of syrup; the farmer kept six and I kept six. It was terrific."

"Why'd you stop?" She thought she knew the answer but couldn't resist asking.

"Just lost interest, I guess." He moved two wooden arm-chairs in front of the window and said, "Sit down. I'll fetch the drinks."

Aziz picked the one with the high back, which reminded her of the chairs by the fireplace in old English pubs. The trees were even more impressive from a lower angle, stretching into the distance like proud columns before diving down the slope of the hill towards the highway. She rested her head against the back of the chair and looked up. The canopy was alive with birds, hopping from one branch to another or shooting into the sky.

MacNeice returned with a tray. On it were two tumblers of water with lime wedges and two glass cylinders that looked like shot glasses, only taller. The glasses had thick bases that, when she lifted hers, made the contents—a clear liquid—seem heavier and more impressive. He set the tray down on a small wooden table, sat down and handed her a glass.

"Cheers, Fiza—to life and better days." He watched her study, smell and swirl the grappa. "Best to sip it slowly."

"Is that your best toast?"

"No, my best is 'Here's to us. Wha's like us? Damn few—and they're all dead.' It was a Gaelic toast popular among Scottish airmen in the Battle of Britain."

"I see. Well . . . cheers."

MacNeice drank his in one gulp, holding it in his mouth for a moment before swallowing. His attention was on the trees but he was aware of her gaze. "I can make you tea or coffee, if you'd prefer," he said.

"No, this is perfect. I'm just savouring the moment." With that she tasted it, held it in her mouth, then swallowed, wincing slightly.

"Too strong, I guess. Let me—" He leaned forward as if he was going to get out of the chair.

"It's just a new sensation. I like it. I think I like it a lot. I was expecting something that burned more, but this is just warming me up."

"There are many grappas that burn, but this isn't one of them."

They sat in silence looking out into the forest. Every so often their heads would turn, like people at a tennis match, when a bird flew by. "What was that last one?" she asked.

"A chickadee. They'll eat seeds out of your hand if you go out there."

"You're not serious."

"Oh yes, I am. They'll land on your arm, your head or your shoulder, make their way to your hand, pick up some seeds and fly off. Then they'll come back for more, often with friends." They sat watching the chickadees for some time before he added, "After they get to know you, they follow you, waiting to see if you're going to feed them."

Within minutes of finishing her grappa, Fiza had slid down in the chair so she could put her feet up on the radiator under the window. The conversation slowed, then stopped, and soon she was asleep.

MacNeice cleared away the grappa glasses and the untouched water, then returned to the window. Fiza's head had tipped sideways. He helped her up and over to the sofa. Laying her head on a cushion, he lifted her legs and took off her shoes. He took the Glock from her belt and placed it on the coffee table, then lifted the soft grey throw from the back of the sofa and draped it over her. She nodded slightly and smiled, but didn't open her eyes. MacNeice closed the curtains.

When she woke, she found a folded note on the coffee table. *Gone to get some provisions. I'll make dinner. Back in one hour.* She loved notes. Notes like this one, which gave a return time but no departure time, especially amused her. Sitting up, she took in the room for the first time. Though she'd been fascinated by every detail as she came into the house, the moment the curtains were drawn back, her attention had been focused on the view outside.

On the desk she noticed shreds of poems scribbled on pads or tucked into the books like bookmarks, some several stanzas long, others just a line or two. Scanning the bookshelves, she saw volumes on birds, art, architecture, photography, poetry, gardening, cooking, history and biography. *The Complete Diaries of Samuel Pepys*, books on John Donne, John Aubrey and John Evelyn, anthologies of music from jazz to classical, but no books on criminology and no crime novels. There were more photographs, some framed, others just lying neatly in stacks. The subject matter varied but most were from nature: close-ups of trees, several of tree trunks carved with messages, still others of telephone poles riddled with rusting staples, shot so the sun made them seem golden and beautiful—and they were beautiful. There were studies of flowers in their full-bloom glory, but more glorious by far, she thought, were those of the same flowers dying.

Fiza pulled the curtains open and sat down in her chair. The light had changed while she'd been asleep, and she wondered for a moment what the view was like in the morning, in autumn, in winter, under a foot of snow. She felt utterly at home here, safe and comfortable, even though she had no real idea where she was, other than in his house. She realized then that the source of the comfort was MacNeice himself.

Her thoughts returned to the hotel—the chaos, the smashed glass, the spectacular, unnecessary death of a young man. On her pant leg were several narrow blood splatters, now almost black on the grey fabric. Holding out her blouse so she could see it, she noticed mascara tracks from her earlier tears. Suddenly needing to pee, she pulled herself out of the chair and went in search of the bathroom, which she found by tracking a spill of light from the master bedroom.

Sitting on the toilet, Aziz scanned the room. With the skylight over the granite shower stall and the window beside her that looked out to a row of mature cedars, it felt as if the bathroom were part of the forest. Flushing, she stood and stepped out of her pants, then slipped off her panties and reached into the stall to turn on the shower. Without undoing her blouse, she slid it up and over her head, shrugged off her bra and stepped in.

Placing her hands flat on the back of the stall, she leaned in, her head under the flow. The heat and force of the water seemed to wash away more than dirt and tears. If she stayed there long enough she might be able to wash away the memory. When her breathing slowed, she picked up the soap, turned it over, saw how the original form had melted away—and marvelled at the intimacy of taking a shower in someone else's bathroom. This soap had been formed by his hand and his body, like a river stone smoothed by the current. She rubbed it slowly over her arm, imagining his arm, slowly over her stomach, imagining his— and then she laughed out loud, shoved the idea out of her mind and soaped herself down.

When she got out, she looked in the mirror and noticed a large bruise on her hip. She must have got it when MacNeice pushed her out of the way of the falling Marcus and the glass. Aziz picked up her panties and put them on, then put on her bra. Staring down at the heap of clothing on the floor, the pant leg flecked with dried blood, she lifted the clothes, folded each piece and went into the bedroom, turning on the light. Inside the closet everything was hung neatly, jackets and trousers together—mostly grey or black—and shirts to the right. She took out a pale blue cotton shirt and slipped it on, rolling up the sleeves and buttoning it. She stood in front of the mirror that ran the length of the wooden chest of drawers, ran her fingers through her hair and thought, *What is it about a man's shirt on a woman? Now there's a question for Bo.* She leaned closer to look at her face. In her dark eyes she saw the pooled sadness, and turned away.

There were photographs in this room too, mostly, she assumed, of his parents. Two were of himself, one as a teen— diving off a dock, caught in mid-air, his long, slender body captured beautifully against the black stillness of the lake. In the other he was a toddler wearing a white knit top; his smile was wide in a way she couldn't remember ever seeing. Maybe that joy had been beaten out of him and would appear no more, lost to a life of observation.

She could tell which side of the bed he slept on by the wrinkles in the pillow and what was on the night table. The telephone sat next to a small reading lamp beside two books, *The Kilvert Diaries* and *The Collected Works of John Keats*. On the wall behind the headboard was a large painting, a mountain scene reduced to form and colour. Beside the bed was an engraving of a horse's head with its mouth open, but whether it was laughing or screaming like the one in *Guernica*, she couldn't tell. In her current state she assumed the latter.

She carried her neatly folded clothes out to the living room and placed them on a chair. In the kitchen she retrieved the tumbler of water he'd poured for her. She squeezed the lime into it and went back to the living room. She looked at the bookcases again, and up to the top of the shelves, where a stack of objects stood alone. A cream-coloured vinyl zippered envelope, like those used by accountants or insurance agents, sat on top of two photo albums. Aziz knew instinctively that this was where he kept Kate, on the periphery, almost out of sight but not out of mind. She stood on her toes and took one of the albums down, then, leaning against bookcase, opened it to the first page. It revealed a close-up of Kate playing the violin in concert, her bobbed dark hair slightly out of focus. The orchestra was also out of focus, and only the baton and hand of the conductor were visible. It was the expression on her face that made the deepest impression on Aziz: her eyes were almost closed, her eyebrows arching, and her mouth turned upward in a sublime smile. It was an image of pure joy. She suddenly felt ashamed to be snooping, and without turning another page, slid the album back in place.

She heard the unmistakable rumbling of the overpowered Chevy. She smiled for a moment at her agitation about being discovered in her underwear and wearing his shirt. She fluffed out her hair, still wet from the shower. Still somewhat fearful that he might be offended, she was considering making a run for the bathroom to put her soiled clothes back on when the door opened and MacNeice appeared, carrying several bags of groceries. As he stood there on the threshold, his jaw dropped slightly, but then he smiled.

"I'm sorry, Mac. I woke up and looked at myself. . . . I hope you don't mind, but I took a shower and hunted around for something clean to wear."

"I don't mind. But if you're uncomfortable, I can find you a pair of sweatpants."

"I'm not uncomfortable, Mac . . . though perhaps I should be."

"Well, I have to say that seeing you in front of that window brings more beauty to the scenery than I've experienced in a long time. I need to put these groceries away. Come and sit in the kitchen—I've got a real treat for you." She followed him, perching on a barstool while he dropped the bags on the counter.

"What are you going to feed me?"

"Mrs. Provenzano, the matriarch of Provenzano's, has made her gnocchi with ricotta—light as a feather." He lifted out a tinfoil dish carefully, as if it were precious metal, then a bunch of greens. "Sage. A bit of garlic, olive oil, a sprinkle of Parmesan and Italian parsley, and you'll think you're somewhere else."

He doled out equal portions onto two plates, set them on the table and put half a baguette in the middle. Aziz climbed off the barstool and sat down as MacNeice poured two glasses of white wine and took his place opposite her. They had just begun eating when his cellphone rang. It was Swetsky. In the silence Aziz could hear him clearly.

"Just checkin' in, boss. I was up at the marina and went through the tuck shop office—the records were all there. Thompson, the mechanic, knew where the cashbox was and where Gibbs kept the key. There was a marina envelope underneath all the paid invoices and so on. It had thirty-five hundred dollars in it in fifty-dollar bills. Thompson couldn't account for it, said he didn't think the old man had ever seen that amount of cash in his life, since the marina is a cheque and credit card business."

"Did he offer any ideas about why the old man went berserk?" MacNeice had put down his fork and pushed his plate away.

"Yeah. Apparently he was always a handful, but his wife kept him in check and kept the business going. When she died, Gibbs seemed to get much worse—going off at kids and their moms, snapping for no reason at all. Thompson thought he was doing drugs of some kind but never actually caught him doing it, though he did say that Ronnie Ruvola hung around a lot. The house is being torn apart now, so we may find out what he was into."

"Were there any records of the rentals?"

"No, and Thompson said that was weird. The wife and even Gibbs always kept records of their boat rentals. But he couldn't find any receipts on the two boats. I think the money in that envelop was a payoff to Gibbs to keep those rentals off the books. The only thing he hadn't counted on was the boats not coming back."

"And the ice auger. Anything else?"

"The shotguns were on the table where Thompson had been cleaning them. The ten- and twelve-gauge are still in pieces; he'd just finished reassembling the wife's when Vertesi arrived. He'd gone to the back of the shop to get more rags to clean the larger pieces when Gibbs grabbed the sixteen-gauge. That's all I've got until Forensics is through with the house. I'm just coming into town now—where do you want me?"

"I think it's time we had a chat with Gregori Petrescu. Can you meet me at the Chelsea Manor in a half-hour? Park outside on the street, away from the entrance."

MacNeice put the cellphone in his jacket pocket and looked over at Aziz. She was mopping up the sauce on her plate with a piece of bread.

"Let me take you home first." He took the plates to the sink and returned to re-cork the wine.

"No, I'll come too."

"I think you need to rest. Why don't you sit this one out? We'll be fine."

"No way, Mac." Aziz got up from her chair and retrieved her pile of clothes. She went into the bathroom and emerged a few minutes later, snapping her service weapon back onto the belt of her creased and bloodstained pants. "Okay, let's go."

TWENTY TWO

—

SWETSKY CLIMBED INTO THE BACK of the Chevy, which dipped with his weight. "What's the plan, Stan?" he asked, closing the door. Aziz was in the passenger seat but didn't turn around.

Driving off, MacNeice met his eyes in the rear-view mirror and said, "First we'll see if the Range Rover is in the parking lot. If it is, the bodyguards will probably be with him. I'll park the car across the street. Aziz, why don't you stay with the car in case we miss them inside?"

"The hell I will." She was looking out the window but the determination in her voice was clear.

Swetsky was surprised at her tone. "Hey, Aziz, relax. Whatever. I'll stay with the car."

"Just so we're clear," MacNeice said, "we're not looking for trouble. If we were, I'd call in the cavalry. We just want to continue the conversation that was interrupted outside his father's house."

Then MacNeice gave Swetsky a brief overview of what had happened while he'd been at the lake. "Aziz and I think Marcus Johnson was killed by the two bodyguards."

The big man's only response came softly from the back seat. "Christ almighty."

THE CHELSEA MANOR HAD BEEN BUILT on land that was once an apple orchard in the shadow of the escarpment to the west of the city. Because it sat high on a dome-like hill, the orchard's name had been Hilltop Macs, a nod to the McIntosh apples grown there. As a teenager, MacNeice had worked at the orchard every fall weekend, picking fruit or sitting in the plywood shack waiting for customers to come and buy a bag, a box or a bushel. When the farmer died, his two sons, who had long before moved away, promptly sold the land. The house, a small but pleasant century-old brick two-storey, and the nearby red barn with HILLTOP MACS and an illustration of a large, juicy apple painted on it were razed. It took only eight days before the hill was transformed into a bald mound and construction of the Manor had begun.

The approach to it had been designated Chelsea Lane, and it followed the path of the dirt road that had once run up to the farm. The only building on Chelsea Lane was the Chelsea Manor—the road was effectively a cul-de-sac. "Strange choice for Gregori," MacNeice said.

"Because it's bogus colonial?" Swetsky asked.

"No, because it's a dead end."

"Maybe they feel they've done nothing wrong," Aziz said. "Or they're really confident."

"I vote for confident."

MacNeice drove around the circular drive, passing under a three-storey-high canopy supported by four gigantic white concrete columns. The parking lot, to the left of the hotel, was separated from the building by two rows of apple trees. Not the original species—these were crabapples, an ironic barb for all those who had once carried Hilltop Macs in their lunch pails or eaten them in pies or applesauce.

After cruising the parking lot without spotting the black Range Rover, MacNeice backed into an empty spot and turned off the engine. "Let's review. We've got three Romanians, all either military or ex-military. Gregori Petrescu is a microbiologist and not likely to be a combatant, but the other two are fit ex-military types and carry foot-long dowels."

"Excuse me?" Swetsky said.

"Foot-long dowels, shoved into the back of their pants. They weren't carrying any other weapons the first time we met, but it doesn't mean they don't have them."

"We're just going in to talk, though?" Aziz said, looking over at MacNeice.

"That's right. The colonel's smart enough to know we're bound to pay a visit, and poised enough not to be worried about it."

"One thing's been eatin' at me, Mac," Swetsky said. "The first killing—the girl—was so precise—spooky-smart, and so clean. Then we get the guy in the boat—okay, you could argue that was also tidy. But throwing the kid off the balcony? That was very messy and very public. I don't get it."

"Maybe the fact that we found him first took the elegance out of the plan," Aziz said.

"It was a quick fix, you mean?"

"Yes. But here's what's weird for me—Marcus had never

met these guys. He didn't know who paid for the cottage." Aziz unsnapped her seatbelt.

MacNeice said, "I've started to think, what if this was a contract? You come, you complete the contract and you leave."

"And these guys?" Swetsky asked.

"They hired the contractor. What's happened since is their problem, and they're not as subtle as he was."

"Tossing a kid off a balcony, you mean." Swetsky made a diving motion with his hand that both MacNeice and Aziz ignored.

"Whoever threw Johnson off the balcony may have suspected that he ran because he knew something." MacNeice looked down the line of cars. A small rabbit edged out onto the driveway and hopped over to the crabapple trees to nibble on the vegetation below. He pointed it out to Aziz and Swetsky.

"Sweet," Aziz said.

"Dinner," Swetsky replied.

"And here's another thing—these guys are Romanian but the syringe was likely built by a Bulgarian."

"What do we do about diplomatic immunity?" Aziz asked.

"To quote the deputy chief, fuck 'em. If the conversation stays pleasant it won't be an issue. If the sticks come out, assume malicious intent."

"And if these guys leave without you and get into their truck?" Swetsky asked.

"We've all got pagers, and we'll use them. If you feel the buzzer in your pocket, stop them. If you don't, try buzzing us. If we don't answer, it's your turn to be John Wayne."

MacNeice was still watching the rabbit, hunkered down and nibbling at the greens. Suddenly its head popped up, its ears went vertical and it bolted back across the pavement.

MacNeice looked beyond it to the entrance to see the black Range Rover ease around the corner, heading towards them. "Well, perhaps no need to wait. Turn the two-way on, Aziz."

The SUV stopped three feet from the Chevy's front bumper. Several seconds passed before the truck's rear door opened. Then Gregori Petrescu stepped out and straightened his suit jacket. He took a cigarette out of a package, put it in his mouth and lit it. Standing in front of the Chevy with one hand in his pocket, he smiled slightly and waited.

MacNeice told Aziz to stay put, got out of the car and walked towards him. "Good day, Mr. Petrescu."

"It must be embarrassing, Detective, to be approached like this. You, a professional, caught sitting in—how do you call it—a dead end?"

"Caught? I wasn't aware I was being hunted." MacNeice looked through the windshield at the two bodyguards, who stared back at him. The one in the passenger seat was sporting dark rings under his eyes, and neither man was smiling. Turning back to Petrescu, he said, "Do you want to ask these boys to step out of the vehicle, or shall I?"

"It's safer if I do." Petrescu knocked twice on the door panel and moved out of the way. As the two men got out, Aziz and Swetsky emerged from the Chevy.

"Ask them to take those dowels from their pants and place them on the ground." MacNeice put his hand on the grip of his service revolver where the colonel could see it.

"Are you arresting me, Detective?" Petrescu asked, without taking the cigarette from his mouth.

"Do I have reason to?"

Aziz and Swetsky moved forward to stand on either side of MacNeice with their hands on their service weapons. Gregori studied Aziz from head to toe and smiled. "She's a beautiful woman, MacNeice, but she looks so terrible—like she's been rolling in dirt, or blood."

"The dowels?" MacNeice nodded at the two bodyguards, who were standing with their hands crossed in front of their genitals, soccer style. Petrescu smiled, took the cigarette out of his mouth and motioned to the two. They reached behind and took out the dowels, placing them on the ground in front of their feet.

"Push them forward." MacNeice motioned with his hand and the two rolled the sticks in his direction.

"Now what, Detective? I have a plane to catch." Petrescu dropped the butt on the ground and crushed it with his shoe.

"You're not staying for your sister's funeral?" MacNeice asked.

"Sadly, no. Events in Romania are calling me home. So, what do you want with us?" He put his hands in his pockets and again turned his attention to Aziz. "Shall I ask you, lady detective? What do you want with me?"

Aziz did not acknowledge him.

"There are several questions that I'd like answers to, Colonel Petrescu, and until I have them, you'll be staying here. But I'd like to conduct that interview at Division and not here in the parking lot."

"So you *are* arresting me. On what charge?" Petrescu's tone indicated that he was finally in danger of losing his cool. The two bodyguards took a half-step forward, dropping their hands to their sides.

Swetsky and Aziz both drew their weapons and assumed firing positions. MacNeice hadn't drawn his; he simply stepped towards the colonel. "Questioning, in this country, is not the same as arresting. But I think it would be best to keep your boys on a leash, so I'm going to ask my partner to cuff them."

"You called me Colonel—thank you for the respect. By partner, do you mean the fat one or the dirty woman?"

"Fuck you, Jack," Swetsky said, his eyes on the bodyguards.

"Well, I think that's enough." MacNeice pulled his weapon out of its holster, pointed it at Petrescu's head and walked forward till the end of the barrel was touching his temple. He moved behind him, took his shoulder and turned him in the direction of the bodyguards. "Swetsky, cuff Black-Eyes first and then his mate."

Petrescu nodded slightly, and the bodyguard put his hands together and brought them forward. Swetsky holstered his weapon and took out the handcuffs.

"Do you mind, Detective, if I call my consul general?" Petrescu asked.

"Right now, yes, I mind." He tapped the barrel gently against the man's temple. "Aziz, once Swetsky's dealt with those two, search the Range Rover."

"With pleasure, boss." Aziz moved around Petrescu and MacNeice, gave her cuffs to Swetsky and waited till he had cuffed the other bodyguard.

"So you do speak," Petrescu said. "Aziz. . . . You're Muslim, but they let you be a detective. What a country!"

"Like my partner said, sir, fuck you." Aziz holstered her weapon, took the latex gloves from her jacket pocket, snapped them on and opened the driver's door of the SUV.

Swetsky grinned and tapped hard on the bodyguards' shoulders, encouraging them to sit down on the pavement.

"The driver's seat is clear," Aziz said, and walked around to the passenger side.

"Do you not need a search warrant, Detective?" Petrescu asked.

"Not this time. Here, blocking a police vehicle is perceived as a threat."

"Passenger side, glove compartment, under the seats all clear, except for a *Hustler* magazine," Aziz called.

"They get lonely being so far from home." Petrescu smiled.

"MacNeice, come take a look at this." Aziz was on the far side of the SUV, leaning over the back seat. In her hands was a black portfolio. She lifted it up towards MacNeice. "Marcus and Lydia's album."

MacNeice pushed Petrescu over to the vehicle and looked in as Aziz slowly turned the pages. "Where did you pick that up?" he asked Petrescu.

"I've told you before, Detective, I am not obliged to answer you."

"That's right, you did. We'll continue our conversation later." At the end of the driveway, three unmarked Chevys bounced over the ramp and into the lane, followed by a large black van. One of the cars circled around and stopped just ahead of the Range Rover, while the other two pulled up behind.

MacNeice turned over Petrescu to the first cop out of his vehicle. "Cuff him, search him and have the Rover searched stem to stern."

"I demand you inform the consul general. You have no idea what you're doing here."

MacNeice ignored him, addressing the officer who now had Petrescu's arms behind him. "Treat him with respect—he's a foreign national. Get someone to move this vehicle out of the way of my car." All three men were led away and disappeared inside the black van.

"Jeezus, Aziz," Swetsky said, "I was going to whack him when he made that crack about your clothes, but the creep had a point." He was looking at the dried blood on her pants and shoes, her creased and tear-stained blouse.

She looked down in mock surprise and smiled insincerely. "Thank you, Swetsky. So good of you to notice."

"Swets, put your gloves on and get those sticks down to Forensics. I want to know if there's anything on them. Also, photograph the portfolio where Aziz found it and then confiscate it. Can you check whether there was a security breach at Lydia's apartment? If there wasn't, this is another portfolio, and I think I know where it came from."

"Okay, Mac."

"Aziz, come with me." MacNeice led her down the lane to the hotel entrance.

AT THE DESK, MACNEICE AND AZIZ showed their badges. "The key for Gregori Petrescu's room, and those of his two companions, please," MacNeice said. The clerk looked surprised to see them—they were the only people around who weren't in the parking lot gawking at the show.

In the elevator Aziz asked, "What are you thinking, Mac?"

"I was just wondering if the fox hasn't been chasing the hounds. We leave Marcus's room and a moment later someone arrives to kill him. We pull in to the parking lot here and a few minutes later the Range Rover arrives and parks right in front of us."

"Why would he follow us when he knows we're coming for him?"

"Good question. If he's got nothing to do with the killings, it doesn't make sense. If he's responsible for the killings, it also

·doesn't make sense." When the doors opened on the fourth floor, they walked towards Room 406.

Two pieces of Petrescu's luggage were sitting on the floor at the end of the bed, packed and locked. The room had been cleaned, as had the adjoining rooms on either side, each with a full duffle bag sitting beside the bed.

Back in Petrescu's room, MacNeice took out his cellphone and called Wallace. "I need clearance, sir, to open the bags of three Romanian nationals who are claiming diplomatic immunity."

"Where are they now?"

"They're in custody, sir, being brought in as we speak."

"On what charges?"

"Obstruction, being in the possession of stolen materials, littering."

"Littering? Are you serious?"

"If I have to be. Petrescu dropped a cigarette and ground it into the pavement in front of three police officers."

"Christ, MacNeice, do you have a charge that has a hope of sticking?"

"Possession of stolen materials. He had the photo portfolio of the girl in the back seat of the car. It could have come from only one—or maybe two—places."

"So open the bags. I'll call upstairs and get Ottawa on side. But do it quickly in case I get turned down. Good work, MacNeice."

"We're not there yet, sir, but thanks." MacNeice put his cellphone away. They both pulled on their latex gloves, then MacNeice pulled out the Leatherman he had tucked into his belt.

"Were you anticipating this?"

"Yes and no. I knew he'd be too cocky not to push it, but I had no idea he'd give us an excuse to handcuff him." He unfolded the tool, turning it into a pair of wire cutters, then snapped the woven-wire locks on both cases and lifted them onto the bed.

"The portfolio coming from one of two places . . . What are you thinking?"

"Marcus was an artist. He would have created a set of prints for his own portfolio, a copy of the one he gave her. When he ran, I think he would have abandoned everything but that. It was a talisman—a reminder of her and the promise of his talent." He flipped open the large suitcase. "You take the smaller one. Before you touch anything, shoot it as is." He took out his digital camera and snapped two shots of the folded clothing, on which a grey envelope with a Romanian flag rested, before handing the camera to Aziz.

"Which would place them in his room at the hotel."

"Precisely."

"It's creepy to think of those goons going through that album."

"It is. On the other hand, it's a significant cut above *Hustler*, so maybe they wouldn't get it. Then again, if their fingerprints are on those pages along with Marcus's, there's something delicious about it."

"How so?"

"Marcus and Lydia are both dead—and they died horribly— but the photos document the story of their love and their art. I think there's something delicious about capturing the people who did this to them by using the portfolio as evidence."

"You're a romantic, boss."

"I suppose I am."

Aziz turned back to the task at hand. "Papers, lots of papers. All of it in Romanian, I guess."

"Shoot them all. Lift them out neatly and shoot as much detail as you can, page after page."

"What's in yours?"

"He comes from a country that's on the ropes, but Mr. Petrescu wears only the best—Italian mostly, even down to his underwear. Wait a minute—hand me the camera again." He took out a folder with several images inside, all black and white but for two badly faded coloured prints. They looked like they had been taken in Romania before the fall of communism. Two were of a young boy in a military uniform squinting into the sunshine as he stood at attention; the other showed a family vacation: a trip to the beach, the mother and father sitting on a blanket, the boy—clearly Gregori—in the foreground with a bucket and shovel, digging in the sand. In addition there were two photos of Antonin in a laboratory and three of sadly deformed young children lying on metal cots and staring vacantly at the camera. For modesty, a narrow cloth had been thrown over their genitals, as if the obscenity of their bodies wasn't more than enough.

"Grotesque," Aziz said as she looked over his shoulder at the images MacNeice was framing with the camera.

"I wonder if these were given to Gregori to show his father or given to him by his father."

After they had taken everything out of both pieces of luggage, they felt through the linings, which were untampered with, then photographed any item they'd missed and put them all back. Next they went through the duffle bags. In Black-Eyes's bag they found a stash of porn, several XXL black T-shirts and a bottle of Jack Daniels. In the driver's there was nothing but clothing, everything neatly folded, military style.

By the time they returned to the Chevy carrying the

luggage, everyone had gone, along with the Range Rover. They drove slowly out of the parking lot, and just before turning down Chelsea Lane, MacNeice remarked, "I liked it better when it was an apple orchard."

TWENTY THREE

—

BEFORE THEY HEADED BACK to Division, Aziz persuaded MacNeice to drop by her apartment so she could change into clean clothes. When they got to the station, a Romanian was ensconced in each of the three interview rooms. Swetsky was leaning against the wall outside the one containing Petrescu. He looked over at Aziz—now wearing a blue suit with a crisp white shirt—and said, "Much better. There's pizza waiting for you two upstairs—at least what's left of it. I was starved."

"Maybe later. Swets, you take the driver. Let Black-Eyes stew for a while. Aziz and I will interview Petrescu. No word yet from Wallace?"

"Nope. Petrescu's been demanding a phone call and generally being a pain in the ass. The other two just sit in their rooms staring at the wall."

MacNeice looked through the wired-glass window at the

colonel. Williams was standing in the corner behind him, and nodded to MacNeice and Aziz as they entered the room.

"Are you comfortable, Mr. Petrescu?" MacNeice said. "Were you offered coffee or tea?"

"You know what I want. Unless you're willing to make this an international incident, you'll give me my phone and let me make a call." Petrescu laid both hands flat on the table as if to emphasize his point.

"I hadn't realized you weren't given that opportunity. Aziz, ask the desk sergeant for Mr. Petrescu's cellphone."

"Certainly, sir." Aziz left the room.

"How did you come into possession of that photo album?" MacNeice said as he sat down.

"I don't know what you're talking about."

"The portfolio of images of your sister. They were on the back seat of your vehicle. Where did you get them?"

"You have no idea what you're dealing with, do you, Detective? You're just flailing about hoping there'll be something to catch hold of."

"Perhaps you're right. I'm not a scientist like yourself."

"No, certainly not. But you could—if you'll excuse me—benefit from scientific study." He was still looking down at the table as if studying the grain.

"Was it upsetting for you to see those images of your sister, Gregori?"

"I'd like a cup of tea. No milk, two sugars." It was the first time he'd looked at MacNeice, and his eyes betrayed no emotion.

"I'll get that for you." MacNeice stood up. "Oatmeal cookies with that?" Petrescu didn't look up. "I'll take that as a no."

Outside the door he met Aziz returning with the cellphone.

"They've recorded all the calls from and to," she said, "but haven't analyzed them yet. Where are you going?"

"I'm going to get Mr. Petrescu a cup of tea."

"Leave that. I'll go."

"No, you go in. See what you can get out of him. Williams has your back, and Petrescu's not a man of action. Give me that." He took the cellphone from her.

As Aziz sat down across from Petrescu, he leaned back in his chair. "Are you going to rough me up, Detective?"

"I'd like to ask you some questions."

"Yes. You know, that colour blue is very beautiful against your skin—your Arab skin. You're from Turkey?"

"Did you know your sister well, Mr. Petrescu?"

"Iran, perhaps?"

"We understand she was your half-sister, but did you see her often?"

"Your accent is British, so I'd guess you're either Iranian or Turkish."

"Are you aware of how your sister died?"

"No, I have it—you're Lebanese. Your parents were among the *petite bourgeois* who left Beirut to its fate. Yes? Am I right?"

"Tell me about your work in microbiology."

"Do you know microbiology, Detective?"

"No, that's why I'm asking. What do you do?"

"I . . . do things that are too complex for a pretty woman such as yourself to understand."

"You mean things like chemical warfare?" Aziz hoped her face hadn't flushed with the contempt she felt for the man.

"The memory capacity of the human brain, Detective, while unknown exactly, has been estimated to be the equivalent of two million home computers. But it does much more than that, doesn't it?"

"Are you speaking about the way your sister died?"

"And yet when a computer dies, its memory doesn't die with it."

"Unlike your sister's." Aziz could feel her forehead getting moist and couldn't bear the thought that the perspiration might be visible to Petrescu.

He turned his attention to the mirrored wall on his right. "I'll wait for my cellphone."

Aziz turned towards the door. Williams caught her eye from the corner of the room and mouthed the word *asshole*. She smiled.

The door opened and MacNeice stepped in and handed Petrescu the cellphone and his cup of tea. As Petrescu was dialling, he said, "She's very pretty, MacNeice, but not that clever."

"I've never had too much respect for clever, Colonel. I prefer depth and intelligence." He touched Aziz's shoulder lightly as he sat down, hoping that she'd realize he'd been watching through the mirror.

Petrescu's urgent conversation in Romanian was being recorded. They'd find someone to translate it, but MacNeice knew his time with the man was running out. He decided he'd simply carry on until he was forced to stop.

When Petrescu ended the call and set his phone face down on the table, MacNeice asked, "You were in the possession of a portfolio of images—nude images—of your sister and a young man. Where did you get them?"

"My consul general has been on the phone to your deputy chief. He was very upset that I missed my flight and is on his way here now. I think, or rather I believe, that this pathetic charade is quickly coming to an end."

"Your family deserted you, left you behind in a military boarding school. Why didn't you join your parents after the fall of the communist regime?"

"My father told you that?" He put the paper cup down hard on the table.

"They had to leave in a hurry; they couldn't reach you, not even to tell you they were going." MacNeice's voice was calm, even sympathetic.

"Did my father tell you that? Tell me!" Petrescu's fists were clenched and his neck veins stood out for a moment, but then he forced himself to relax, sat back and smiled. "Is that what you wanted, Detective—some Oedipal rage that would fit your tiny picture?"

"That was very good, Colonel. Not entirely convincing, but nonetheless very good."

There was a knock on the door. Williams looked over at MacNeice, who nodded for him to open it. Two men came in ahead of Wallace. The first was clearly the Romanian consul general, flushed with anger; the second, most likely a Canadian diplomat, had a look of weary detachment. He spoke first.

"Detective Superintendent MacNeice, I'm Farrelly from External Affairs. This gentleman is the consul general of Romania, Alexandru Banica. You are to release Colonel Petrescu and his men immediately into his custody, along with all their possessions."

"All except one—a portfolio of images that is part of an ongoing homicide investigation," MacNeice responded. "I might as well ask, since we're all here, could you compel Mr. Petrescu to tell us how he came to be in possession of that portfolio?"

Farrelly shot a look at the deputy chief, who was staring at the floor. Stepping closer to MacNeice, Farrelly said, "You must have misunderstood me. I said release this man and his associates immediately."

Petrescu was on his feet. Stepping around the table, he turned to MacNeice. "Even in the Wild West, it appears, there are limitations, Detective. Pity. I was enjoying our conversation."

"Where did you put the syringe, Gregori, when you were finished with it?"

"MacNeice, that's enough," said Wallace as he moved aside to let the three men out of the room. Farrelly gave MacNeice a weary parting glance.

"What the fuck was that?" Williams said.

DC Wallace swung around. He hadn't noticed the tall black officer standing in the corner. "Who are you?"

"Williams, sir. Detective Inspector Montile Williams."

Wallace nodded and turned back to MacNeice. "How far did you get?"

"Not far at all, sir. But we managed between the two of us to paint a picture for him—one he may or may not have expected. What's our next move?"

"Nothing, unless you're prepared to charge him and his bodyguards with something beyond littering. You've got very little time before they ship him out to New York, then on to Romania."

"I apologize if this has put you in the meat grinder."

. "Fuck that!" Wallace swore, startling even himself, it seemed. Looking at Aziz, he said, "Sorry, Detective, I can't seem to shake the street." Aziz raised her hand as if to say *no problem*, and he continued. "MacNeice, I am having a fucking ball. You just keep going. Get something on that devious shit, and fast. When you do, I'll make the call to Farrelly, and trust me, that's a call I'm looking forward to making." With that he turned, nodded to Williams, who smiled and nodded back, and was gone.

"Well," MacNeice said.

"He's an impressive little fucker, that one," Williams said. Then, "Sorry, Aziz, no offence."

"Don't be a smartass, Williams. Boss, it's twenty minutes to midnight. He's not going anywhere tonight. What do you want to do?"

"We visit Antonin Petrescu first thing in the morning, but before we do, I'll send Swetsky to check Lydia's bedroom closet to see if her album is still there. Cold pizza, anyone?"

TWENTY FOUR

—

SHORTLY BEFORE EIGHT ON Wednesday morning, as the hospital staff were clearing away the breakfast trays, Aziz walked into Vertesi's hospital room carrying half a dozen magazines, from *Sports Illustrated* to the *New Yorker*. She wasn't sure what he liked to read, so she was trying everything. He was asleep with a newspaper on his lap. She put the magazines down on the table and gently rested her hand on his shoulder to wake him.

In the moment it took his eyes to open, she took in his pallor and the new hollows in his cheeks. The stubble looked so black against his skin that it seemed dyed. Then he saw her and smiled, embarrassed, it seemed to her, to be in this fix.

Aziz pulled up a chair and sat beside him. "I brought you some magazines, enough to keep you going for a while. Are you feeling better, Michael?"

Looking at the stack on the table, he said, "Thanks, Fiza, that's great. I've mostly been reading about you guys in the newspapers every day." He gathered up the paper and set it on the table to his left. "I still feel pretty weak, but yeah, I'm better."

"Have they said how long you'll be in here?" She scanned the room, noticing the many flowers and get-well cards, including those from Division.

"Not yet." He looked down at his left side. "All the buckshot's out, but it was torn up in there. They're worried about infection."

"Are you able to sleep?"

"Sleep is what I do best. The drugs are great—it's like you're in pain one minute and it's getting worse, then you get this pill and slowly you're drifting off to dreamland."

"I feel like I could use one of those about now." She smiled wearily.

"How are things with the case? Wallace is doing a great job at not saying much to the media." He winced as he shifted a little towards her.

"We're making headway, but I didn't come to talk about that. I don't want you thinking about work." She put a hand on his wrist above the bandage that secured the intravenous tube.

"But I really want to know what's been happening."

Changing the subject, Aziz said, "I met Rachel. She seems lovely, and she was very concerned about you."

"I'm so ashamed, Fiza. I feel like I let you all down."

"You couldn't have known that the old man would snap."

"Yeah, I could have. I knew there was something seriously off with the guy."

"So why did you go out there alone?"

"I don't know . . . I wanted to do something that would bust open the case, I guess. Does Mac know you're here?"

"No, I'm meeting him in an hour or so. Has Rachel been back to see you?"

"Every day after school. She brings me oatmeal raisin cookies. Want one?" He pointed to the bulging paper bag on the bedside table.

"No, thanks, I just had breakfast. When you sleep, do you have nightmares?"

"Fiza, what's going on with you?"

"Do you have nightmares?"

"If you mean do I see Gibbs comin' at me with the shotgun—yes. If you're asking about my shooting him—no. Truth is, I can't remember it."

"Maybe that's a blessing, Michael."

"Not according to the department shrink. She wants me to dig deeper and she's insisting that I open up; she won't sign me ready for duty until I do."

"Makes sense, I guess. Do it when you're ready, though. Especially if you feel you went out there to prove something—"

"Christ, I've been 'proving something' since I went into the academy—before, even—maybe since I was a kid. I know I cranked the old guy up after he called me a wop. I was playing with him. Worse, I humiliated him in front of his mechanic, and he could see I was enjoying it. It was like I was back on Barton Street showing off in front of my friends."

"Did you tell the shrink that?"

"No . . . this is the first time I've been willing to admit it."

She met his eyes then, and they were serene. He knew he'd

brought this on himself, and he didn't mind her knowing too.

"Thank you for trusting me, Michael."

"What's happened to you, Fiz? And please don't blow me off."

"Excuse me?"

"C'mon. I know you, at least a little, and you don't look like your usual impervious self."

"We failed to stop the death of a young man yesterday. It was horrific—and we could have stopped it." She shrugged slightly and her eyes filled with tears.

"You and MacNeice?"

"Yes. It was Lydia's boyfriend, Marcus Johnson. He was thrown off a balcony twenty-one storeys up. He smashed—" She cleared her throat. "He landed a few feet away from me . . . and we'd been with him only minutes before."

"You blaming yourself, or Mac?" He raised the bed's back higher.

"Me. Well, both of us." Aziz grabbed several tissues from the bedside table and wiped her eyes.

"Don't shit me. You're blaming MacNeice. You've found out he's fallible."

"Maybe." Now tears were streaming down her face, and she reached over for more tissues. "And here I am telling you to talk to the shrink."

"Aziz, nothing in my life has ever scared me before—nothing. But that old man bearing down on me with a shotgun is deep-in-my-head scary. The shrink knew that; she said something about PTSD, though I don't think I was listening. I am now, though. And I think you should too. You can't have that happen to you without damage up here." He tapped his temple several times.

"I know."

"What I'm getting at is, don't blame yourself, and don't blame MacNeice—he's human. And no matter what happened yesterday, he may be the finest cop this city's ever known."

She cleared her throat. "I had a message on my phone when I got home last night. It was from my professor in Ottawa. He's now the department head and he wants me back to teach criminology."

"Mistake." Vertesi reached over carefully, picked up his juice and sipped through the straw.

"I'm not so sure. I thought I was okay last night, but I feel. . . ." Aziz put the clump of tissues into the plastic bag hanging off the bedside table.

"You're not in any shape to make a decision like that. Have you told Mac?"

"No. I need time to think."

"When do you have to get back to your professor?"

"Soon. He wants me to start in September."

"Then you don't have time to think. But as far as I'm concerned, it's a mistake, Aziz." He put the cup down and eased the bed back down to a sleeping position.

Aziz stood, leaned over and kissed him on the cheek, once again touching his shoulder with her hand. "Sleep, Michael. I'll see you soon."

"Thanks for coming. Do you want to take some cookies for Swetsky?"

"Nah, he's a doughnut man. You have them—they're good for you."

"You asked about dreams earlier. You know what I dreamt about last night?"

"No, what?"

"That MacNeice was here, sitting in that chair." He nodded at the one she'd just gotten out of. "He was just sitting there looking at me. It was like he was watching over me or something. So weird. . . . Next thing I knew they were waking me for breakfast."

"Nice dream. Rest now. I'll see you soon."

She was already at the door when he said, "You're a cop, Fiza—like me. Go and be a cop."

ON HER WAY OUT AZIZ STOPPED at the nursing station and waited for someone to notice her. Finally a big woman with a soft black face smiled and said, "Can I help you, miss?"

"Yes. I'm Detective Inspector Aziz, and I want to know if my colleague, Detective Michael Vertesi, had a visitor late last night. Can you check for me?"

"Certainly." She swung her chair around and lifted a clipboard off the wall. Putting on her glasses, she turned over a page to read the entries from the night nurse. Looking over the glasses she said, "Yes, he did. A Detective Superintendent MacNeice. He arrived just before midnight and he left at 1:46 a.m."

TWENTY FIVE

—

MADELEINE ANSWERED THE DOOR at 9:16 a.m. Wednesday morning, but instead of opening it wide she merely held it tight to the length of the security chain. "You have an appointment?"

"Madeleine, please let him know we're here." MacNeice's cellphone rang as they stood on the steps. He looked at the small screen. "This is Richardson. Fiza, you get us in there," he said, nodding towards the now closed door as he moved back down the walk to take the call.

"Will do."

Richardson sounded weary. "Well, MacNeice, you wanted to know if there were signs of blunt trauma on that young man before the impact of the fall."

"That's right. The weapon, I believe, could have been a twelve-or thirteen-inch-long hardwood dowel, approximately an inch and a half in diameter. There may have been two of them going at him from different directions."

"You understand, the face of this young man was so damaged by the impact that it's very difficult to draw conclusions
about any prior blunt trauma there. But there are signs on the
back of his skull, just above the neck. As well, on his upper
right shoulder and spine there are several bruises about one to
one and a half inches in diameter. Two contusions indicate a
shaft of some kind, though it's difficult to determine anything
exact from glancing blows. I'd be willing to say they're within
the range you're talking about. Most telling of all, though, and
the blow that likely rendered him unconscious prior to the fall,
is the circular contusion we found near his intact temple once
we shaved his hair off. That one—very nasty—is exactly one
and a half inches in diameter."

"These marks couldn't have been caused by the fall?"

"Not possible, even if he had bounced. He hit a flat surface, and then moments later he rode that flat surface down to
land on another flat surface. No, these were inflicted prior to
the first impact."

"Anything else?" His phone beeped with another call.
"Excuse me, Doctor, while I put another call on hold." It was
Swetsky checking in, and MacNeice asked him to wait. He went
back to Richardson. "So, anything else?"

"I think I've answered your most pressing question,
MacNeice. I can also tell you that the fellow had ingested large
amounts of cannabis and some alcohol, but I don't think that's
what you're after."

"No."

"Incidentally, your cellphone number was scribbled on
some hotel notepaper in his pocket. I thought you'd like to
know that."

"Anything else?"

"Eleven dollars and thirty-nine cents. No wallet and no ID. Quite sad, really. . . ."

"Thanks, Doc," he said, and picked up the other call, holding up a finger to Aziz to let her know he'd be tied up a little longer. "Swetsky, what have you got?"

"The portfolio in Lydia's apartment—it's still there. Do you want me to leave it or pull it for safekeeping?"

"Leave it. Thanks, Swets." Aziz was waiting in front of the open door, Madeleine behind her in the foyer.

"One more thing. Going through Gibbs's house, Forensics discovered a crack pipe and a small stash. Turns out that his wife was one of Ruvola's customers. When she was dying of cancer, she got seriously into smoking dope to ease the pain. Gibbs went for the heavier stuff after she passed."

"This may be some comfort, however cold, to Vertesi. And it explains the financial incentive for Gibbs in this."

"Yeah, that's one unlucky wop. Later, Mac."

TEA HAD BEEN SET FOR TWO in the window, empty cups and napkins waiting on the tray. Madeleine told them to make themselves comfortable, then picked up the tray and left the room, closing the door behind her.

They saw Antonin Petrescu out in the garden, pruning dead blooms off the lilac tree. When Madeleine walked across the lawn to speak to him, he looked over his shoulder in the direction of the library, put down his gloves and garden shears and turned towards the house. "Here he comes, Mac. What's our strategy?"

"I don't really have one other than to be blunt. We're running out of time. We've been very gentle with Mr. Petrescu, and while I still feel great sympathy for him, there are answers we need right now."

"I'll follow your lead." Aziz stood by the chair nearest the window, took out the small recording device and placed it on the table.

"Detective," Petrescu said as he entered the room, "what can I do for you?"

"Several things have occurred since we last met, Mr. Petrescu, and we believe you may be able to explain a good number of them. Do you mind if we sit down?"

"Sir, if you don't object, we will be recording this interview," Aziz said, and pushed a button. A small green light came to life on the silver panel.

"Object? Not at all. Shall I ring Madeleine for coffee or tea?" He sat down opposite MacNeice, settling wearily into the chair.

"That won't be necessary—we are very short on time."

"I'm afraid I don't follow you, Detective."

"We detained your son, Gregori, and his two bodyguards."

"On what charges?"

"On suspicion only, no charges. He and his colleagues were released when the Romanian consul general arrived."

"But what do you suspect him of doing?"

"We believe your son was involved in Lydia's death, as well as in the deaths of her boyfriend and a local drug dealer."

For the first time Petrescu looked old and frail. He turned his eyes vaguely towards the garden and mindlessly began folding over the crease in his trouser leg.

"Your daughter's boyfriend, the father of her unborn child, died yesterday after being thrown out of a hotel window," Aziz said softly, leaning slightly towards the older man.

"My daughter's boyfriend? Who would— Why on earth would Gregori do such a thing?"

"We don't know, but we believe you may." Aziz achieved just the right tone—accusation wrapped with such compassion that Petrescu wasn't offended.

"Me. Why? I don't—"

"When we apprehended your son, he was in possession of several documents and photographs. Do you know what I'm referring to?" MacNeice asked.

Again Petrescu's eyes drifted off to the garden. "You know, I was just trimming the lilac . . . such a pretty tree for two weeks. After they bloom, they're just a dreary green till autumn. Beauty is so fleeting."

"The photographs and documents appear to be yours. You haven't told us that you were a microbiologist in Romania, or that your daughter's father was Ceausescu."

The older man stared at them, then clearly gave up at the effort to hide his secrets. "I was her real father. I loved her as if she were my own. I gave her everything I had and encouraged her in every way I could. My joy—my only joy—has been in protecting her and watching her flower into this extraordinary creature. She was magnificent, do you understand?"

"There are many things I'm uncertain about, but I do know how magnificent your daughter was. But you left your son when you fled Romania, even though he could have joined you then or after the fall of the regime. You could have brought him out—but you didn't."

Petrescu stood up, stepped behind Aziz and stood in the bay window with his arms crossed as if he were keeping his torso from coming apart.

"The photographs. . . ."

"The photographs!" Petrescu snapped, turning around to face MacNeice. "I know those photographs. I took them!" He was shaking with rage. "You think you know something now, and perhaps you do, but I suspect not." The blood was back in his face and his stance was combative.

"Did you release poison into the Danube?" Aziz asked.

"Did I? Oh, my dear, what a tragic diversion this is. . . ." He sat down again and looked from MacNeice to Aziz and back again. "I developed chemicals, yes. I pointed out that they would be devastating to use—not just for our neighbours along the Danube and the Black Sea, but also for Romanians."

"But you did release them into the waterway—the industrial effluent and your fertilizer formula?" MacNeice's tone was pressing.

"Yes, both. The first flight followed by the test barrels, all twelve of them. Then I waited—fourteen days. I drove down the river and saw the dead fish and waterfowl, the lesions and exploding flesh on children and fisherman, on a dead dog's legs and jaw. . . . I photographed it all."

"Why did you do that?"

"Because I wanted to show him—Ceausescu—that if he wouldn't stop it, I would show the world what I had been forced to do on his orders."

"Your wife was having an affair with him. Was that why you turned against him?"

"You are an ugly man to ask such a question."

"I am short of time, sir, and I am desperately trying to find the killer of your daughter. I apologize for being abrupt."

"I alone knew how to make what went into those barrels. Yes, my wife was pregnant with Lydia, and yes, I hated the man who had impregnated her, but I loved my wife very much.

I don't know that you can understand such love, Detective. Half of the daughter who would be born to my wife was hers, hers alone, and I could live with the other half because of the love I had for her."

"Why didn't you bring Gregori with you?"

"Gregori . . . even at that young age he was already a stranger. He had been indoctrinated as a communist, one of a virulent breed that mixed ancient beliefs about Romania and destiny into their politics. Even so, I wanted to take him. I believed I could deprogram—I think that's the word—remove the stain of communism from him. But he was told who Lydia's father was—not by me, but by someone over there—and after that he thought I was a coward, a weakling who had been cuckolded by Ceausescu. Instead of seeking revenge, I simply ran away."

"And did that hate find its way to Lydia?"

"I don't think he hated her. I don't recall ever hearing him speak of her. As far as I know, he never accepted that he had a sister."

"Were you prosecuted for what you did to the water systems?"

"No. I was charged but I was never prosecuted."

"Why is that? You admit that the twelve barrels mutilated hundreds, killed dozens and had a devastating effect on the Danube and Black Sea that lasted for years. . . ."

"Because I was forced to do it and I had the documents to prove it."

"Was that all?"

"What do you mean?"

"You left Romania with that formula. Did you use it as insurance in the event that you were going to be prosecuted?

Unless you went free, you would release it to any psychopathic despot in the world to recreate?"

"He threatened to kill all of us, did you know that?"

"I do. But hundreds of lives were ruined and you were left to walk free."

"Walk free! I see those pictures in my sleep, I see them when I'm in the garden, when I'm— when I was watching Lydia play. I see them now, with you. I am not free!"

"Did they drop the case because you still held the secret to what was in those barrels?"

"Yes."

"And they kept the details from getting out to the media and the families of Romanian and Bulgarian victims by making it appear that it was Ceausescu's doing."

"Yes."

"Do you have those documents here?"

"No."

"Where are they?"

"They're gone."

"Gone with Gregori?"

"Yes."

"Is that why he came back?"

"Yes."

"Why did he want them?"

"What do you mean?"

"Romania is a member of the European Union, on the verge of collective prosperity—"

"Romania has a deeply rooted siege mentality. It knows only conflict and impending conflict."

"Meaning Gregori wanted your documents as a potential weapon?"

"A weapon of defence. Gregori told me that it was the Bulgarians who killed Lydia, that it was an act of retribution against me, and against Ceausescu."

"How did you support your wife after you left Romania?"

"You have asked a very good question. How did I pay for the German lawyer, how did I make a living, who would hire a disgraced microbiologist? You know, even though the case was thrown out of court, the scientific community is very small . . . with a long memory."

"Who paid the bills?"

"Ceausescu. Not for me, no. He believed the time was coming when he'd leave Romania, and he looked forward to it—yes, he did. He was convinced that his baby—my Lydia— was part of a new future for him. I would disappear. You know, many still remained loyal to him. He put two million American dollars in a Swiss bank account in my wife's name to ensure that Lydia would have the best of everything, paid for by her father."

"Did she know who her father was?"

"*I* was her father!" He slapped his chest hard with the flat of his hand. His eyes welled up, then he turned away. "I was her father. . . . No, she never knew."

"She had a ticket for a flight to Turkey. Why do you think she'd go there?"

"She wanted a vacation after graduating, and like many young people, she wanted to get back to her roots. I told her she wouldn't be safe in Romania because of my role in the communist government, so she settled on Turkey and being able to put her feet in the Black Sea, to breathe the air of her ancestors. She was a romantic, like her mother. Her best friend from childhood, Margaux Deviers, is in Istanbul on a fellowship. Lydia was planning to stay with her."

"Have you been threatened before?"

"Have I. . . . Ah, I see—your question is have I been hunted by the Bulgarian state?"

"Yes, or for that matter, by the Romanian state?"

"Four years ago a brick was thrown through the front window of my shop. The police said it was vandals, but I thought it was a warning, a reminder that I wasn't forgotten. The brick had three dots on it—red, green and white, the colours of the Bulgarian flag."

"Yes. Or someone wanted you to believe it was Bulgarian." MacNeice took out his camera and handed it to Aziz, saying, "Find the images you took in the hotel room."

"Give me a minute," Aziz said.

"Why didn't you destroy those documents when you left Romania?" MacNeice asked.

"I don't understand your question."

"If you were opposed to deploying the chemicals and took the time to record their impact on the people and the environment, why didn't you burn them when you escaped?"

"They were my insurance against Ceausescu."

"But soon after you got out he was executed. Why didn't you destroy them then, or after the case was dropped?"

"I had created something evil, but I had created it. It's difficult to destroy a creation. I also thought that one day someone would come after me and I could use them to trade for Lydia's life."

"And your own?"

"I was for the most part dead already. I was only alive when I was with her. . . . Now I am truly dead."

"Your son persuaded you that a Bulgarian killed Lydia. How did he do that?"

"The syringe. He showed me documents about the individual who had created it. He's a KGB weapons engineer from Nessebar, a town on the Black Sea—a specialist who designs lethal instruments for torture and espionage. He was avenging the spill, but Gregori said it was just the beginning. This Bulgarian, he said, was acting on behalf of the state."

"But, as a former KGB man, isn't it possible he's a free lancer?"

"Entirely."

"Here you go, sir—this one and the next nine images." Aziz handed the camera to MacNeice, who carried it over to the older man and held it so he could see the display.

Toggling slowly through the images, MacNeice asked, "Are these the documents you're referring to?"

"Yes, but how—?"

"These are photographs taken of the contents of Gregori's luggage." He turned the camera off and tucked it back into his pocket.

"I see."

"I still don't understand why you gave him the documents you'd protected for so long."

"He convinced me that Romania remains vulnerable to threats from the former Soviet satellites to the north, west and south, as well as from the south and east, where Muslim nations are intent on solidifying and expanding Islamic fundamentalism throughout the region. And, of course, Russia never forgave Romania for going its own way with communism. Gregori convinced me that they will be his insurance policy, just as they have been mine."

"How would they provide him with insurance?"

"As a microbiologist, he's been researching various crop

enhancement programs—increasing yield and so on. He discovered certain properties of plants that, when enhanced by exotic
chemical formulae, could become lethal—"

"For chemical warfare, you mean."

"Of course. But before you get too self-righteous, Detective,
this is a nation threatened on all sides. Gregori had created a
deterrent for any land incursion but still needed one for the sea.
He pointed out that, God willing, neither would ever be used."

"What had you originally intended to do with the
documents?"

"They are in my will, bequeathed to the United Nations for
safekeeping. I now have two reasons to change my will. There
is also a missing link, a critical component of the formula that
I've kept separate for safety."

"Did Gregori take that document too?" MacNeice asked.

"No. What he has is incomplete, but he doesn't know that."

"You don't trust him." MacNeice didn't expect a response,
and he didn't get one.

"Mr. Petrescu," Aziz said, "did Gregori show you the portfolio of images of your daughter?"

"No. Why would he have images of my daughter?"

"They were photographs taken by her boyfriend. Intimate
photographs. He never mentioned them?"

"What do you mean, 'intimate'? My daughter was a good
girl."

"Nude photographs, with her violin. They are beauti—"

Petrescu interrupted her. "I want no more of this, please.
I want you to leave my house." He lifted his head, staring
directly at MacNeice.

"One last question, sir, and then we'll go. Do you know
when your son is leaving?"

Standing up to indicate that the interview was truly over, Petrescu said, "He called to say that his original schedule had unexpectedly changed and that he was catching the 1:30 p.m. flight to New York."

"Why was he calling?" MacNeice asked.

"He wanted to know if the formula was complete. . . ."

MacNeice picked up the recorder and turned it off. No further words were spoken until they were on the other side of the front door, where MacNeice turned to say goodbye. Before he could get a word out, the door slammed with such force that the bronze knocker jumped and clacked twice. He caught Aziz's eye and shrugged, and she briefly put a hand on his shoulder.

BACK IN THE CHEVY, MacNeice hit the speed-dial for his boss. "Sir, here's the situation. We have a growing body of circumstantial evidence that Gregori Petrescu and his two bodyguards are responsible for the girl's death and that of her boyfriend, as well as the dealer in the boat."

"How circumstantial?"

"The strongest evidence we have is that the pathologist has identified the marks on Marcus Johnson's head and shoulders as being consistent with the sticks the two bodyguards were carrying. Forensics haven't processed the sticks yet, but Richardson's evidence is pretty sound."

"That's it?"

"We have a portfolio of images of Lydia Petrescu taken by her boyfriend. It was in the Range Rover with Gregori Petrescu, and I believe his fingerprints and those of his bodyguards will be on it. The only way he could have gotten that portfolio was from Johnson himself. We believe it was just before or after throwing the boy off the balcony."

"How much time do we have?"

"Three hours before their flight."

"You have my backing. Get it done."

MacNeice got Swetsky on the two-way radio. "Get the New York flight schedules from the international, regional and Buffalo airports. Find out which flight Petrescu and his body-guards are booked on."

"Where are you headed?"

"Aziz and I are going back to the Chelsea Manor. If the Range Rover is there we'll sit tight near the entrance to the hotel. I'll call you when we get there. Grab Williams and come over as soon as you can."

"We'll be there." Swetsky broke off contact and the car fell silent for a moment.

"What if he's not there?" Aziz asked.

"We'll determine which airport they're flying out of and put up a roadblock. If it's Buffalo, we'll get Wallace on it."

They drove through the tree-lined streets where it seemed that nothing bad ever happened. The dappled light played on the hood and windshield, causing Aziz to screen her eyes with her hand.

"I saw Vertesi this morning. He's doing better." Looking over at MacNeice, she added, "He had a dream that you were there last night."

"That would be the Demerol talking."

"Right." She smiled, and a moment later asked, "What do you think will happen to the old man now?"

"Honestly? I think he'll be dead by tomorrow."

"Should we be doing something about that?"

"You mean like a suicide watch? No. He's already lost every-thing that meant anything to him, and today we told him that his own son had Lydia murdered. But I could be wrong. He's certainly a strong man, and he's suffered losses before now. . . ."

"When he suggested that you hadn't known love like that he felt for his wife . . . I half expected you to correct him."

"That's good, Aziz." He glanced over at her.

"I didn't mean—" She turned to lean towards him.

"I'm serious. It's a legitimate . . . observation. And true. I certainly thought about it, but there wouldn't have been any point. That was just grief venting," MacNeice said. "You weigh everything after the death of a loved one, including life. Petrescu has experienced a tremendous amount of pain in his life. I believed him when he said that joy had narrowed to the point where he could find it only in Lydia. Add to that the potential or likelihood that his son was responsible . . . The rest of the journey is bleak. I think he's a proud man who's seen enough. But I may be wrong. I sincerely hope I'm wrong."

"Were we too hard on him?"

"Not at all. There were questions that needed to be asked and we asked them. Did you notice his eyes, though?"

"I'm not sure I follow—"

"He looked directly at me when we talked about Lydia, but when we got on to his son, he'd look away, sometimes to the table, or off to the garden."

"What do you take from that?"

"He's lying."

"If it's all over, what's left to lie about?"

"I'm not certain, but I think Gregori will know. Right, here we are." He turned into the lane to the Chelsea Manor. "We'll do a quick circuit of the parking lot."

The radio barked to life as they passed beneath the columns. "MacNeice."

"The little shit is booked out of two airports. He's got tickets on flights leaving from Dundurn Regional and Toronto International," Swetsky said.

"Smart. What times?"

"International at 1:30 p.m., Dundurn at 1:10 p.m."

"Where are you?"

"Ten minutes away. Do we take him down if he's there now?"

"No, we wait till they leave the hotel."

"Don't start this party without us."

MacNeice hung up. Aziz nodded to the doorman, who had stepped out ready to open the door of the Chevy, but MacNeice drove slowly past, leaving him standing on the pavement. After a complete circuit of the lot without seeing the Range Rover, MacNeice came back to the doorman. Rolling down the window, he asked, "The black Range Rover and the three men who travel in it, have you seen them?"

"Yes, sir. They left here about a half-hour ago. Gave me a ten-dollar tip."

"You mean they've checked out."

"That's right, sir. Two of them had duffle bags and the leader—I mean the guy with the nice suit—he had suitcases and a briefcase. They wouldn't let me load them in; they did it themselves."

"So why the ten-spot?"

"I dunno. I mean, I was nice to them like I am with everyone. They wouldn't even let me open the car door for the guy in the suit. The first time I tried, this big guy gets out of the front and puts a hand up, like it was a crime to open the door for the guy in back. So I never tried again."

"Did you happen to see which way they were headed?"

"I did, because the driver laid some rubber as he turned onto the street—that caught my attention. They went left, towards downtown."

MacNeice thanked him and pulled away from the hotel.

"What's downtown that would interest these guys?" Aziz asked as MacNeice turned left too.

"I bet Gregori's figured out there's a missing link. He's either gone back to his father's house or he's at the antique shop looking for it." MacNeice reached for the radio. "Swetsky, come in."

"We're a half-block from the intersection. What's up?"

"They've checked out. I have a hunch that they've gone either to the old man's house or to his shop. You two go to the house, but don't engage. Just let us know if you see the Range Rover there."

"We're on it."

"Check around the back of the house too. They may have parked in the laneway."

As MacNeice came to a stop at the intersection, he saw Swetsky's unmarked car making a U-turn south. Williams waved to them from the passenger side as if he were Queen Elizabeth. MacNeice turned right towards the shopping district, speeding past the parked cars and smartly maintained lawns of the quiet west-end neighbourhood.

Twelve minutes later Swetsky was on the radio. "MacNeice, we're just approaching the house now. Nothing on the street out front. . . . Wait a minute. . . . Nope, nothin' in the back lane. Do you want us to hang in here or come to you?"

"We'll be at the shop in five minutes. Hang in, but stay on that side street so you're not spotted if they do show up."

"Turning now. I'll leave the radio on."

"Thanks, Swets."

"I don't know what we're worried about, though. I mean, these guys fight with sticks and I'm sitting here with a forty-four on my hip." MacNeice heard Williams laugh.

"Don't underestimate them," he said firmly. "Now, sit tight."

TWENTY SIX

—

THE WEST VILLAGE HAD BEEN CREATED to meet the needs of an expanding city and of Brant University, whose campus hugged its edge on one side and the ravines of the escarpment on the other. Over the decades, the main-street restaurants, galleries, gourmet emporiums and antique shops had multiplied to reflect the affluence of the surrounding neighbourhood.

"There it is, ahead on the left. Nothing in front, though." Aziz was craning forward, her hands on the dash.

"We'll check the street to the east." MacNeice slowed as he passed in front of the shop. There was no sign of anyone inside. He paused at the stop sign and scanned the vehicles parked along the cross-street. "There it is."

"Where?"

"Six cars down, tucked behind the green van."

He went through the intersection and did a U-turn

halfway up the block. "Swetsky, get over here now. We're a half-block to the east of the shop. Just pull in behind us and get into our car."

"Be there in a jiffy."

From where they were parked they could see the front of the shop and its side door. A woman pushing a stroller was coming towards the shop and an older couple was walking on the other side of the street, but other than that it was quiet. Several minutes later, Swetsky eased in behind them.

Both rear doors opened, and as Swetsky and Williams climbed into the back seat, MacNeice was vaguely aware of cologne—Williams, he assumed. When the doors closed, he said, "That's the shop up on the right. Front and side doors. The Range Rover's a hundred feet or so down the side street."

"Got it. So what's the plan, Stan?" Swetsky leaned forward, his bulk filling the rear-view mirror.

"We're making it up as we go. To a certain extent it's driven by the Romanians, but it will come together fairly quickly, I suspect."

"Do we call in the troops?" Williams asked.

"No. We're trying to be effective but discreet. We've got Wallace's support, but beyond him are External Affairs and the Romanian consulate. If we do this right, we can shortcut their involvement till we have so much evidence they can't spring them."

"So we're Jesuits, and we'll seek forgiveness afterwards," Williams said.

"Exactly. See the Vanilla Bean ice cream shop across the street?"

"Yeah," Williams responded.

"Go get yourself a cone and wander down the street like a

gentleman out for the day. Cross over beyond the antique shop and casually do some window shopping while you enjoy your ice cream. If we're lucky, Petrescu won't recognize you from the interview room, and his bodyguards have never seen you."

"Do I get to choose the flavour?"

"Anything your heart desires, Williams. Take your time, but keep wandering. When you've checked out the window, cross the street and call me."

"Chocolate."

"Figures," Swetsky said as Williams got out of the car.

"I heard that, cracker." Williams pointed at Swetsky and smiled.

When he came out of the ice cream parlour, he held up the cone, and it was indeed chocolate. He turned away and began to walk casually down the street.

Swetzky laughed. "Don't worry," he said. "He's got a sense of humour, but he's a good cop."

"I'm counting on it," MacNeice said.

In a few minutes Williams had crossed the street and was sitting on a bench just outside Petrescu's shop. With one arm stretched out along the back of the bench, he really did look like a guy with time to kill. A drop of ice cream fell onto his shirt; he took a tissue from his pocket and tried to wipe it off while licking around the cone to stay ahead of the melting chocolate. To get a better view of the damage to his shirt, he walked over to use the shop window as a mirror. He kept wiping at the stain and licking the ice cream before giving up and turning away. He dropped the ice cream in the waste bin on the corner and slowly crossed the street. On the other side, still checking out his shirt in the shop windows, he took out his cellphone.

Pushing the hands-free button, MacNeice said, "That was brilliant, Williams."

"I worked in improv before I went to the academy, sir, though the stain wasn't planned. . . ."

"That's why they call it improv. What have you got for us?"

"There's movement in the back. You can't see anyone clearly, but the lights are on back there and I could see maybe two or three shadows. I guess it's the office. You'll love this, though—the front door is slightly open. Caught on the frame so they thought it was closed, but it's definitely open. In my old neighbourhood that place would be cleaned out in three minutes flat. In the middle of the back wall, which is all bookshelves, there's a panelled wood door to the back room. On the right side there's a narrow horizontal window between the shelves, a kind of peek-a-boo slider, to see into the store from the office behind. It's made of translucent glass, and that's where you can see the shadows."

"Anything else?"

"No, that's it."

"Williams, take a seat on that bench to your left. I'll get back to you."

"Why would they leave the front door open?" Aziz asked.

"Don't know," MacNeice said.

"Maybe it has something to do with the security system. They must've disarmed it," Swetsky said, but without conviction.

"Or it's as Williams said—they shoved it, but it's an old door and it stuck without closing. Whichever it is, you can bet there's a buzzer or bell that sounds in the back room when it opens wide."

"What's this?" Aziz said.

An old woman with a tiny dog on a leash had stopped at the bench outside the shop. She sat down and began feeding the dog something that looked like popcorn.

"Swets, there's a pair of small binoculars in the seat pocket beside you. Can you hand them to me?"

"Sure thing." He picked them up; they looked tiny in his hand. Swets winked at Aziz. "These are the opera glasses the boss uses for all the uptown cases."

"They actually are, smartass." MacNeice unfolded them and looked towards the shop. The dog was on the woman's lap and a bag of PuffyPop was in her hand. She was feeding the kernels one by one into its tiny snout. The dog munched each one quickly, then looked up at her face and then to her hand in the bag.

MacNeice called Williams, who was tracking a young woman walking along with her toddler. "Williams, look over at the shop. See her?"

"The old lady? Pink twinset? Yup."

"I want you to go over there and, as gently as possible, get her to move along. There's another bench down a block. Tell her that's the one everyone favours because of the sun or something."

"What if she don't wanna leave?"

"Be persuasive and gentle."

"I'm on it."

MacNeice, Aziz and Swetsky watched as Williams crossed the street, a little more purposefully than before, though he slowed as he got close to the woman. Through the binoculars MacNeice could see that she was aware of Williams, and she seemed to hug the dog closer to her chest as he approached. What followed was a Charlie Chaplin movie. Williams reached for her arm and the woman pulled back, horrified. Undeterred, Williams put his large black hand on her thin pink arm. MacNeice could see the woman's mouth open wide as the dog seized Williams's wrist with its nasty little jaws. MacNeice rolled the window down in time to hear her scream.

The dog was still locked on Williams's right wrist. When he turned towards them with a look of *What now?* it hung in mid-air, its tiny legs clawing at nothing. The woman was scream-ing, "Help! Please help me!"

Williams looked stricken when the door to the shop opened and the heavyset blond with the black eyes came out. He was smoking a cigarette and had one hand in his pocket. He was also laughing. Williams instinctively turned away from the Chevy. The lady was now on her feet. She threw the bag of PuffyPop at Williams and looked over to the Romanian, yelling, "Help me!" The blond was laughing so hard now he was coughing. He flicked his cigarette into the street and walked over to Williams.

"This is it," MacNeice said. "Aziz, head for the side door but watch out for the Rover. We don't know if the driver's still in it or inside the shop. Swetsky, come with me. We'll go through the front door. Quickly now." The three got out of the Chevy and didn't bother closing the doors.

Williams was trying to pry the dog off his wrist, which was bleeding—another stain to deal with—when the blond tapped him on the shoulder.

"Leave lady alone, Sambo." The blond's back was to MacNeice and Swetsky as they approached.

"Sambo? Who the fuck do you think you're talkin' to, white boy?"

"Leave lady." The blond reached out to grab William's shirt front.

"I'll tell you what, motherfucker—get your hand off me, and after I deal with this rat-dog, you and I will have some special fucking time together."

The F-bomb in all its glory was too much for the old lady, who hit the deck beside the bench. Her pink wrist was still tethered to the dog by its leash, and the dog was still locked on Williams's wrist, its little legs clawing at the air.

"You kill lady, Sambo."

"That's it." Williams whipped his right arm forward as if throwing a pass downfield. The dog became airborne—till it reached the end of the red leather leash and lurched to a halt in mid-air. The old lady's arm flopped for a moment, then it and the dog fell to the ground, after which neither moved.

As Williams crouched to check on the woman, he was hit on the side of the head by a wooden baton and knocked to the sidewalk, then kicked in the ribs. Before the blond could launch a second kick, Swetsky wrapped his arms around him.

MacNeice stepped quietly into the shop.

"About time," Williams said as he got up on all fours.

"Mister, I've got you," Swetsky managed to say to the struggling blond. "Now just settle down, ya hear me?"

"Fuck you." The blond leaned forward, lifting Swetsky's feet and impressive bulk off the ground, then pushed back with such force that he hit the brick wall of the building with a crack that knocked the wind out of him. But Swetsky hung on, and tightened the bear hug.

Williams was all the way up now. The blond swung Swetsky towards him, causing Williams to back up.

"That's one crazy fucker you got there, Swets. Do you wanna keep dancing with him, or how do you wanna handle this?"

"Tackle the fucker!" Swetsky shouted.

Squaring himself, Williams launched forward in a perfect football lunge, slamming into the two men at knee height. All three flew into the window, which exploded inwards. The impact knocked Williams off the two bigger men, who were now draped over the window frame. He landed on his back in the shop and sat up, just as a large section of glass broke free from its caulking ten feet above and sliced into the blond's stomach, leaving a giant triangle sticking out of him. Swetsky was still holding tight.

MacNeice was at the door to the office when the window blew in. He turned towards the noise, then hit the floor when the distinctive *ping* of a silencer sent a bullet whizzing past his head. Glass and ceramic statuary and vases blew apart, as did the window on the other side of the front door. MacNeice rolled clear and sat up against the bookshelves. More shots struck the heavy table in front of the three downed men; its antique veneer splintered and flew about.

MacNeice drew his weapon and got to his feet. As he turned towards the office, he saw a long tubular silver barrel extending from the doorway—a custom-made weapon, as menacing and powerful as it was strange.

"Uri? Uri!" Moving further into the shop, the driver didn't notice MacNeice standing against the back wall.

"Put the weapon down. Drop it now," he said.

The driver didn't move, nor did he lower the weapon. He looked over his shoulder and saw MacNeice with the pistol pointed at his head, but kept moving forward towards the storefront.

"Last time—put the weapon down." MacNeice stepped forward with both hands on the pistol to steady himself.

The driver looked down to see the blond trying to pry the glass wedge out of his stomach, his eyes raised pleadingly towards his comrade. He was trying to say something but seemed to have no wind left in him. Swetsky was still beneath him, and the driver recognized him from the parking lot.

The driver looked back at MacNeice, then over at Williams, who was leaning against the door frame struggling to get his gun out. The driver slowly shifted his weapon towards Williams's head.

"Put the weapon down now," MacNeice said.

The driver looked at Uri, then back at MacNeice before turning again to Williams. Just as his finger tightened on the trigger, a gunshot from outside the shop snapped his head back. Hair and brain tissue hit the bookcase, and he fell back, dropping the weapon.

Williams looked at MacNeice. MacNeice said, "Wasn't me."

Aziz came into view, her arms outstretched and her Glock still at the ready.

"Where's Petrescu?" MacNeice asked.

"I don't know. Nobody came out the side door."

MacNeice turned towards the office. "Williams, come with me. Aziz, make sure Swetsky's okay."

"I'm fine," Swetsky managed to say. He had finally crawled out from under the blond and was sitting against the wall picking glass out of his bleeding hands.

"I'm coming with you, Mac," Aziz said.

MacNeice went through the door, followed by Aziz and Williams. Petrescu wasn't there. They opened the closet and bathroom doors—nothing. The filing cabinets were all open, as was a wall safe. There were papers and books on the floor.

"The Range Rover. Come on, we've been distracted by these two." MacNeice opened the side door, but the black SUV was gone. They went back inside the shop.

"Swetsky, you okay?"

"I'm fine. This guy ain't doin' so good, though." The blond's breathing was shallow and his eyes glassy. Several sirens could be heard in the distance.

Looking at the blood streaming from Swetsky's hands, MacNeice said, "Give Williams your keys. You stay and handle this. You okay with that?"

"No problem." Swetsky found himself a chair, brushed it off and sat down. "Messed this place up pretty bad." He threw the keys to Williams.

"It could have been a lot worse," Williams said. He put his right fist on his chest over his heart, then pointed at Swetsky.

"Yeah, yeah. Go on, get outta here."

People were gathering on the other side of street. Maybe it was because the dog was licking the rouge off her cheek, but the old lady woke up just as MacNeice and Aziz came out of the shop, followed by Williams. She was about to scream again when MacNeice said, "He's a police officer, ma'am, and a very good one. Do you need any assistance? Can we help you up?"

She shook her head, and as Williams walked by, she stared at him. He smiled and said, "You have a nice day, ma'am."

When they got to the Chevy, MacNeice said to Williams, "You take the international airport, we'll take Dundurn."

"You knew, didn't you?" Aziz asked as they drove away.

"Knew what?"

"That the old lady would freak out when she saw Williams."

"I figured it was fifty-fifty, and that either way, it would work to our advantage." MacNeice switched on the radio.

"Give me your position, Williams."

"Just turning onto the Queen E. No sign of him so far."

"When you get to Pearson, go to Departures. There's no place for him to return the Rover there, so he'll likely dump it outside. We're fifteen minutes away from Dundurn Regional. If you see the vehicle on the way, stay back, call immediately and we'll come to you. Understood?"

"Yes, sir."

"Put your shoulder harness on," MacNeice said as he hung up. "We're going to do some driving." MacNeice took the cherry from under the dash, put it on the roof and switched his headlights to flashing. He gathered speed and began weaving through the traffic.

He glanced over at her. She was looking out the window to the right.

She felt his gaze and said, "I thought you were hit, Mac. I couldn't see you from the corner, but I saw Williams and that guy pointing the gun at his head. I didn't think about it; I just took aim and fired."

"That was impressive shooting, Aziz. How about now? Are you feeling steady?"

"I think I am . . . but I may be in shock. I've never shot anyone before."

"We've been playing catch-up all through this case, always arriving after the fact. Now Petrescu's on the run and we don't know how he'll respond to that."

"What are you getting at?" She looked over at him.

"He's not a man to get his hands bloody. But he sacrificed both those men, and now he has to deal with us on his own. I need to know that you're steady, Fiza. There's no shame if you're not—I just need to know."

"I'm a little shaky, but my adrenalin's pumping. . . . I'll deal with the repercussions later."

"Right. He's got perhaps eight to ten minutes on us. We can reel him in before he reaches the airport."

"And if we don't?"

"He'll be among hundreds of people, and that could get ugly. Alert airport security."

"What do I tell them?"

"Tell them we've received a bomb threat for both airports and they should take the necessary precautions. Let Williams know you've done that, then call the DC and tell him. Use my cellphone." He took it out and handed it across to her.

BOTH LANES OF THE ACCESS ROAD to the regional airport were fairly busy. MacNeice hit the outside shoulder, raising a cloud of dust. He sped past the vehicles, watching the adjacent lanes for the Range Rover. A quarter-mile from the terminal, he spotted it on the inside lane, several cars ahead. He stopped, but not quickly enough—the Range Rover suddenly pulled out of line and across the shoulder onto the grass, where it halted for a moment.

"Call Williams. Tell him to turn around—we've found him."

Aziz called and then quickly stepped out of the Chevy. She slammed the palm of her hand on the window of a Lincoln town car that had stopped in the confusion and motioned to the driver to pull out of line and onto the shoulder. "Do it now!" Then she ran to the inside lane and waved at a frightened woman approaching in a Toyota to pull out of line onto the opposite shoulder. The woman hesitated until Aziz ran up and bashed on the hood. "Now move!"

With a gap opened up across the two lanes, she held up both hands to the vehicles beyond and motioned for MacNeice to drive through. After he got across the road, he stopped, and Aziz got in the car and did up her seatbelt.

The Range Rover was skidding along the grassy slope, trying to make it up to the highway again. MacNeice pursued it from above, using the gravel shoulder for traction as both vehicles raced towards a culvert less than a hundred yards ahead. Suddenly the SUV swung to the right, heading for the chain-link fence that separated the highway from the airport. On the tarmac a commuter plane was slowly taxiing away from the terminal.

"He's going to try to crash the fence," MacNeice said.

The black SUV tore down to the bottom of the slope and up the other side, hitting the fence with force. The shock of the impact rippled down the line of fencing and bent the two supporting poles, but they didn't give way. The Range Rover's front end was suspended on the mesh, its back end tearing at the sod and kicking up dirt as the engine screamed and the wheels spun.

MacNeice brought the Chevy to a stop to the left of the Range Rover. He couldn't see through the tinted windows, but stepping out of the Chevy, he pointed his handgun at the driver's side, moving slowly forward. Aziz got out and ran to cover the other side.

"It's over!" MacNeice shouted, not certain he could be heard above the racing engine and screaming tires, which were digging deeper into the dirt. "Shut it down!"

Suddenly the brake lights came on and the wheels stopped spinning as the engine returned to idle.

"Get out of the truck, Gregori," MacNeice ordered. The door didn't open.

As if he'd thought of a new strategy, the engine came to life again. The gearbox clanked as the Range Rover rocked violently forward and then backwards.

"Aziz! Stay clear." Once she'd moved out of the way, MacNeice shot out the driver's-side rear and front tires and motioned to her to do the same. The engine continued to howl, the wheels spinning on their rims, the vehicle rocking harmlessly back and forth. And then it stopped, the motor dying.

For a moment the sound of a birdcall filled the void. *Redwinged blackbird*, MacNeice thought, *trying to chase these intruders away from its nest.*

Holding his weapon before him, he approached the driver's door. "Open the door, Petrescu."

Moments passed, and then the window slid down to reveal Gregori leaning back against the headrest, something classical playing on the radio, so softly that MacNeice couldn't make it out.

"I have no weapon, Detective. Join me in the car, please. I wish to make a statement." The dark glass window closed again.

Motioning to Aziz, MacNeice said, "Get the recorder from the glove compartment and bring it over to the passenger's side. Call off the bomb scare and get the airport police and an ambulance out here fast."

Aziz ran to the Chevy, its headlights and cherry top still flashing.

Keeping his gun trained on the driver, MacNeice opened the passenger door and stepped into the Range Rover.

"I told you, I'm not armed. You don't need that."

"No offence, but I like to take precautions when I'm arresting a suspect on murder charges." He listened for a moment to the music. "Beethoven—Piano Concerto number one."

"Just so. MacNeice, I have approximately nine and a half minutes left. I'll answer any questions you have."

"What do you mean?"

He held up a small steel cylinder and handed it to MacNeice. "There was a capsule in here. I created it for just such an occasion. Check the pockets of my bodyguards and you'll find two more. It takes about ten minutes, depending on your stress level."

"Why did you kill your sister?" MacNeice heard a tap on his window and rolled it down. Aziz handed him the recorder, silently mouthing, *It's on.* He set it on the black leather dashboard.

"Hello, Detective Aziz," Petrescu said. "I'm sorry we don't have more time to chat about the Old Country."

"Your sister?" MacNeice asked.

Petrescu rolled his head towards him. "She was not my sister. I never knew her. She was an orphan."

"Your father feels otherwise."

"My father is dead, Detective." MacNeice looked up at him. "Yes, I see you're surprised. An hour ago he sent Madeleine for strawberries and cream, and when she came back he was dead, sitting by the garden window of the library. That's when she called me. He put a bullet through his mouth and emptied his skull. My method is much more civilized." Glancing down at the clock on the dashboard he said, "Eight minutes."

"Why kill Lydia, and why that way?"

"Elegant, no? There is only one person who could do that with such finesse. He's Bulgarian, and a former KGB specialist. He was also born on the Black Sea. His five-year-old son was one of those deformed for life by my father. Because of that he gave me a discount for Lydia. He's left the country; you'll never find him."

"The boyfriend and Ruvola?"

"Collateral damage. I believe that term was invented over here. The boyfriend was a pornographer. The other was trash, a drug dealer."

"Did you show those images of Lydia to your father?"

"No. You don't understand—I didn't do this to hurt my father. He's nothing to me . . . was nothing to me. Yes, I was his blood and she wasn't, but I did this for my country."

"Are you saying the Romanian government was involved in this?"

"Not at all." Gregori managed a short chuckle. "We are a poor country, very weak militarily and economically. I was doing research on my own. Had I the documents that are back there"—he motioned towards the back of the SUV—"I could have ensured that at least we were not defenceless."

"That was once your father's plan too, it seems."

"Do you play chess, Detective?"

"Some."

"Antonin Petrescu was not a pawn but a rook. He could move on certain limited paths. He imagined himself as much more—a bishop, perhaps."

"You presumably have more power?"

"I do. . . . I did. We are trying on capitalism like a new suit, but the ones learning fastest are the ones who learned to survive in the old suits."

"Why didn't you just ask your father for the formula? Why did you have to kill the girl?"

"My father was righteous and repentant. He felt guilt for what he had done, even though it was Ceausescu who forced him to do it. He would have gone to his grave without handing over those documents. But the one thing he feared—call it the sentiment of the region—was a Bulgarian invasion of Romania. He thought that Lydia's death—the manner of her death—was a message from Bulgaria. Compared to the clumsy poisoning of rivers and beaches, this was a precision-engineered death. He had no choice but to give them to me."

"What about Lydia?"

"We have thousands of beautiful girls, talented girls, in Romania. None of them will ever have the privileges she enjoyed. The money was dirty. The father, Ceausescu, was filth. My father pretended to be a father—he never was one, not to me and not to her. The girl meant nothing. I wanted the formula, and I wanted to settle accounts."

"And yet he withheld one piece of the puzzle."

"Yes. It was foolish of him to do so, and when I realized what he'd done, foolish of me to go looking for it. I'm sure that within a year I could have worked out the last piece. I am— I was a better microbiologist than my father. By far. He was privileged, of course, because of my mother. What did he do with that privilege? He couldn't keep his wife faithful, and if he had stayed in Romania, he would have lost all his privileges, along with his head."

"Is there anything else you want to tell me?"

"The rest is details, best left alone. You have the basics." Petrescu looked at the clock again. "I have perhaps two minutes or so. Do you mind, Detective, leaving me alone to look at the sky?" A series of mild convulsions rocked his body; he belched several times, and his face suddenly lost its colour. He looked over to MacNeice and smiled weakly, his eyes shining with sudden tears that reflected the sunlight and blue sky. "I may have miscalculated." He coughed, and a stream of blood-red spittle rolled down his chin. "Next time, I'll—"

A tear spilled out of his right eye and slid down the swiftly greying cheek.

MacNeice took his recorder and got out of the vehicle, quietly shutting the door behind him.

Speeding towards them over the grass were two airport cruisers and an ambulance. "Intercept them, Aziz," MacNeice said. "Keep them away for a couple more minutes."

Raising her hand to the oncoming cruisers, Aziz stopped them just beyond the Chevy. Two police officers exited the lead vehicle and came towards her, one carrying a shotgun and the other with his hand on a holstered sidearm. Aziz switched off the cherry on the Chevy and waited for them.

MacNeice listened for the red-winged blackbird, but it was gone. He looked at the tinted window of the Range Rover, thinking about how, once again, Gregori Petrescu had dictated the pace of the game. The vehicle shook briefly, as if the man inside was moving about violently, and then it was still. He walked around the SUV towards Aziz and the assembled cops and paramedics.

"His name is Colonel Gregori Petrescu. He's a Romanian national. Shield the vehicle from traffic"—he waved towards the airport-bound commuters without looking at the road—"then take him out with as much dignity as you can manage. Put the contents of the SUV in the trunk of my car. I'll call the pathologist and tell her to expect him. There'll be a report in your hands by tomorrow morning."

As soon as the trunk was loaded, MacNeice climbed into the Chevy. Once again Aziz opened up a path through the traffic before climbing in beside him. He drove across the two lanes, then slowly over the grass infield before turning onto the airport exit lane. They passed people in cars laughing and sharing their stories of holidays and honeymoons and graduation back-packing trips to exotic places. For some time they said nothing. There was, it seemed, nothing left to say.

"I never got to Lydia's emails."

"Leave them. They had nothing to do with her death."

They continued on in silence for several miles, passing the flat unfolding suburbs, then climbing slightly till they reached the crest of the escarpment.

"I don't know how I should feel now that it's done," Aziz said.

"Not entirely done. There's still a Bulgarian to find."

He eased to a stop outside her apartment, put the Chevy in park and let the engine idle. Aziz was looking out the window towards her building. "I've just been asked to go back to university—as a teacher," she said.

"I see." His voice was as flat as he felt. The day couldn't end without more bad news. "You're considering it, I take it."

"Yes."

"Because of Marcus Johnson?"

"Because of everything, Mac. I never thought I'd shoot a man." She looked over at him, both wanting and fearing his response.

"I won't do anything to stop you if it's what you need to do." He rested both hands on the steering wheel as if he was ready to drive off.

She wanted to say *I wish you would*, but instead she said, "I'll see you tomorrow," and opened the car door.

EPILOGUE

LEAVING THE HOUSE EARLIER than usual, California
state trooper Sergeant First-Class Calvin Mendez, a
fifteen-year veteran of the highway patrol, turned
towards the Interstate from his neighbourhood outside Salinas
and headed west towards Highway 1, where his day would
officially begin. He stopped at a roadside diner south of
Carmel, and after ham and eggs, buttered toast and a cup of
coffee, he climbed into his cruiser and turned south onto the
two-lane stretch known as America's most scenic drive, the
Pacific Coast Highway. Sections of the highway, like this one,
were so far above the sea that the only way to detect surfers
was by the white trails their boards made cutting through
the waves.

Mendez believed he was blessed, not only to earn a decent
wage but also to be so close to the ocean every working day.
He studied the wave patterns on the sea as he drove, scanning
for the dawn patrol of serious surfers, who always arrived
early. He knew some of them from his own decades of

surfing—an obsession that his father, a former migrant worker from Mexico, believed would ruin his life.

It being so early on a Sunday morning, the radio was quiet, and Mendez knew that for the most part his presence was more a visual reminder than anything else. Cars slowed down when they saw him coming, but as he and every other trooper knew, it was the kids on the supercharged Italian and Japanese motorcycles—crotch-rockets, they called them—who were often the problem. On the weekend they'd come screaming out of L.A. heading north, or south from San Francisco, to test themselves on America's most challenging highway. So far, however, this morning seemed peaceful.

Somewhere south of Big Creek Bridge at 7:39 a.m., he became aware of a Mustang convertible ahead that seemed to be weaving slightly but rhythmically, the way people on Rollerblades do when they listen to music while they skate. Several oncoming vehicles, including a large RV heading north, flashed their headlights and eased towards the shoulder to avoid the car.

Mendez called it in and began hop-scotching his way towards the vehicle. When he was directly behind it, he kept pace, assuming the driver would slow down the way most people do when they see a trooper in their rear-view mirror. This one didn't. Then one weave caused the car to hit the shoulder, spitting up gravel that clicked off the cruiser's hood and windshield. Mendez hit the switch for the light bar and gave him several *whurp-whurp*s from the siren. He called it in again, reported the Mustang's licence plate and his location, and said he was pulling the vehicle over.

The Mustang hit the shoulder again and ran along it for several yards, enveloping Mendez's cruiser in dust. When it settled, he could see that the car was a foot or so from the cliff edge, angled towards the ocean. Mendez asked over the radio if they had anything on the plates.

"Roger that," the dispatcher said. "It's a rental out of San Francisco International. Nothing yet on the driver."

"I'm getting out now. Have the unit south of me—I believe it's Lane Montgomery—stand by."

"Roger that. Be careful, trooper."

"Roger."

He took the restraining harness off his service weapon and, with his hand firmly on its grip, Mendez moved slowly to the driver's side of the Mustang. The Beach Boys' "Good Vibrations" was blaring from the stereo. The driver's head was resting on the headrest, but it rolled to the left to watch Mendez approaching in the side-view mirror.

"Throw the keys out here, sir, and then step out of the vehicle with your hands behind your head. Do it now."

The music stopped, the keys were tossed onto the gravel, and a tall man who looked to be in his late forties stepped out of the Mustang, still singing the tune.

"Turn around, sir. Put your hands on the car and spread your legs."

The man gave a slight bow and turned almost theatrically towards the car. Searching him, Mendez noticed how silky the suit was; other than two hundred dollars in fifties, there was nothing in the pockets of his pants. In the left breast pocket of his jacket was a small leather wallet with no credit cards but a driver's licence and some plastic ID in a language Mendez couldn't identify. From the other pocket Mendez retrieved a passport—Gheorghi Borisov, mechanical engineer, Sofia, Bulgaria.

"Have you been drinking, Georgie?"

"It's Gheorghi—*yor-gee*. No, I do not drink; it upsets my stomach. Without alcohol I have only good vibrations."

"You were weaving back and forth on the highway. Why was that?"

"Oh, the music, the view . . . It's beautiful, no?"

Mendez looked in the door pocket—nothing, nor was there anything under the driver and passenger seats or in the back.

"Get back in the car and stay there. I'm going to check the trunk. How long have you been in America, Gheorghi?" He was beginning to enjoy saying the name.

From the front seat Borisov said, "Three days only. It's beautiful."

There were two black metal cases in the trunk, both locked and bearing a tag with his name but no address, except for *Bulgaria*. "What are the codes to these cases, Mr. Borisov?"

"Same code—1-2, 1-2, 1-7. Keep it simple, stupid."

Mendez dialled the code and popped the smaller of the cases to find it packed with brand-new clothes, all still wearing their shop tags, all very expensive. "Nice threads, Gheorghi."

"Ya, sure. Though not American, only European. Americans make crap clothes. Hawaiian-shirt shit."

"That so."

Mendez reached below the pale grey and blue shirts, the charcoal and black jackets and pants, to find the entire bottom of the case layered with stacks of fifty-dollar bills. "You've got a lot of money back here, Gheorghi. Can you explain that to me?"

"Sure. I'm an engineer. I accept only cash payment. No credit, just cash." He returned to singing the Beach Boys.

Mendez rotated the little wheels of the lock on the second case, but before he could open it, the drivers passing by started honking their horns and yelling from their windows. He looked around the trunk lid to see Borisov standing with one foot on the hood and the other on the fender above the right front headlight. His arms were outstretched as if he was doing the "king of the world" scene from *Titanic*. Mendez quietly shut the trunk, retrieved the key and then walked slowly along the side of the car, once again with his hand on his weapon.

"Get down from the vehicle, sir. Get down now."

"I don't know where but she sends me there. . . ." Borisov sang as he looked out to the ocean, the updraft from the cliff face whipping his pants and jacket.

Several cars had slowed to watch the spectacle, and a pickup truck with three surfboards in it pulled off the road just ahead of Mendez. Three young men, tanned and blond, stepped out of the truck but stayed by its side.

Borisov waved to them and crooned, "Oh my, my, my, what a sensation. . . ."

"Get down from the car, Gheorghi. Get down now." Into his shoulder radio he said, "Ah, I need support right now. Send Montgomery. And I need medical assistance. Please confirm. Over."

"Roger that. Will call for support and paramedics immediately."

Borisov looked back at Mendez and smiled, then looked over to the surfers and did a semi-bow before he turned seaward, still singing. "Got to keep those lovin' good vibrations a-happening with her. . . ." He dipped his knees, swung his arms like Greg Louganis on the ten-metre platform, then pushed off, launching himself into a perfect swan dive before he disappeared from view.

"Sweet Jesus!" Mendez rushed over to the edge, followed by the surfers.

The perfect dive broke when Borisov hit the side of the cliff. He cartwheeled downward and slammed into the beach with a delayed, muted thud, ending up draped over one of the rock formations that jutted up from the sand.

"No fuckin' way, man. That was way too cool—him smiling, singing and all."

"Fubar. Truly fu-bar," another surfer said slowly, emphasizing the two syllables. "That stoner could fly, man—but gravity wins."

Below, surfers began to gather around the body. Mendez retrieved the megaphone from the trunk of his cruiser. Several more vehicles had now stopped on the shoulder, emptied of the curious, who lined the edge of the cliff.

Pressing the button of his shoulder radio, Mendez said, "Status, please?"

"On their way, Sergeant. Should arrive shortly."

Through the megaphone, Mendez called down, "Stay away from that body. Do not touch it. There is a medical team arriving shortly. I repeat, stay away from the body." His hat flew off in the updraft, skidding across the gravel, where it was picked up by a large woman in a yellow tank top, Lycra cycling shorts and flip-flops who'd stepped out of a camper. He thanked her when she returned it, placed it snugly on his head, raised the megaphone again and, looking down the line of people gawking over the edge of the cliff, said, "Okay, folks, there's nothing left to see here. Please get back in your vehicles and leave immediately."

Turning to the three surfers he said, "I'll need your IDs so I can call you as witnesses." Each dug something out of his baggy cargo shorts and handed it to him. Mendez wrote down the information and handed their cards back. Stuffing the notebook into his Kevlar vest, he said, "You guys can go too. But catch your waves farther down the beach. I don't want to see you below. Understood?"

"Right on, dude. Seriously bad karma here anyway," said the tallest of the three as they climbed back into the truck. Just before they pulled away, the driver reversed to get closer to Mendez. The kid with curly hair was leaning out of the window. "Hey, officer, what'd you say to get him up on the hood in the first place?"

"Damned if I know, son. Damned if I know. Buckle up now, drive safe and ride some waves for me."

"Rock on." The truck pulled ahead slowly to minimize the kick-up of dust and gravel before powering onto the highway.

For several moments afterwards Mendez could hear only the wind and the calls of seabirds. He looked down again. A crowd of people was standing some yards away from the body, and it included a yellow Labrador that was slowly, warily edging closer. On the sand was a dark starburst of blood and brain matter from Gheorghi's exploded head. The dog was sniffing the end of one of the splatters.

"Get that dog away from the body!" he shouted through the megaphone. Its owner stepped forward, grabbed it by the neck and pulled it away towards the shore, where he let fly with a Frisbee. The dog took off after it, snagging it before splashing down into the surf. Mendez returned to the trunk of the Mustang.

The second suitcase contained more new clothes, two pairs of Prada shoes in soft beige bags, and a large manila envelope. Inside were two sheets of blotting paper, each with a grid of eighth-inch brown dots. *Old-style acid*, Mendez thought. The corner of one sheet had been neatly torn off and two dots were missing. Underneath the envelope were two black cases, one that looked vaguely like his daughter's flute case, the other four inches or so longer and slightly wider.

Opening the smaller one, he discovered a stainless steel syringe, which he assumed would be used for large animals, maybe elephants or rhinos. It was nestled in black Styrofoam that had been cut to its exact shape. He snapped the case shut and laid it back in the suitcase before opening the other one. Inside he found a similar Styrofoam nest but with nothing in it. In the foam were two long, slender slots an inch wide and deep, one slightly longer than the other. There was an oddly shaped section that he couldn't identify, and another that sent a chill through him—the shape of a pistol grip, angled back and scalloped with four finger-sized grooves.

Mendez closed the trunk and went back to the edge of the cliff. The crowd was smaller now and still staying several yards away from the body. He pushed the control on his shoulder radio. "How far away is the support?"

"Close. What's the condition of the injured party?"

"Roger. Well, he likely took one brown dot too many and did a swan dive off the cliff. At the moment he's four hundred feet below me on the beach. I'd say he's feelin' no pain. Over."

"Ah, roger that, Sergeant. The medical team will arrive momentarily."

"Let them know they can slow down; this is now a retrieval. Get the coroner's office and the crime-scene boys down here. Send a tow truck for the Mustang. As soon as Montgomery gets here, we'll secure the area upside and down."

"Roger that."

He could hear sirens approaching from the north and the south. He switched off the two-way on his belt, squatted down and watched the surfers. The waves had picked up, and three were hitting the peak to get a decent ride. The surfer on the lead board was squatting with his arms out, ripping along the lip of the wave.

"Keep cutting that edge, son."

The dog was racing along the shoreline, barking and jumping through the foam, trying to keep up with the surfer. When the kid finally slid down the wave and his board slowed, the dog bounced into the waves to meet him. "The American dream," Mendez said to himself, without a hint of irony.

ACKNOWLEDGMENTS

—

The first three chapters of this book appeared to me in dreams over the course of eight or nine months. I scribbled them down in the dark as Shirley slept beside me. A year or so passed from the time of the first dream to the moment when my wife read through them and thought they formed a narrative. She challenged me to continue: "There's a book here. Why don't you write it?"

Shirley is my first reader and reality check. David Young promised to read the first draft ruthlessly, "as if it was my own." Margaret Atwood brought Bruce Westwood of Westwood Creative Artists into my life, and Kristine Wookey, Chris Casuccio and Bruce read *Erasing Memory* before agreeing to represent me. Bruce then passed it along to Anne Collins of Random House Canada, who swiftly became the book's champion. She and her colleagues Marion Garner and Louise Dennys agreed to publish this first-time mystery novelist in their World of Crime series—something akin to three lightning strikes on a dime.

It has been an extraordinary education working with Anne; I am deeply grateful for her editorial guidance, and even her occasional "huh?!!" Thanks also to my close friends Shin Sugino and Roman Borys, my daughter-in-law, Christine Tizzard, and my colleagues Kirk Stephens and Mark Lyall, for helping me create a cover in forty-eight hours. Thank you, Scott Richardson of Random House of Canada, for contributing so selflessly to its realization.

My desire to write and draw was encouraged by my beloved uncle Wesley G. Woods, OBE, of Woodbridge, Suffolk—priest, classical scholar, bomber navigator, cultural diplomat, artist, linguist and bird-watcher. Whoever I am as a storyteller began in the lessons learned through our decades-long correspondence. He was, and remains, my hero. Robert Morrow, Doctors Dody and John Bienenstock, and Rae Lake all answered questions that I'm certain seemed bizarre at the time. Thank you, Sarah Jane Caddick, PhD, for introducing me to neuroscience, a journey I could never have imagined taking. I'm grateful to Marcello and Chris Barone, who always save my seat at the bar, and to my colleague Carmen Serravalle and my friend Tim Seeton for saving a place for me in their hearts. I want also to thank my family for their patience through this period of my distraction—Marsh and Andrea, Ian and Christine, Sophia, Ozzie and Charles. And to end with a confession, the dreams continue—even while I'm awake—and they've grown more intense.

SCOTT THORNLEY has had a diverse career, from designing the Gemini Award for the Academy of Canadian Television to the logos for *Mary Poppins* and *The Little Mermaid*. As president and creative director of Scott Thornley + Company (a strategic creative firm that defines, builds and maintains the brands of clients in Canada, the United States and Great Britain), Thornley has worked for twenty years with the pillars of the Canadian and international cultural and scientific communities in the field of applied storytelling. Having won over 150 international awards for design, he was inducted into the Royal Canadian Academy of the Arts in 1990. His interests also include drawing and photography—both of which he has exhibited.